The Knees of
Gullah
Island

The Knees of Gullah Island

DWIGHT FRYER

sepia™

THE KNEES OF GULLAH ISLAND

ISBN-13: 978-0-373-83119-7
ISBN-10:   0-373-83119-6

www.kimanipress.com

Printed in U.S.A.

My wife Linda—you are intertwined with my every adulthood success and memory. Thanks for sharing my life and helping make it the wonderful existence it is.

Amanda, my child—I have loved you with the best I have from the moment I knew you were conceived. I am so proud of who you are and look forward to who you will become.

Mary D. Fryer, my mother—Thank you for being the wonderful lighthouse and watchtower you are for me. My every accomplishment in life began on your lap and standing at your knee. It is a privilege to be your son.

Adri, Pops thinks of you every day. As God increases my platform, I will continue to tell all I meet to consider immunization to protect themselves and their loved ones against the bacteria and viruses that cause meningitis and to learn its symptoms.

ACKNOWLEDGMENT

During my study of Gullah culture and its language, a Creole mixture of African dialects and English, I found eye-opening facts that pointed back toward the wellspring from which I have come. I recalled a favorite college speech teacher's efforts to help me not use "d" at the beginning of many words that start with "th." This is a Gullah speech trait. During my upbringing, one of my favorite great-aunts, Mrs. Emma Sue Prewitt Buntyn, often said "ooman" instead of "woman." My mother always says "swimps" for the word "shrimps," despite the most gentle but persistent efforts of her eight children to use the English word we considered more correct.

Swimps and ooman are Gullah words formed and steeped in a rich Sea Island culture of the Carolina Low Country. I do not know when, where or how, but everything within me speaks that some part of the forced migration of my maternal forebears traveled through Charleston or the Atlantic barrier islands along the eastern coast of this country where the Gullah-Geechee culture was formed. I would like to thank Linda Gill, general manager of Kimani Press, my editor Glenda Howard and the teams at Harlequin and Kimani Press for their support, advice and counsel.

I appreciate the kindness of U.S. Congressman Steve Cohen, Reverend Chester Berryhill, Jr. and Mrs. Vivian Vance Berryhill. I applaud the work being done by House Majority Whip James Clyburn of South Carolina and his wife, Emily, in their efforts to document and preserve Gullah-Geechee culture.

Many thanks to Reverend Edward Chatman, pastor of Emmanuel Episcopal Church. It was wonderful exploring the sanctuary and the basement of your church in Cumberland, Maryland, which had been dug by British regulars, and feeling the spirits of those who escaped on the Underground Railroad—through the work of Reverend David Hillhouse Buehl and others—using the tunnels beneath the church.

Reverend Joseph Darby, pastor of Morris Brown AME Church, and Mrs. Darby—Linda and I appreciate you taking the time from your schedule to meet with two strangers. Kelly Curnell, you blessed us with the gift of your Gullah baskets. I pray for you every time I look at them and thank God for your ability and willingness to preserve Gullah culture.

Dr. David and Angela Hiley, I am still thankful for the God-cidence of dinner with you in Charleston. Roy Golightly, you are always so encouraging. Thanks for giving us a Charleston connection. And John Pelletier, I cannot express how you helped us by introducing us to several Charlestonians. Archdeacon Jack Beckwith and Dave Souter, you are two outstanding gentlemen and your time with us was invaluable. John and Patti Sosnowski, God bless angels like you for welcoming us to your Wadmalaw Island home and allowing us to spend some time on a Low Country Sea Island. John, I did put the opossum in the book!

Mr. Alonzo Brown of Gullah Tours, you know Charleston, Gullah life and the Low Country so well. Your flowing description of the culture in this area touched me in ways I cannot describe. Thanks for introducing me to world-renowned Charleston blacksmith Mr. Philip Simmons. Mr. Simmons, you are a gentleman and a saint, and your legend lives on in all you have met. To Sean Ahearn, a young blacksmith in the Charleston tradition, keep on making music in your shop.

Reverend Walter Peggs, Evangelist Wilma Peggs and Fullview Baptist Church, your love and encouragement heal me a bit more each and every day. Melverta Scott, Bridgett Rawls, Laurie Tucker, Karen Smith and Richard and Barbara Williams, thanks for reading my work and giving me candid feedback. Nelson, Mitchell, James, Ernest, Bobby, Marion, Carol, Don, Carl and Kevin, you are my brothers and sisters and I love you.

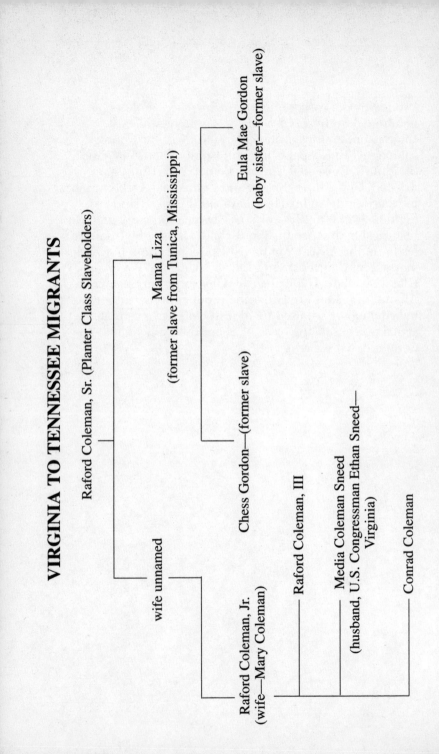

VIRGINIA TO TENNESSEE MIGRANTS

Raford Coleman, Sr. (Planter Class Slaveholders)

Mama Liza
(former slave from Tunica, Mississippi)

Eula Mae Gordon
(baby sister—former slave)

Chess Gordon—(former slave)

wife unnamed

Raford Coleman, III

Media Coleman Sneed
(husband, U.S. Congressman Ethan Sneed—
Virginia)

Conrad Coleman

Raford Coleman, Jr.
(wife—Mary Coleman)

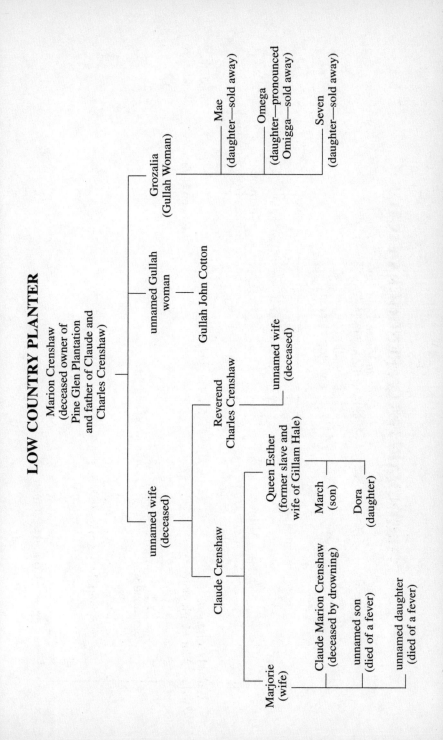

LOW COUNTRY PLANTER

Marion Crenshaw
(deceased owner of
Pine Glen Plantation
and father of Claude and
Charles Crenshaw)

unnamed wife
(deceased)

unnamed Gullah
woman

Grozalia
(Gullah Woman)

Gullah John Cotton

Mae
(daughter—sold away)

Omega
(daughter—pronounced
Omigga—sold away)

Seven
(daughter—sold away)

Claude Crenshaw

Reverend
Charles Crenshaw

unnamed wife
(deceased)

Marjorie
(wife)

Queen Esther
(former slave and
wife of Gillam Hale)

March
(son)

Dora
(daughter)

Claude Marion Crenshaw
(deceased by drowning)

unnamed son
(died of a fever)

unnamed daughter
(died of a fever)

CHARLESTON PENINSULA FACTOR

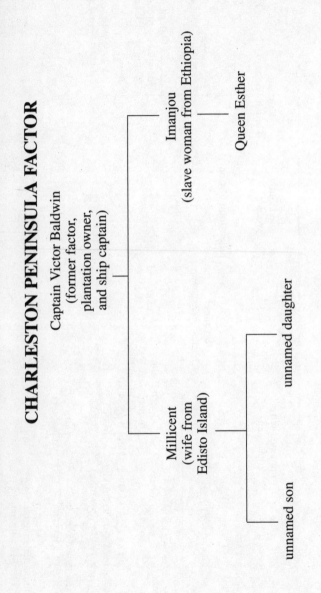

Captain Victor Baldwin
(former factor,
plantation owner,
and ship captain)

Imanjou
(slave woman from Ethiopia)

Queen Esther

Millicent
(wife from
Edisto Island)

unnamed daughter

unnamed son

VIRGINIA SLAVES TO FREEDMEN

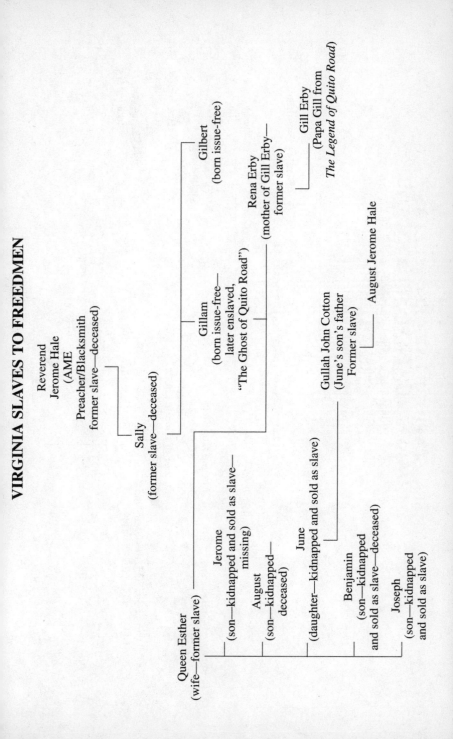

Reverend
Jerome Hale
(AME
Preacher/Blacksmith
former slave—deceased)

Sally
(former slave—deceased)

Gilbert
(born issue-free)

Gillam
(born issue-free—
later enslaved,
"The Ghost of Quito Road")

Rena Erby
(mother of Gill Erby—
former slave)

Gill Erby
(Papa Gill from
The Legend of Quito Road)

Queen Esther
(wife—former slave)

Jerome
(son—kidnapped and sold as slave—
missing)

August
(son—kidnapped—
deceased)

June
(daughter—kidnapped and sold as slave)

Gullah John Cotton
(June's son's father
Former slave)

August Jerome Hale

Benjamin
(son—kidnapped
and sold as slave—deceased)

Joseph
(son—kidnapped
and sold as slave)

SEA ISLAND GULLAH-GEECHEE CLAN

Pine Glen Plantation
Edisto Island, South Carolina
Slave Family
Unnamed Gullah
Slave Woman and Slave Man

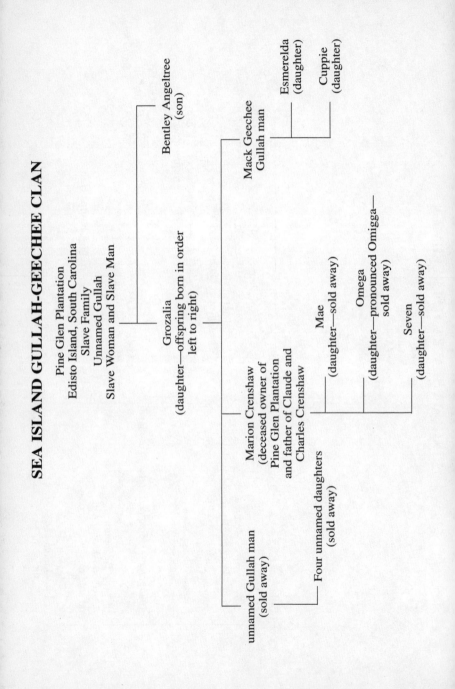

Grozalia
(daughter—offspring born in order
left to right)

Bentley Angeltree
(son)

Mack Geechee
Gullah man

Esmerelda
(daughter)

Cuppie
(daughter)

Marion Crenshaw
(deceased owner of
Pine Glen Plantation
and father of Claude and
Charles Crenshaw)

Mae
(daughter—sold away)

Omega
(daughter—pronounced Omigga—
sold away)

Seven
(daughter—sold away)

unnamed Gullah man
(sold away)

Four unnamed daughters
(sold away)

For the love of money is the root of all evil: which while some coveted after, they have erred from the faith, and pierced themselves through with many sorrows.

1 Timothy 6:10
King James Version of the Bible

Cause de lob ob money da mek a poson do all kind ebil ting. Some people cause dey wahn money bad, done stop trus een God, an dey haat git broke.

1 Timothy 6:10
De Nyew Testament—The New Testament in Gullah
Sea Island Creole
The Sea Island Translation Team with Wycliffe Bible
Translators
Copyright American Bible Society 2005

KEY GULLAH WORD TRANSLATION

English	Gullah
brother	bubba
daughter	daa'tuh
devil	debble
evil	ebil
father	fada
for	fuh
horse	haas
give	gib
living	libin'
love	lob
make	mek
mother	mauma
of	ob
over	ober
shrimp	swimp
that	dat
the	de, duh
they	dey
this	dis
thing	t'ing
want	wan
white man	buckruh
woman	ooman
you	oona

PART ONE—

PRECIOUS CARGO

1

CATTLECAR DISCOVERY

Joseph lay on his side atop piles of prickly straw inside a cattle car. His eyelids were heavy, but the pungent smells transported him to consciousness. The train had stopped and was not moving. Something was burning nearby and the smoke permeated the openings near the top of the walls.

Joseph rested his head on his emaciated biceps that cradled his head. His gaze wandered to his traveling partner Pete sitting across the rail car. Pete's direct but blank stare pointed at Joseph. Joseph smiled. "What you looking at, old man?" Joseph asked. During their thirteen years on the road Pete had talked every waking moment. Now, Pete did not reply so Joseph said, "Reverend Peter Johnson, how's my favorite preacher doing today?"

Pete coughed. "Young preacher man, I'm aching today." He groaned and repeated his cough several times. Pete harked and jerked his head back to spit toward the end of the car. "What's burning? Where are we?"

"I don't know what's on fire. I just woke up and can't tell exactly where we are either," Joseph answered.

"That smell and how I feel takes me outta 1883 and to the marches across the South with Sherman's Union army."

Joseph asked, "Pete, how was that?"

Pete paused. He tried to get up, but could not rise. He rolled onto his right side, placed his bundle under his head. His eyes never left Joseph's. He coughed and spit out what came up. "This cough's killing me." He looked away then returned his gaze to the young man. He said softly, "You ever seen a cotton fire?"

Joseph nodded. "As a boy on Edisto Island in South Carolina."

Pete said, "I saw plenty during that part of the war. If it was windy, that dry cotton burned like kerosene was on it." He wiped sweat from his brow. Pete sighed and rolled onto his back. "Joseph, when I encountered you and your mother on Edisto, you were a young boy. You told me you wanted to minister to folks. During our time together, I've taught you all I could about what it takes to do that, right?"

"Sure, Pete," Joseph said.

"When you going home to that girl of yours?" Pete asked.

Joseph shrugged.

Pete continued, "We ain't gone find your father. It's time you head to Charleston to that girl you always talking about and to Queen Esther. You hear?" He stared at Joseph.

"Yessuh," Joseph replied.

"I need you to go home. We've been a strange pair

traveling around for thirteen years now. You colored and I'm white. Sometimes we slept in places like this. At other stops, we were in barns, under bridges, at almshouses or even in jails."

Joseph coughed a few times.

Pete said, "Must be something serious we got. I've never had a cough like this in the summertime. We better see 'bout it or it's gone kill us." He stopped talking and breathed deeply.

"You ought to stop speaking that," Joseph warned.

"Over and over during the War I went from being chaplain to a madman," Pete stated.

Joseph gave him a quizzical look.

Pete continued, "Every day of that ugly war I smelled and witnessed death. I hated what it'd done to our country, pitted the North and South. Most of all I regretted your family's kidnapping from Cumberland and my hand in it."

Joseph shifted in his place. He used both hands to push himself up from the filthy floor. "Pete, you never said you had a part in what happened. Why've you never tol' me that before? What'd you do?" Anger resonated with each of his loud words.

Pete did not answer. Finally, he said, "Joseph, you remember I used to visit your pastor, Reverend David Hilhouse Buehl, in Cumberland?"

Joseph said, "Yes sir."

"That wasn't the only reason I came." Pete stared at the ceiling. "Reverend Buehl and I were part of a network, the Underground Railroad. We helped runaway slaves get North."

"Pete, really? Why didn't you say so before?"

"Joseph, hear the rest. After I preached, I'd always head back over the National Road to Pittsburgh. We'd hide the slaves in a false bottom under my wagon." He laughed several times before a coughing spell hit him. It ended with a deep wheezing sound that resonated with every breath he took. Pete laughed again.

Joseph said, "What's so funny?"

"I bet helping Southern human chattel escape was never on the mind of slave-holding President Tom Jefferson when he ordered the building of that road."

"Papa always said that was why my grandfather moved to Cumberland from Philadelphia—the blacksmith business from all the travelers heading west," Joseph stated.

Pete said, "Your grandfather went there for another reason he couldn't know. It was for his son's wife, your mother, to some day be a conductor on the Underground Railroad."

"My mauma," Joseph said.

Pete nodded several times. He looked at Joseph and said, "The night they took your family—" He paused to wheeze and had trouble getting his breath. "Some slave catchers stopped me about five miles outside of town. It was around ten o'clock. There were two of 'em and they were from Tennessee. The tall one named Rafe Coleman did most of the talking. He kept asking me about a group of runaways—they were in my wagon all the time. I kept saying I hadn't seen any Negroes. They didn't believe me.

The other one was shorter and fat." He paused and stared at Joseph again. "The moon wasn't up that night and you could see every star. We were down in a valley just before you head into the mountains toward Pittsburgh. The stout guy didn't talk much, but the big fellow ran off at the mouth. His hair was so red that I could see its color in the dark. He jumped off his horse and pulled me from my wagon. He hit me with a whip." Pete stopped speaking and did not begin again.

Joseph held his breath and waited. Finally he said, "Pete, what happened?"

Pete wheezed again. When he resumed, his words came slow and were slurred. He said, "He hit me over and over. The tall one said, 'U'm gone beat you like I would the niggers you been stealing.' He hit me in the jaw with his fist so hard that I fell to the ground on my face. That blow knocked out several of my teeth." Pete touched his left cheek. "He kicked me in my side and started in with the whip again. It cut right through my shirt. I was bleeding from everywhere he hit me. My back, shoulders, arms, face, and even my hands were cut up. He just kept on and on hitting me." Pete paused for a few moments. "I thought he…he was going to kill me. The fat fellow laughed every time that whip connected."

Pete stopped talking and his breathing became more shallow and slower. He said, "Joseph, I told 'em that your mother used her quilts to signal when the runaways should come to Emanuel Church. I'm so sorry. I, I told him about Queen Esther, Reverend Buehl, and our network in

Cumberland." Pete was crying. "He hit me again and I gave up the runaways under the boards in my wagon."

Joseph stared at Pete. Neither said a word.

Joseph finally broke the silence. "Is that why you been trying to help me?"

Pete nodded. He said, "I'm sorry. I, I, I been trying to fix it since we left Charleston in 1870." His last words came out in a barely audible whisper followed by two deep sighs.

"You shoulda tol' me dis befo'. Why didn't you?" Joseph asked, his tone full of pain.

Pete did not answer and just stared at Joseph.

Joseph said, "Pete, you all right?"

Pete's frozen stare spurred Joseph to move quicker than he had in a long time. He crawled toward his friend but stopped a short distance from Pete's motionless body. He reached out, touched him, then pulled back to stifle the hacking cough they had both suffered for months.

"Well, Pete, you said whatever we had would kill us— guess you were right."

In the distance, a voice shouted, a nearby rail car door rolled open along its track, and Joseph struggled to his feet. His eyes stayed on Pete while he backed away. Joseph knew death well.

"They coming, Pete. Pete—" he paused "—I—I—I gotta go." He bent down to grope for his bundle. Joseph's eyes never left Pete's body and he moved toward the end of the rail car, the place they'd called home for the past few days. He walked back, lifted the dead man's head, and removed

Pete's bundle. Joseph gently placed Pete's head on the floor. Joseph struggled up the ladder steps to the roof trapdoor, his tear-filled eyes still on Pete. He pushed open the exit and raised his head through the opening to squint at the daylight before ducking below the roofline for one last look at his friend. "Pete, t'ank you for all oona done," Joseph whispered. "I'll keep looking for my papa."

He wiped both eyes with the back of his hand and pulled himself through the trapdoor, gained his bearings on the roof, and climbed down the ladder at the end of the rail car. Joseph jumped to the ground on the side of the train away from where he figured a car-by-car search for tramps was taking place. His feet hit the ground and, two bounds later, Joseph crossed a dusty road and entered a well-worn path through a briar patch.

He moved through the blackberries like a cottontail and disappeared into the thick brush as the door to his and Pete's rolling bedchamber banged open on the other side of the freight train. He paused to listen for the railroad workers' discovery of the body of the Reverend Mr. Peter Johnson, Joseph's friend since childhood and father-figure during their long years of travel.

"Come on out of there!" drawled an angry Southern voice.

Another man said, "He ain't coming nowheres." The man paused before adding, "Can't you see that fella dead?"

"Damn if he ain't," the first man replied a few seconds later.

Joseph whispered in prayer, "See you sometime, Pete." He continued his silent escape through the brush, his aching, empty stomach roiling. A steam whistle blew three short blasts and he looked up at the noonday sun cascading through a break in the canopy above.

2

A KINSMAN REDEEMER

Gillam Hale walked through the red sands of Tippah Street along the tracks in Lucy, Tennessee, several times each day. Five days a week, and often on Saturday, Gillam left the shanty he shared with Rena Erby and their son Gill to go to and from his job at the Marble Yard. But along these journeys, his memory haunted him.

He'd been born issue-free—he had never been a slave, until he, Queen Esther and their five children were kidnapped from a home he, his father and brother had built along the tracks of the Baltimore and Ohio Railroad, near the end of the Chesapeake and Ohio Canal. The residence, with Gillam's blacksmith shop in the rear, overlooked downtown Cumberland, Maryland, and was northwest of Washington, D.C.

"Where are you, Queen Esther?" Gillam spoke aloud to the woman he'd married and loved, whom he had not seen for twenty-five years, not since the auctioneer's men dragged him away. They were black men, Negroes like him.

"Baby girl." Gillam often called her that. He spoke to

her as if she could hear him and he was going home to her in their house. "Where you today? How you doing?" In this fashion, his days began, progressed, and ended. He thought of his wife Queen Esther and their children, but he walked home to Rena Erby, his woman now, and their son, Gill.

After the war ended in 1865, Gillam sent inquiries to the Freedmen's Bureau in Charleston, South Carolina. Each letter and telegram drew a similar reply, if any response came. "We have no record of a Queen Esther Hale or the five children you seek." His letters to his parents and brother in Cumberland received an even worse reply—they had died during the war. So, Gillam Hale remained trapped in a life foreign to him, dwelling in a home he did not build, living with a woman he could not fully love, and rearing a son whose existence reminded him of the children he lost.

Gillam recalled the time he first saw Queen Esther. She was thirteen, already a beauty. He had just turned eighteen, an upcoming young blacksmith, not quite a man with a wisp of a mustache under his broad nose, across his dark, narrow face.

When Gillam's eyes met Queen Esther's for the first time, he'd smiled wide and showed every tooth in the front of his mouth, including the gap, top-row center. But even now, at age sixty-three, Gillam yearned for Queen Esther, the love of his life.

Instead, Rena waited and served him dutifully. She prepared dishes he taught her to make. Rena eventually bore his son, but even that event, the birth of a child physically like Gillam in every way, did not erase the anguish in his heart.

"Boy!" someone said from between two rail cars Gillam was passing. Gillam did not hear him, preoccupied by his daydream. "Boy!" Gillam kept walking. "You hear me! U'm talking to you, nigger!"

Gillam snapped from his trance. He stopped and turned toward the tracks. It was the train's brakeman. Gillam looked at the white man but offered no reply.

"Boy," the much younger white man repeated, "go get the town constable. We just found a dead man in this car over here." The man's voice with its distinctive rural west Tennessee drawl echoed among the silent train cars.

The hair stood up on the back of Gillam's neck and he turned to face the man. Gillam's hand fondled a small .32 caliber revolver he always kept in his pocket. All in Lucy knew he carried and would use it. This man who now stood on the couplings between the cars was a stranger.

"Is it a white or a colored man?" Gillam asked.

"He white," the man replied.

Gillam turned from the road and stepped into a path worn through the underbrush, mostly by him. "Get the constable your damn self!" he shouted over his shoulder. He walked toward a dinner meal prepared to his specifications by hands and a heart that couldn't replace his first wife.

"Nigger! Get back here!" the white man shouted. "Come here right now, niggah!"

The railroad man's partner pulled on his pants leg from

where he stood on the rock-covered ground below. "Let him alone. Don't pay to fool with him."

Ahead, Gillam blew under his breath and moved toward his home and noonday meal. "Today'll be no different," he said aloud. He remembered the argument with a white man on the day his life changed forever. The night riders had come to his Cumberland home. They'd burned it before taking him and his family away in chains. "It's gonna be just the same," he said when his shanty appeared in the clearing ahead.

Gillam Hale had never been more wrong. That July 1883 day would be more different than any during his twenty-five years without his Queen Esther.

In the kitchen of her home near the Lucy railroad tracks, Rena Erby turned from her black-and-white wood-fueled cookstove. "Negro boy," she said, her free left hand moving to its normal perch on her full-sized hip. "When you get in from school today, you gone he'p me pick dat okra."

"Yessum," her son replied. He raised his head from the earthen pottery bowl over which he hovered. "Ma dear, ain't no meat in dis stew."

"Gill, it got corn, okra, tomatoes, butter beans, potatoes and onions."

"But, Ma dear, I want some meat."

"I made many days on cuzghat."

He looked up from shoveling the contents of his bowl into his face. "Cuzghat, what's that?"

"Negro boy." She stopped stirring her pot and half

turned to look at her only child. "The stew you eating's called cuzghat! How many times I got to tell you 'bout dis stew 'til you remember." She laughed at his disinterest in her oral storytelling.

"Ma dear, did yo' mama teach you how to make it?"

"Papa Gillam showed me how to cook cuzghat."

"Ma dear, why you always call me Negro boy?"

Rena frowned before she turned her back on him. She retrieved a big metal spoon from the cast-iron pot and stirred her stew. The strokes clanged against the sides before her smooth motions returned.

The boy waited for an answer. He lowered his face over his bowl and placed another heaping spoonful into his open mouth.

She turned to face him; a side view talking wouldn't do. "I call you Negro boy, 'cause you needs to know what you is."

The stove popped and whined from the burning wood inside. The ticks from the mantel clock in the front room echoed into their space. Rena looked her boy straight in his light-brown eyes, inherited from his father.

"Gill." she paused to think about her answer, wiped the beads of sweat from her forehead, wide nose and thick lips with her apron. She turned toward the stove to close the damper in the soot-covered exhaust pipe. The racing fire slowed, ending with a double pop-pop and a slow whine. Rena wiped her hands on the checkerboard blue-and-white apron tied around her thick waist. She raised the tail of the thin cloth to her face again, dabbing the corners of her eyes in a dainty manner not befitting her girth.

"Gill," she began again and spooned her measured words to him, "I gotta make you know what you is, and—" she looked at him "—what you ain't." She edged closer until he looked up from his meal. "You not a nigger, no matter what you heard growing up on the Coleman place." She looked into his face until his nod confirmed he understood.

Rena turned to her stove. She opened the small oven and did something that folks living a soft life could never do. Her years of hard work cooking for others along with long days chopping and picking cotton had prepared her. With her bare hands, she pulled out a cast-iron pan filled with corn bread sticks. Her leathery fingers were immune to burns from brief exposure to hot items, except from the most intense heat.

Rena placed her left hand on top of the bread sticks, grasped the pan with her right, and banged it against the countertop next to the stove. After inverting it, she removed her fingers from underneath and the bread emptied into a pan, black from past use. Rena picked up two bread sticks and turned toward Gill. She placed these morsels, golden brown on the bottom and yellow on top, across the sides of his bowl. He picked one up and broke it, but the heat forced the bread from his hands.

"Mama, how you hold that hot bread?" Gill asked.

She laughed. "These old hooks—" she rocked onto her heels and chuckled again "—like leather from all the hard work I done over the years." As usual, Rena spoke in her cadenced rhythm.

The family dog issued a low growl and she heard the handle of the old pump out back of the house squeak as it flew up and down. The beast broke into an intense barrage of barks and snarls. Rena broke another piece of corn bread in half. She blew on it and gobbled down her handiwork, sucking in air to cool the mouthful. She licked her fingers on her left hand, then patted Gill's head when she walked past him toward the back door.

"Gill, you know Gillam don't like no dog barking at him." She stared at the boy. "Dat dog gone come up dead for barking at your papa."

Rena chewed the bread, savoring its rich buttermilk flavor and opened the door to peer outside. Instead of her man, a stranger was bent over the water trough under their pump. He raised the handle with his right hand and used his left to wash his face and head with the cool water. She looked back at Gill—he nibbled his second piece of bread, oblivious to the outside activity.

The man issued a hacking cough. He rose up from his midday washing at the trough. Still unaware of Rena's presence, he hacked to clear the mucus from his chest and spat onto the bare ground next to the water trough. The spittle was laced with blood. Rena stopped chewing and swallowed her bread down.

He wobbled and she surveyed him from head to toe. His right shirtsleeve was torn at the shoulder; he was thin and gaunt-looking. He wiped the water from his face with both hands and a swipe of his left forearm across his eyes and brow. His shoes were a type she remembered from her slavery days. He wore pants of homespun cloth held up by braces improvised from old cotton string. His clothes were filthy; it was difficult to tell their original color.

He looked up and their eyes met. The tramp wobbled again.

"Howdy," he said. He smiled, showing front teeth with a natural gap between his two large ones in the top front.

Rena returned his greeting with a stare.

"Missus, can you spare me some food? I'm powerful hungry." He put his left hand on top of the pump to steady himself.

"My man coming home soon. Get on 'way from here!" Rena tasted her prized corn bread when she spat her refusal at the beggar. She half closed the door; their dog continued his barks and snarls.

"Can you spare me a piece of dat bread before I go?"

She opened her mouth again to deny his request, but he interrupted by waving his left hand in a sweeping motion.

"Is it corn bread? Missus, it smells like corn bread." The man spoke his drawled words like a child begging for cake.

For a brief moment, Rena Erby continued to close the door. She pulled it almost shut and placed her hand on the bolt to secure the opening. She peeked at his face again and paused to look back at Gill before returning her gaze to the tramp. There was something she knew about his eyes. His salt-and-peppered gray hair did not fit with his thin young face.

"Please, missus, u'm starving." He released the pump and wobbled again. "I'll work fuh you, if you feed me. You...you got work? I can do it." He wavered again on his feet.

"Didn't you hear dat dinner whistle blow a while ago? My man gone be home directly." Her interest in this familiar stranger drew her to inch the door open a bit more. Rena glanced back at Gill again and the boy looked up from his food when she turned back to the homeless wanderer. "Where you come from?"

The wanderer said, "U'm not from here. Just traveling through."

"But where is you from?"

"Well." He paused and took a few steps away from the pump to stand next to the back porch steps. "I finished growing up in South Carolina, but I'm from up in Maryland. That's where I was born."

Rena said, "What you doing in Tennessee?"

"Trying to get to Memphis." He grabbed his head. "Where's this place?"

Rena scratched the matted, short hair on her head. Thick furrows formed in her broad forehead. "You don't know where you at?" A frown formed on Rena's round dark face.

The man grinned. "No ma'am, me and a friend hopped a freight train in Mississippi and fell asleep. I woke up in this town and got off."

"Well, y'all rode all the way through Memphis. You on the north side of Shelby county and past the city." Rena opened the door wide and looked around her backyard. "Where's yo' friend?"

The man held on to the rail next to the steps with his right hand and scratched his head with his left. "I...I...ah..." He stared at the ground. "He left me during the night. 'Cause, ah, he was, ah, gone." He raised his eyes into the distance, "after I woke up, he jus' left." His voice trailed into a raspy whisper.

Rena searched the crevices of her mind for where she'd seen him before. She said, "You'll see him again. He probably 'round somewhere."

The man shook his lowered head. "Can I just have a little of that bread? I'll eat outside." Their eyes met. "If you spare me some."

Rena Erby had never let the tramps from the rails enter her home. So her next words surprised her. "If u'm gone feed you, I'll do it inside! Duh white folks whose place I come from fed all the Negroes outdoors. I hate seeing somebody hand food out a back do' tuh folks. Come on. We got stew and corn bread." She stepped back, opening the rear door wide. "But, you 'member now—my man on the way fuh his dinner right now."

"Yes, ma'am, and thank you, ma'am," he replied. He gripped the rail to climb the steps and followed Rena inside.

The man stepped into her little kitchen and gazed around the room. Rena pulled a bowl from an open cupboard along the walls just past the entry door. She moved to the stove and filled the dish above the brim with the thick cuzghat. She stuck two corn bread sticks on each side of the red, yellow, white and green mixture. Rena turned to the stranger. He looked around the room, discomfort showed on his face.

"What's wrong?" she asked.

"Been so long since I been in a house—it seems strange."

"Dis my boy," she pointed at thirteen-year-old Gill. "And," she reached across the table to place the stew before him, "dis yours."

He barely glanced at her boy Gill. Instead, his eyes bulged when he saw the food. "Lord, thank you," he coughed, covered his mouth then hacked again. "Thank you very much, ma'am." He spoke just above a whisper with sincerity laced throughout his raspy voice.

The man sat down and grabbed a piece of the bread with each hand and broke it. He raised the piece in his left to his mouth, but stopped just short of his lips before putting it back in the bowl. He bowed his head. "Lord, we thank you for this food to nourish our bodies," he paused before whispering, "for Christ's sake."

"Mama," Gill said, "he say blessing just like Papa."

The tramp used his left hand to grab a piece of the broken bread and ate half of a corn bread stick in one bite. He retrieved the spoon with his same hand and shoveled the hot stew into his mouth.

Rena turned to stir the stew. She looked back, watched him eat the rest of the corn stick. He picked up his spoon, again left-handed, and scooped the utensil full.

This time he blew on it before he shoveled a heaping spoonful into his mouth. His throat issued moans of approval and a smile appeared on his medium-sized lips. The tramp pushed two more loaded deposits into his mouth, chewed a few times, and gulped it down.

"Man, slow down befo' you make yo'self sick," Rena said.

He smiled and continued his attack on the stew at a

slower rate. "A friend of mine's mama, Miss Grozalia, on de place in South Carolina where I grew up, cooked a stew jus' like dis."

Gill said, "Mama, he left-handed like me and Papa."

"Gill, get finished so you can get back to school after Gillam gets here."

The stranger mumbled under his breath at the same time Rena spoke. "She called it cuzghat." His face twisted when she finished speaking her man's name.

Rena did not hear him say the name she used for her stew, but young Gill did. The boy dropped his pewter spoon to the wooden floor. The tramp stopped chewing and looked at the boy for the first time. He turned to Rena and then back to her son. The three exchanged stares.

"Missus," he said through a mouth full of food, "what you say yo' man's name is?" The tramp trembled; he swallowed hard.

"Gillam," Rena whispered, "his name's Gillam Hale." She stepped forward and pointed over young Gill's head. "His picture on de wall in the front room."

The man gazed at Gill again and stared past the boy into the next room. He saw a black-and-white portrait in an ornate wooden frame on the opposite wall across the floor. The tramp wobbled to his feet. His chair fell over behind him, but he did not pause. He rushed past the boy.

"Where he at?" he shouted. "Where can I see him?"

His vigor startled Rena. She moved around Gill. "Where's who? Who the debil you talkin' 'bout?" She stopped in the doorway.

He turned to face her and, before either spoke again, she knew why this stranger was so familiar.

"Where's my papa?" the man said. "Where is Gillam Hale?"

The back door burst open and a thin, older Negro man stepped inside. His skin was the color of dark chocolate. There was a thin gray-filled mustache beneath his wide nose and just above his medium-sized lips. He was five foot ten inches tall. The man hung his hat on a hook next to the door and scratched his head of salt-and-pepper hair. He noticed the chair on the floor, Rena in the front room doorway, and the stranger in the next room.

"What the hell's going on?" Gillam asked. He placed his left hand inside the front pocket of his loose-fitting britches.

Rena turned her back on the stranger and looked into Gillam's scowled face. The vagabond pushed her aside and stepped inside the kitchen toward Gillam.

Gillam pulled his pistol. The stranger ignored the weapon and inched forward. The gun clicked when Gillam eased the hammer back.

"Papa?" the tramp trembled and placed his hand against the wall while stepping forward. "Papa Gillam," he squealed like a little boy. "It's me, Papa Gillam. U'm Joseph, yo' boy. It's me, Papa! It's me!"

Gillam froze when the man stumbled forward. The tramp collapsed into the arms of Gillam Hale. Sobs mixed with Joseph's words.

"Joseph?" Gillam whispered. "Boy, how can that be you?"

For a few moments, they paused. Rena Erby put her right hand over her mouth and walked toward the two. Gillam Hale spoke the question she never wanted him to have answered.

"Joseph, where's Queen Esther?" Gillam said. Joseph offered no reply and changed to dead weight in his father's arms. "Boy!" Gillam shouted at the thirty-two-year-old man he held like a baby, "where is your mama?" He shook Joseph once, dropped to his left knee, and laid the unconscious younger man on his back. Gillam released the hammer on his pistol and pocketed it. He attempted to rouse his youngest child by Queen Esther Hale with a second firm shake.

Joseph opened his eyes while Rena hovered over the two men.

"Boy!" Gillam said, "where's my wife?"

Joseph's eyes bulged. He stared around the room, jerked when he looked again into Gillam's face. "Mauma, Mauma, she...she in the Low Country," he said. His eyes rolled back before he closed them again.

Gillam paused, then shook him hard. "You talking out yo' head. Ain't no damned Low Country."

Joseph looked at his papa, whom he had not seen since just after his seventh birthday. "But, Papa, yes it is, Papa!" Joseph said in a low voice. "The Low Country in Carolina, near Charleston, Charleston, South Carolina."

3

GOODBYE MEANS FOREVER

In Charleston, South Carolina, Queen Esther removed a postcard from a small wooden box. She turned the card over. The note opened with the rural South Carolina name for mother.

April 15, 1883
Mauma,
I hope this card finds you well. Me and Reverend Johnson been sick, but we praying for strength. We'll catch a train to Memphis soon. Give my love to Uncle Bentley, Cuppie, June, Dora and March.
   Truly yours, Joseph Hale

"That boy still think he'll find Gillam someday. I wish he'd just come home," Queen Esther said. She removed a bundle of letters and postcards from the box and slid this recent one under the blue silk ribbon that bound them.

Gripping the stack in her small hands, she said, "He's searched for Gillam thirteen of his thirty-two years. I'd much rather have him home and helping out our family."

She returned the bundle to its keeping place and put the box in a cupboard along the back wall. Pausing in front of the wall mirror, Queen Esther observed her light brown skin, the color of coffee with too much cream. She smoothed her reddish-brown gray-tinged hair tied in a knot at the nape of her neck, and pursed her medium-sized lips. They were a slightly darker tan than her skin.

Dora said, "Mauma, why does Joseph send you postcards, but Cuppie gets letters?" Other than Dora's lighter skin and sandy-brown hair, her every feature copied Queen Esther's, even her high forehead and large eyes. She even stood five feet eight inches tall, like her mother.

March said, "Joseph wants her to stay his sweetheart and keep waiting for him to come back. Same reason that white man sent the note to you last month. U'm gone bust his brains out if he bothers you again!"

Queen Esther's eyes narrowed—they were an exotic reddish-brown, the color of fire. Her dainty eyebrows arched and she said, "March Crenshaw, hush that type of talk. Dora, finish counting that money. I need to go to the bank soon."

"Mauma, tell us what Gillam Hale was like," Dora said. She continued arranging the coins and paper money into like stacks.

"Dora," March interrupted before Queen Esther replied, "don't talk about that man!"

Queen Esther approached her adult son from behind— she gave him what she always did when he acted up, a well-placed thump with her middle finger connected to the back of his head through his kinky brown hair.

"Mauma, how many children did you have by Gillam Hale?" Dora asked.

Queen Esther said, "Four boys and a girl. The two oldest were boys and then June was born. After that, two more sons came." She looked sad and said, "My oldest, Jerome, was sold away when we were brought to Charleston. I've never heard from him again. August was my second child. He drowned on the trip here." She whispered, "The boy just younger than June was named Benjamin. He and June were sold to the same plantation on Sullivan's Island. Benjamin died out there the next year. Joseph was our youngest." Her last words were barely audible. "I wish I had them back again."

"Mauma, you think Gillam's deceased?" Dora asked.

March turned to face his sister. "He's not coming here so he's good as dead to us," he spat.

A second thump connected to the still-tender spot on March's head. He turned around again. "Mauma, stop doing that!" His complaint sounded child-like. The twenty-three-year-old opened his mouth, but Queen Esther placed a finger to the middle of his lips. The furrows in his brow deepened and his complexion reddened.

"Mauma, is Joseph dead too?" Dora's soft voice rang through the small and narrow restaurant dining room.

Queen Esther moved to March's left. She turned him in his chair by placing her hands on his shoulders. In a voice identical to her daughter's, she answered the question no mother wants asked about her child. "I just don't know, there's been no word from him since the spring." Her next comment came in a barely audible whisper. "Dora,

I birthed seven children, five by Gillam and you and March by your father, but only you two are with me."

March put his arm around her waist and leaned against her, like he had done when he was a tender boy.

"You still got June," Dora said. Her lips moved in silence while she counted the restaurant receipts from the day before.

Queen Esther's eyes searched the walls of 64 Broad Street, her rented restaurant. She looked at the paintings, tables and chairs she owned. Her gaze rose to the two identical chandeliers that anchored the ends of the single dining room. She smiled at Dora across the table before looking down into March's pale-gray eyes.

"I got what the devil left of June," she said of her daughter, the middle child of her five fathered by Gillam Hale. She finally did what Dora loved, but what their mauma would rarely do—Queen Esther spoke about Gillam Hale.

"I met Gillam when I was just thirteen years old. His father was already preaching when we got to the worship meeting. I knew he would become my husband the moment we looked at each other." She paused and smiled. "Gillam was a free man and he saved the money to buy me in less than a year. We were married and I moved to Cumberland. He taught me to read and write and count money. Gillam Hale showed me most of what I know." Her voice trailed off. "I never met a man so capable in so many ways."

March piped up, "He's not as good as our father."

March despised being a Negro and any reminder of his mother's previous life.

Ignoring March and his comment about Claude Crenshaw, she whispered again, "It's been so many years, but he's not dead."

"Mother," March deepened his voice, "how can you know?"

"Huh," Queen Esther replied, "I know 'cause I know in my heart what you don't."

4

THE CAROLINA LOW COUNTRY

The Crenshaw brothers, Claude and Charles, sat on the back porch of their ancestral home. That once one-thousand-acre plantation, Pine Glen, was built by slave hands at the end of a man-made tidal creek. Pine Glen was just south of the first deep crook in Dawhoo Creek above where it emptied into the North Edisto River.

The two men looked down on the North Edisto and the marshland surrounding it. There was a dock that was used to load crops onto the family schooner for shipment to Charleston each year. Workers under the bondage of Low Country slavery produced Sea Island cotton and indigo. Later, a small rice culture flourished, even among the high salinity of the creeks, tributaries and tidal pools of the Edisto waterways.

The brothers were smallish men, each about five foot seven in height. The similarities in appearance for these fraternal twins included their light brown hair, blue eyes, and lips so thin that they were barely noticeable. But Claude was slim and always wore a well-groomed goatee.

Charles, chubby since his childhood, had rounded cheeks and a clean-shaved face.

The three-story house was elevated from the ground to handle high water and tidal surges if a hurricane came ashore. The white plank mansion was built with cypress from the Edisto marshes. Pine Glen had a sweeping second story porch on all four sides. The floor was painted red to match the flat-tiled roof. The first floor had rounded portico windows and doors, both with matching crimson hurricane shutters.

In the distance, from their left, a woodpecker issued his haunting call amongst the dense trees. From their right, another bird answered with an identical call. The dove-sized woodpecker flew across the flat and open lawn. Flashes of yellow showed with each flap of the wings of the Eastern Flicker, mixed with a clear view of a thick white patch just above his tail feathers.

Claude Crenshaw set his glass down and pointed at the bird. He struck a mock hunting pose. The fowl landed on the main trunk of a live oak and clung there with its specialized four-toed feet. Claude pretended to fire a shot from his imaginary weapon.

"Bubba, let that go," Charles said. He moved his right hand to arrange the few strands of comb-over that remained on the top of his bald head and then patted the closely cropped hair around the sides of his head with his chubby hands.

"Don't you give me that this fine evening," Claude said. "And, don't call me that Gullah mess; I'm yo' brother not yo' bubba." He placed a short, thick cigar between his teeth and swung his arms wide. As he puffed, the billow-ing smoke cloud surrounded his face and moved toward Charles.

Charles said, "Bubba, oona fada say dat fuh oona name." He laughed and his brother's scowl deepened.

Claude ignored the Gullah speech he and Charles grew up using in play and later in work commands with Negroes.

Claude said, "It still burns me up that them damned Yankees took almost every stick of furniture and valuable item out of this house during the war. All I got left is Daddy's plantation record book." He placed his left hand in his thick hair and mussed it to the back in the direction he always combed it.

Charles said, "You know why Dah Grozalia saved that, don't you?" They called the Negro woman who raised them by the Low Country term *dah* for favorite female servant.

Claude nodded and frowned even harder than before.

Charles did what only he and one other person could when his sibling reached such an irritated state. He reached over and touched Claude's scowling forehead right between his bushy eyebrows.

"Claude, the War for Southern Independence ended eighteen years ago. Put all that behind you. Let it alone and it'll be fine. Press it and you'll regret your actions." Charles's plump cheeks shook while he spoke.

The elder brother yanked the cigar from his mouth and put it on a dish in front of him. His brow furrowed like crop rows. Claude said, "We wouldn't be sitting here

drinking this nice wine if I hadn't decided to 'press it.'"
He coughed hard several times. The last ended with a
rasping sound and the wind escaped his lungs in several
wheezing breaths.

Charles laughed and sipped from his glass again.

"Hell, Charles, the Crenshaws fought Indians, the
Spanish, pirates and the British to keep this land!" He
shook his head and stared at his brother. "You glad I
didn't let it alone when the Yankees decided to sell off the
remaining half of Pine Glen."

Charles nodded and smiled at his brother's observation.
"Claude, you're the heir, but I'm happy for you."

Claude glowered at his brother's reference to the good
fortune provided by his earlier birth. "Marion Crenshaw
was a Low Country traditionalist. It's not my fault he
believed that the eldest living son should get his entire
estate."

Charles said, "Does that mean March will receive your
property?"

Claude looked away toward the Dawhoo and ignored
Charles's question.

Charles waited a few moments and raised his glass.
"Mister, we both know you enjoyed doing what had to
be done when the Yankees tried to take the last part of
this place. And, when you press, you really know how."

Both brothers laughed.

Charles said, "Claude, bet you glad you sold the Edings
Beach place to that fellow from up North before that
storm hit in '81."

"Yeah, but that carpetbagger lost big time on that one."

A smirk crossed Claude's face. "I feel terrible that he had several houses over at Edingsville when that hurricane and tidal surge wiped Edings Beach off the map." Edingsville was a historic group of resort homes owned by area planters on Edisto Island at Edings Beach. Edisto Island was about forty miles southeast of Charleston.

Charles laughed and said, "I still have a hard time believing Edingsville's gone." He shook his head. "Boy, what memories I have from there as a child."

Claude smiled and said, "I got Yankee buyers signed up to buy every house I can build on Edisto." Claude paused and looked at Charles. "I just need more property out there at the ocean."

"Claude, you're working your way up to go after the colored folks' Seaside land on Edisto. You got plenty. Leave those folks alone."

Claude chuckled and then laughed. His humor ended in another series of rasping coughs. He wiped the water his eyes produced during his coughing spell.

"Are you after Dah Grozalia's place?"

Claude did not answer Charles, his only conscience.

Charles took a sip from his glass. "This isn't nearly good as the Madeira them damn Yankees stole during the war."

Claude placed his trained nose over his glass. He inhaled the liquor's aroma and calculated an answer. "That's not all they stole. They stole our slaves—they wasn't theirs to free!" He glared at Charles. "Then they gave the niggers half the Pine Glen land. That was Crenshaw land for a hundred and fifty years." Claude said, "I still can't believe

Queen Esther put that nigger's name on her piece of property."

"You talking 'bout her husband?"

Claude nodded and sipped again.

Charles said, "You figure he's dead?"

Claude shook his head.

"How would you know that?"

Claude performed an action rare for him. He smiled. "I paid a fellow over at the Freedmen's Bureau before it was closed. He got several letters from one Gillam Hale looking for a Queen Esther Hale."

Charles said, "What was done about the letters?"

"I had the man reply there was no Queen Esther Hale in the Charleston area." Claude laughed and drank from his glass. "Crenshaw is her surname!"

Charles shook his head. He said, "How many years ago did the Yankees take that land?"

Claude drank more of his wine before answering. "1864, two years after Dora's birth. She came in 1862 while I was away in the fighting. She's almost twenty-one now, so it's been nineteen years."

Charles paused before catching his brother's eye. "Father used to track time based on our ages."

Claude said, "Father also marked years with the age of his darkies. That's how he got on his slippery slope."

Charles decided to let his brother's double-standard remark pass. He took another sip from his glass and asked, "What're we drinking?" He picked up the bottle and read the label aloud. "*Vin Mariani,* popular French tonic wine. Restores health and vitality." He picked up the three-ounce glass of wine and held it up to eye level to examine the reddish liquid. "Where'd you find this stuff?"

"My dear wife brought a few cases of it back from her trip to Marseille last year. She thinks it'll cure me." He chuckled. "Maybe even us." Claude twitched as he spoke and circled both hands in the air. "Her beloved Catholic pope recommends it for all that ails you." He laughed and coughed twice before puffing at his cigar. It was out and he placed it in the ashtray.

Charles said, "Is it helping you any? How's your consumption?"

Claude shook his head. "It's 'bout the same."

"You need to slow down. Have you been to the physician?" Charles looked into his brother's eyes.

Claude shook his head. "No reason to go, Reverend Mr. Charles Crenshaw. He always has the same news."

Charles said, "Claude, I'm your brother, but listen to me now as your priest. Your health is not good and you planned all your life to leave your resources to your progeny. It's the Crenshaw way."

Claude did not reply.

Charles said, "I don't have children and yours happen to be Negro."

Claude said, "It's also not the Crenshaw way to leave property to our colored offspring."

Charles said, "I wonder how John C. Calhoun felt about Negroes as he stepped from this world into eternity." He hoisted the wine to his rounded face. An aroma like red grapes and light smoked meat greeted his long nose.

He drained the last of the reddish-brown liquid and asked, "Does this have opiates in it?"

Claude smiled. "Naw, it's harmless. It contains cocaine."

5

COW SENSE

"Is Joseph gone die, Doc?" Gillam handed the physician the buggy reins for his drive to his office in Lucy town square.

"Gillam, he's definitely consumptive."

"What's that mean?" Gillam paused to untie the horse's reins.

The doctor climbed aboard his buggy. "Tuberculosis, that's its official name. They also call it Wasting Away Disease." He paused. "Little by little, it consumes a victim's body until their ability to function ceases."

The white and the black men made eye contact. The doctor said, "Gillam, consumption usually means a death sentence."

Gillam dropped his head. "But, we just found each other again," he whispered. His hand rested on the buggy's side rail.

The doctor performed an unusual but brief cross-race act of open intimacy—he patted Gillam's hand. They eyed the contrast of their appendages, but the white man spoke of their similarities. "Gillam, my boy died in the war at the siege of Vicksburg. You know that?"

Gillam nodded and their eyes met again.

"I've never got the straight of it, but I sent for his body after I heard he was dead." The doctor's gaze wandered in the distance. "I examined him. There wasn't a bullet or sword mark anywhere. I hate to tell you, but, best I could tell, my boy died of the same thing your son's got."

"But—but, what can I do? There's got to be something!"

The physician said, "You need to stay prayed up on this."

Gillam ignored his comment. All who knew him understood he did not go to church or pray.

"Gillam," the doctor said, "everybody 'round here knows how you are not about church and God." He paused. "But, even cows got enough sense to get on their knees before they bed down. Gillam, you want this to work for you. You need to bend your knees this time."

Gillam looked sad and shook his head.

"Keep doing what you already are. Give him plenty of good food, rest and care." The doctor paused. "There's one more thing. Get him away from here before winter. I've read of some success in warm ocean climates and pine forests."

"Like The carolinas?" Gillam asked.

The doctor nodded his head. "I'm told they've had particularly good success there against consumptive disease near Charleston, South Carolina. They think it's something about the combination of resinous air, ocean and moderate climate that does the trick, along with proper rest and care."

Gillam moved his lowered head side to side in disbelief. "Doc, how much I owe you?"

"Ah." The doctor smiled and looked around to ensure their privacy. "You got anything like what you paid me with when Rena had Gill?"

Gillam Hale laughed, "I got some much better than that. It's been aging for over a year in a white oak barrel with peaches and charcoal in the keg."

"Half a gallon of that would settle us up."

"Wouldn't you rather I bring you a gallon, Doc?"

"No, no," he smiled. "I might like it too well." They laughed. The doctor took the reins firmly in his hands. "Gillam, give a little of that sipping whiskey to Joseph. And," he paused to point a finger in the Negro's face, "limit the time Joseph spends with everybody. Consumption is contagious on contact and proximity." He popped the reins and his horse pulled the buggy from the yard into the dusty road and sped away.

The train whistle blew long and loud, signaling their departure. Smoke mixed with water vapor and soot billowed past the windows. Gillam heard the steam-driven locomotive wheels spin. He looked down at his sleeping son just before the train jerked several times, spinning its wheels before taking hold and lurching forward. Joseph awoke to look out the window just as a sign flashed by, Collierville, Tennessee.

"Papa, how far've we traveled?"

Gillam laughed. "Some things never change. That was your favorite thing to ask when we used to go somewheres when you were a boy."

Joseph smiled, ignored his daddy's reference to his constant flow of questions as a child. "Where's Collierville? How far east are we?"

"We in a little town just outside of Memphis," Gillam replied.

Joseph looked at him and sat more erect. He stretched his arms skyward before slumping against the wooden trim around the passenger-car window. The train swayed gently from side to side and the young man yawned. Joseph said, "Papa, you gone be all right 'bout leaving?"

Gillam nodded. "I feel like I did when they carried me away from y'all in Charleston. U'm tore up inside and I feel like somebody been beating me all over."

Joseph patted his father's shoulder and the old man dropped his head.

Gillam said, "That boy hollered like you did when I was taken out the house."

"Think you might ever come back?" Joseph asked. He looked away out the window.

Gillam shook his head. "If Queen Esther don't want me, I think I'll just live somewhere alone."

Gillam drew quiet and, in his mind, he journeyed back to the evening of July 1858. The last one he would spend with Queen Esther before they were torn apart.

Gillam leaned against the doorway to his and Queen Esther's bedroom. He watched her make the final preparations for their picnic.

Queen Esther said, "June Hale, I done tol' you once, you ain't going. Now sit down over there and hush before I take yo' daddy's strap to you."

June plopped into her seat at the dining room table and pouted. Benjamin and Joseph snickered.

Queen Esther said, "Hush," and raised her foot onto one of the dining room table chairs. She pulled her light tan skirt up to her knee and laced the strings around the metal posts on her black high-top shoes. She lowered her leg and dropped the ruffled material of the garment to its full length just above the floor. Queen Esther looked in the wall mirror and straightened her peach colored peasant blouse about her shoulders. She adjusted the neat ball her hair was pulled into behind her head and touched one of her high cheekbones with the fingertips of her hand.

Gillam had watched her every move and he walked over to her. He said, "You want me to help you do that?"

She smiled and one of the boys giggled. He leaned near her and picked up the tan picnic basket from the table. She lifted a near-new quilt made from white backing with green colored maple leaves from one of the chairs and folded it over her arm.

Gillam said, "The weight of this basket says there's a quilt a'ready in here. Why we need two?"

She said, "I'm airing this one out on the front fence this evening." She moved from the dining room toward the front door. Over her shoulder Queen Esther said, "You three stay inside the yard while we gone."

The boys chorused, "Yessum." June's pout continued and a scowl crossed the young girl's face.

Gillam patted her head when he moved past. He smiled and followed Queen Esther into the front room. His eyes captured her every motion. She moved through the screen door and held it for him. He stepped over the threshold and walked across the porch. She closed the door and took his waiting hand while descending. They followed a bricked path to the front wooden gate. Gillam opened it. Queen Esther stepped through and spread the quilt across the split rail fence while Gillam latched the entrance. She took his hand and they crossed a dirt road into a thick grove of maples. Neither spoke while they descended one hundred feet along a well-worn path to a flat, gravel road bed below.

Gillam moved from the woods. He set the basket down. Reached up and lifted her the final two feet to the canal path. Queen Esther placed her hands on his shoulders and smiled wide the moment he touched her waist. He returned her gesture and picked up their dinner. They turned south, away from Cumberland.

Ahead, two young white children sat atop a mule harnessed to a canal boat. A second animal was connected in tandem to the tan-and-brown ark-like vessel. It was fourteen feet wide and ninety feet long, a perfect fit for the canal locks. It rode high in the waters of the Chesapeake and Ohio Canal. Cargoes of flour, corn, iron ore, lime, coal, rock, lumber and grain were carried south, but as usual its return trip northward from Washington, D.C., contained items not as dense.

A girl of eleven sat behind her brother, younger by at least four years. She said, "Hey, Gillam. Hey, Queen Esther." Her smile radiated across her thin face and she brushed her stringy blond hair back while fanning at a large horsefly. Her brother did not speak, but he offered a broad grin, toothless at the top and bottom.

Gillam and Queen Esther stood to the side and the mules eased past. The couple watched and listened to the gurgling sounds of the greenish waters as the boat glided along. A white man stood near the rear of the vessel. He waved and said, "Howdy, Queen Esther. Gillam, how you?"

Gillam said, "Mighty fine, mighty fine!"

Queen Esther waved and the boat traveled on. Gillam took her hand again and they continued their journey south while the craft moved around a bend and out of sight. In a short time, they arrived at their destination. It was a large round rock. They walked to the south side of it. Gillam opened the basket and unfurled the blanket over the thick grass. The maple leaves on this one were all red and the backing was a dingy off-white from use.

Gillam lay down on the quilt and Queen Esther picked up the container. He looked up at her and used his index finger to signal that she draw near. Queen Esther walked over and sat down next to him. She turned away and began to unpack the food items she had prepared, but Gillam pulled her to him. She turned toward him and they kissed.

After a long embrace, Gillam whispered into her ear,

"Baby girl, I been thinking 'bout that all day whilst I stood over that hot iron and fire."

The sound of Joseph's cough interrupted Gillam's thoughts. "I hope Cuppie's still in Charleston," Joseph said.

"You mentioned her befo'. Tell me 'bout this Cuppie."

Joseph smiled wider than anytime since he had found Gillam. "She's dark as a chocolate drop and sweeter to boot!"

Gillam said, "Talk to me now!"

They both laughed.

"Papa, we grew up together on Edisto. The folks that bought me and Mauma always owned her people. Cuppie's got dimples in both cheeks. Her hair's jet black, long and straight like a white woman's."

Gillam said, "Sound like Indian's in her lines. Probably Geechee blood, too."

Joseph said, "T'ink so 'bout the Indian blood." He smiled. "She's a sho' 'nough pretty Geechee gal tuh me!"

Gillam said, "Yeah, man. Them Geechee gals all right. Jet black dark with long straight hair!"

They laughed together.

Gillam rubbed his chin and asked, "Joseph, why that preacher go with you all them years?"

Joseph opened his eyes, but he looked out the window instead of at Gillam. "Pete said he did some things in the war that made him promise God he'd never get in a pulpit again."

"But, that don't explain why he stayed wit' you all them years."

Joseph shrugged. He said, "Papa, he owed us, our family."

A puzzled look crossed Gillam's face.

Joseph looked at Gillam and then past him out the right side of the train. "Papa, you remember Mauma's pretty quilts?"

Gillam said, "They were the best in Cumberland, probably anywhere." His chest expanded. "My Queen Esther used to put them maple leaf designs on 'em. They'd be the color of every season."

"Did you know Mauma helped slave folks escape on the Underground Railroad with her quilts?"

Gillam shook his head. His eyes found the floor. "I didn't know," he said. "I forbid her to even feed 'em!"

"Well, she did that and more. Pete and Pastor Buehl arranged for Mauma to signal the folks when it was safe for them to cross Wills Creek just where it emptied into the Potomac at Cumberland."

Gillam said, "Right there below the church?"

"Uh-huh," Joseph said. "Mauma would put her quilts on our fence line and the runaways knew that was the night to cross over and go up under Emanuel Episcopal."

"Damn," Gillam said, "they used the tunnels, didn't they?"

Joseph nodded.

Gillam said, "Everybody in Cumberland knew there was always runaways around. Some white folks liked it, but others would turn 'em in."

"Yeah," Joseph said, "it almost split Emanuel."

"Y'all great Emanuel Episcopal Church with the upper

balconies on each side—one for the choir and the other for the niggers."

"Papa, Mauma stayed there to help the slaves escape. She did that for years."

"What you say?" Gillam said. He shook his head and looked at Joseph. "How long was that going on?"

"Pete told me he arranged it with Pastor David Hilhouse Buehl way before I was born."

"My papa never let us help 'em," Gillam said.

"Why wouldn't Grandpa help the runaways?" Joseph asked.

"He was scared of what would be done to us if the white folks found out."

Joseph shook his head.

Gillam said, "He'd been a Virginia slave and lived with the threat of being sold south, away from all he knew to cotton country and cotton-mouth moccasin snakes." He shook his head, looked at Joseph, and then out the window. "I tol' Queen Esther to never help 'em!" He pounded his left fist into his other palm. He paused and looked at the floor. Gillam said in a whisper, "I was scared, too."

"It's all right, Papa." Joseph rubbed his father's back.

Gillam said, "All these years I thought they took us 'cause of jealously and greed for slave money, but it was over helping escaped slaves." He turned to Joseph. "How did you and Reverend Johnson hook up?"

"Pete came to Edisto with the Yankees early in the war. He saw to it that we got what we needed while he was there. He got reassigned to General William Sherman later on as a chaplain. After he mustered out of the army at the end of the war, he came back to Charleston and we left together five years later in 1870."

Gillam said, "Good ol Charleston, ugh!"

Joseph laughed. "Everybody loves Charleston."

"Ain't nothing I love 'bout it!" Gillam worked his mouth and raised his tin-can spittoon to his lips. He deposited the wad of tobacco he'd worked on since they'd boarded the train at Buntyn Station, just east of Memphis. "White folks sold more Negroes at auction in Charleston than anywheres else."

A white man in a blue flannel suit, sitting across the aisle at the front of the car turned to look back, indicating he'd heard Gillam's words. Gillam pulled a pocket knife and popped the five-inch-long blade open with the thumb of his left hand in a motion resembling a snap of the fingers. He made a production of letting the man see him slice a healthy plug from the chunk of tobacco in his right hand. The passenger turned toward the front and looked out the right side of the train, away from where Gillam and Joseph sat.

Joseph placed his hand on Gillam's leg and moved both hands palms down, indicating for his father to lower his voice. "Papa, on the road, it's better to be humble and silent. You never know what you gone run into and how these folks'll react to a colored person just showing up, let alone what you say or do once you there." He looked at Gillam's glistening weapon.

Gillam closed the knife in a smooth one-handed motion

of his index finger and thumb. Obviously, he had executed this move many times before.

The train passed a cotton field full of black hands on the right side of the track. A large white man on a horse rode through the crop rows toward the train, waving his hands at the workers, instructing his charges.

Gillam looked back while the typical Southern scene moved from sight. "That overseer back there look just like the leader of the men that took us, Rafe Coleman." He paused and then frowned. "You know what they done...done it in front a you and me." He paused again. "The fat slave catcher lived in Grand Junction, he sold me to a slave dealer in Memphis, even though they knew I, we was free—he sold us anyway. They paid him to deliver me to Memphis. I come back here. Hoped he'd tell me where you and Queen Esther and the others was sold." Gillam looked at Joseph. "I figured wrong." He looked down at his hands again and stretched them open, palm down and rotated them to face upwards.

"It's all right, Papa," Joseph whispered. He'd heard many confessions before. "Go on," the young man encouraged.

Gillam's fingers wove together again, like strands of grass and straw in a Gullah basket struggling to find the right strength to hold something inside, stretching for the give and take needed not to burst from its load.

"I knew where his house was. He kept me there for six weeks for my back and face to heal up some," he paused, "from where they beat me."

"Papa, is dat when you got duh spider web on yo' back?" He spoke of Gillam's extensive scarring.

Gillam nodded. "It started on the canal boat. I got more from Rafe Coleman in Lucy after the fellow in Grand Junction was through." Gillam shook his head. "Them men and some fine folks in Cumberland kidnapped us. And, you and me know what they done to Queen Esther. They took her. They done it in front of you and I vowed then to take care of both of 'em. We was at war when I went back. White folks 'round here won't see it that way, but that fellow needed—he deserved what I give him!" Gillam picked up speed with his story—he seemed to want to finish before the train stopped again.

"I had gotten myself on with Sherman's army as a blacksmith. Sherman had his men 'stablish camp next to the rail yard in Grand Junction. The slave trader's place was two miles to the south of the town, almost in Mississippi. I watched his house for two days to make sure he was home. I knew he'd be. He owned too many slaves and, in my experience, most of the rich folks with slaves didn't fight in the war. The po' trash did most of the fighting and dying in the Southern rebellion for the right to get Negroes and land—that meant money." He spat into his cup.

"I left camp late one evening after lights out and went down there. I'd just got there when—" he paused to look up. The white man at the front of the car looked back again. Gillam whispered. "I got lucky. Just as I got behind some bushes, he come out of his house and headed to the privy out back. Guess he had to go outside for a change 'cause Sherman set all his slaves loose and there wasn't no one to empty his chamber pot the way they did when he had me chained to a post." A look of disgust moved over Gillam. "I waited 'til he got inside the outhouse and I was sure he'd sat down and started his business before I busted in on him." Gillam grinned. "I was younger then, stronger. I grabbed that peckerwood by his collar with my right hand. Put my left around that fat throat of his and squeezed. He knew who I was from the first moment I jumped him. I'd heard him say he never forgot a nigger, no matter how many he sold." Gillam looked at Joseph again and smiled. "I shook him. Scared him so bad that he kept on wit' his bus'ness."

Gillam laughed before turning solemn again. "I said, 'Where my wife and my young 'uns?'" Gillam looked back at the floor and opened his hands. "You and I know what he'd done...to Queen Esther, to us. He made sure we saw it." Gillam shook his head and Joseph rubbed his father's shoulders and back. "He laughed at me. He said, 'Nigger, go to hell!' And...and then, he pulled this knife from his breeches pocket." Gillam took the green-handled crabapple switch out again. He popped the blade open with a fluid motion of his left hand. It shone in the sunlight coming through the side of the train. "I done to him what he meant for me. I put his knife in his big belly over and over." Gillam paused. "He took us from each other. I opened the toilet seat and throwed him in there head-first. I heard him moan once after he splashed down." A twisted smile emerged on Gillam's face. "I paid him in full."

Joseph continued to look out the left window. "Papa,

I seen things, fighting like that many times," he sounded for a moment like a child. He cleared his throat and said in a man's voice, "I'm a Sherman cut-loose, too!" That term was used for the many blacks Sherman and his troops freed in their guerrilla warfare march across the South.

The train slowed and the conductor opened the rear door of the car. Gillam closed his weapon and put it away. Neither Joseph nor Gillam looked up as the uniformed man strolled past. He said, "Next stop Rossville!" The white man at the front stopped him. They whispered to each other and the conductor turned back toward Gillam and Joseph. He pulled a gold watch attached to a silver chain from a small pocket of his black vest.

"Boys," he said, "that man up there say one of y'all got a knife." His voice resounded with "R-full speech" like a man from the eastern seaboard, instead of the deep South. "Give it to me and move to the back car or I'll have the town constable on you for vagrancy when we stop in Rossville."

Gillam and Joseph both knew how Southerners in the first wave of the Black Codes tried to control blacks all across the United States, especially those in transit to a potentially better life. Gillam retrieved the knife from his pocket and handed it to the man. The railroad employee looked at it, put it in his britches pocket, and turned to walk away.

Joseph said, "Excuse me, sir. Excuse me."

The conductor stopped and looked over his shoulder.

"Where are you from, sir?" Joseph asked.

The white man smiled. "From where your ticket say

you going, boy, the best place in this world, Charleston, South Carolina." He turned, whistling *Dixie* as he headed toward the forward door. He looked at his watch again when he stopped to smile at the white man in the blue flannel suit.

The conductor said, "Sergeant Mueller, here's a souvenir for you." He handed him the knife; they exchanged smiles.

The conductor looked back at Gillam and Joseph. "You boys be gone to that end car befo' I come back now. You hea'?" The sound of his Charleston brogue, a mixture of Southern drawl and English cadence, dripped from every word. Like a fine English gentleman of his day, he dropped many of the Rs from his words.

Gillam and Joseph nodded. The conductor closed the door and moved toward the next car forward. The man in the blue flannel suit glared at them as they walked away. Gillam pulled their bundles from under the seat in front of them. They stood, walked through the rear exit, and Joseph closed the door behind them.

Outside, the shadow of the coal smoke from the steam-engine boiler blocked the sun and the sounds of the engine echoed like the breaths of a huge but tired beast. The slowing train swayed and wind swirled about them. They stepped across the couplings to the next car.

Joseph said, "Papa, what'd you do with your pearl-handled revolver?"

"I give that .32 to Rena's cousin for him to hold for Gill 'til he's old enough."

Joseph said, "I hope he never gives it to him. You can't get old enough to own a weapon. You'll use it the first time you get mad or scared enough. I'm glad you don't have a knife or a gun for the first time since you got free again."

The train's whistle sounded a succession of blasts, signaling the stop at Rossville to load and unload its burdens of passengers, freight and produce.

6

MEETING BEFORE THE MEETING

Three and a half days later, on a Thursday night, a woman spat out her command from the shadows on East Battery at Calhoun Street in downtown Charleston. "Man, ober here."

He stepped off the curb and moved to the side of her high-wheeled cart. The ox that pulled her wooden vehicle with its metal wheels jerked when the man drew close. But she held the beast fast and the ring in the giant steer's nose ended any ideas of his disobedience.

"Evening," he said.

"How do, yo'self, Mistuh Bentley Angeltree?"

He laughed, shaking his girth in slow motion. "U'm doing mighty fine!" They both looked around to ensure their privacy in this dark spot between the gas lamps along the street. A foggy mist hung in the evening air.

She said, "Just keep putting a few drops of this sea rose tea in his food." She handed him a cylindrical bottle about the size of an index finger with a glass dropper inside. "Be careful to just put a very little—too much'll kill him and we don't want that fool dead!"

He put the bottle in his pocket and nodded in agreement.

"Now, you need to wash real good when you handle that."

He grunted with a jerk, rolled his eyes at her. "Now you tell me my wu'k."

A rare smile covered her drawn face, lined with the wear and tear poverty, hard work, bitterness and desolation bring. She was a tiny woman with lively eyes, bluish black in color from cataracts. Although she was eighty-five years old, her dark-brown skin did not have many lines. Miss Grozalia always wore a white rag tied tightly about her head to cover her matted hair that was now a muddy gray.

She handed him a rolled-up plain brown bag, an inch thick. "Put dis in duh high buckruh's food." She spoke in a cadence filled with English charm, African rhythm, and Caribbean spice. She was Gullah, from Edisto on the South Carolina coast.

He nodded. "Grozalia, you want me to gib de white man the usual amount?"

"Boy, long as you been using this, now you playing dumb puss'n wit' me. You know how tuh do! Especially dis saltpeter 'cause dis one de mos' important to me."

The man shrugged his broad, rounded shoulders. He smiled at her in the moonlight and thought of how much she looked and acted like their mother. "All right, Grozalia Geechee."

He stepped back from the wheel well of the cart.

Grozalia said, "Get up, Rosebud!" She clucked at the

ox twice, popped the reins on his back once, and released them, giving him his head to move free. The beast lumbered away, taking her and the cart along. The metal-spoked wheels clattered over the oblong cobblestones of Calhoun Street and Grozalia hummed a song aloud as she moved into the soft light of the first gas lamp she passed.

Her confidant, Bentley Angeltree, stood for a moment in the street and looked after Grozalia. He moved to the sidewalk and stepped up to it before following Calhoun in the same direction Grozalia rode away. Instead of her westward track, he would turn south on Meeting Street just ahead toward the place where he lived in the rear of Queen Esther's restaurant.

The train cruised through the swampy South Carolina Low Country. Joseph looked around the passenger car. Everyone was asleep. Even his father had finally suc-cumbed to the need for rest after they'd left Savannah earlier the previous evening. The train was ending its run on the Charleston Railroad at the town whose name it bore. For hours now, there had been swamps, marshes, rivers, creeks and ponds in every direction Joseph looked. He was home; if he had one, this was it. It was the Low Country and water was a part of everything.

Joseph peered out the window and wondered. White light was supplied by a full moon. Every living thing had silvery Spanish moss on it. It just hung in lengthy clumps of every size and shape. The plant with its tiny pointed leaves and whitish-gray color gave the entire area an eerie aura—the Low Country could look scary and mysterious, especially just before daybreak. A generous amount of fog hovered over the nooks, crannies and all things in the area like a fluffy cotton blanket covering a ruffled bed.

Even at this time of evening, Joseph recognized the flora he had come to know as a boy walking through woods just like these. He could see the long-leaf pine, cypress and tupelo trees so prevalent here. Joseph had seen their rot-resistant lumber used time and again to build Low Country churches, houses, barns, fences, gates, sluices for rice fields, boats and a hangman's gallows.

Among the lush shrubs was his favorite tree in the world, the palmetto palm. South Carolina was known for this tree with its plain bark, singular shaft-like trunk and pointed evergreen leaves that grew in a clustered center.

The train flew through the bushes at a speed faster than they had traveled the entire journey—the engineer must have heard Charleston calling.

Gillam awoke and said, "Where are we?"

"We'll be in Charleston soon." Joseph smiled. "Papa, I remember folding and weaving roses from those green palm leaves as a boy. We sold 'em to tourists and folks on the streets. You remember I tol' you about Uncle Bentley? He duh Crenshaw family cook at Pine Glen on Edisto Island. In de summer, we all traveled with the Crenshaws to their Charleston townhouse on South Battery in downtown. Uncle Bentley lobed children, but didn't have none of his own. He showed me how to make the palmetto roses."

Gillam said, "What's them things sticking up out there?"

Joseph laughed. "Papa, I'm surprised you don't know. Those are tree roots. They call 'em knees. That reminds me of something. 'Bent knees straighten crooked deeds.'"

Gillam said, "You remember that?"

"Mauma said dat a lot, I got it from her. She always said, 'don't forget to pray.'"

Gillam said, "Your mama loved that saying. She got it from my Papa."

Joseph said, "Mauma said it so much dat Cuppie's mama, Miss Grozalia, picked it up. She said it more than Mauma." He bowed his head and prepared to pray. "Papa, will you pray wit' me?"

Gillam did not answer.

Joseph did not raise his head or his voice. He said, "I must t'ank God for bringing us home to Mauma and Cuppie."

Joseph said, "Papa, dis ain't neber gone work out 'til you talk to duh Lawd 'bout yo' concerns." He prayed from his seat without a sound but his lips, head, and shoulders moved.

In the distance, the train's horn signaled its arrival at Charleston. Initially, Gillam ignored his son's prayer, lost in his own thoughts. He looked at Joseph then moved his gaze to the giant cypress and tupelo trees. Their knees stuck out in the moonlight. Some even rose above the fog and the green moss that covered them was visible, even at this dark early morning hour.

"The best thing about having a child," Gillam whispered, "is when they get old enough to teach you something." For the first time in the years since he last saw Queen Esther, Gillam bowed his head. His lips moved in silent prayer beneath his furrowed brow.

7

WIGGLE IN SWIMPS AND GRITS

Muley Jenkins walked along and sang his vendor's tune. "Swimps, swimps, get yo' fresh swimps from the bay. Fish, fresh swimps, fix-um up yo' way. Hot, cold, spicy, mild, Muley's fresh swimp sho gone make oona smile." He always said *swimps* instead of *shrimps,* but everyone understood this Gullah word meant the shellfish that were a Charleston staple. He paused and listened for any takers.

A Negro woman appeared through a gate below the front door landing of 27 King Street. It was the Miles Brewton House across King Street.

"Morning, Muley, I want my usual," she said. She grabbed the bars with her left hand as if she was in jail and looked at Muley with a smile. She was a heavy woman in her thirties with a blue-and-white rag tied on her head and a white apron covering her black maid's dress.

He swung his two-wheeled cart around in a semicircle and tipped his small ragged felt hat. His skin was the color of light milk chocolate, really a deep tan. The young man's face was long with a wide-nostriled and flat nose.

Muley's large dark eyes sat a little too far to the sides of his face. He resembled the cruel nickname he carried.

Muley moved his scale into place on the pipe mooring that was attached to the side of the cart. The words *Charleston Fish Company* were stenciled on the side in black. He opened his covered cart and filled his scoop with the shellfish.

The metal fence gate groaned when the woman opened it. Esmerelda was her name, and she walked over to his cart and handed him her container. He placed the first load into the rounded pan hanging from the scale by three links of braided brass chain. Muley repeated his effort a second and third time—this was a three-scoop home. He noted the weight.

"Two pounds fuh de lady, Esmerelda," he said. "At least sixteen count to the pound, good size fuh swimp and grits."

She nodded and Muley stepped onto the sidewalk and the side of the cart. He poured the pink shrimp into her container and placed it back into her hands. The shellfish he sold at this dawn exchange would become a part of the household meals she prepared throughout the day.

She looked down at them and smiled at him again. She shifted the container to her left arm and jiggled the coins she held in her right hand. Her movements bounced her heavy breasts inside her white blouse. She handed him his pay.

"Muley, tell me somet'ing today."

He turned each piece in the deft fingers of his right hand, but his gaze hung on her and, for a few moments, strayed to the other items she had shaken, just as she had hoped he would. "T'ank ya' fuh de extra," he chorused in Gullah for the monetary and entertainment tips. He smiled wide, displaying horse-sized teeth. In a seamless motion, polished by years of repetition, Muley put the coins into his apron pocket and tipped his tattered hat to another satisfied customer.

Muley edged closer, looked over his right shoulder and then up at the imposing seven-foot-high iron fence behind them, sharp steel spikes lining the top. He whispered, "Your boss man already ober tuh Miss Queen Esther's place fuh breakfast wit' his brother, Mistuh Charles."

She joined him in his fervent gossip. "Mr. Claude need tuh stay home wit' his own wife and leave Miss Queen Esther 'lone. That what that stupid buckruh ought to do." She swayed her left shoulder into him to make sure he got her message.

Muley smiled and said, "That man tek mos' a his meals ober to dat restaurant, but he ain't doing not'ing else ober dere." He wiggled a little below the waist, side to side.

"Muley, you t'ink you know eberyt'ing. How you know what that white man do and ain't doing?"

"I just know!" He popped the knuckles of his right hand into his left open palm twice.

"Muley, tell me what oona wan'," Esmerelda said mischievously.

He shook his head, showed embarrassment with a grin. He said, "I jus' wan' someone and someplace a my own." It was a whisper rooted in the cries of a slave child whose mother had been sold away when he was twenty months old.

"Come by tonight after supper," she whispered. "My white folks going to dat dance." She stepped away from him, widened her eyes up at him and shimmied her shoulders a bit. "I'll have somet'ing fuh oona tonight dat no girl can match," she looked around. "Oona won't sleep out in duh cold dis ebening." Esmerelda batted the lids on her big clear eyes and turned to reenter the gate to the fortified residence.

She continued to clutch her precious seafood with the other arm and moved quicker than most would think she could to the gate. She swooped low to pick up a folded newspaper and a metal rack that contained four bottles of milk—the rich cream was clearly visible on top. After stepping inside the fence, she swung the double-doored metal gate closed.

Esmerelda descended the stairs and stopped at the wooden basement entrance just long enough to ensure Muley had watched her every bounce and sway. The woman placed the dairy products on the landing and took another peep at her secret suitor before opening the door. She stepped inside and from the secrecy of the portal, Esmerelda retrieved the milk, blew Muley a kiss, smiled wide and pretty at him, and closed the basement-entry door at 27 King Street.

Muley stood still for a few moments and surveyed the imposing front of the Charleston double-house. The generals from the Northern occupying army had used it during the Civil War, as had the British officers a hundred years earlier in the Revolutionary occupation of Charleston. There were stairs on each side of the entrance that led up to an impressive landing surrounded by four large columns. The redbrick mansion was well into its second century.

All that was beautiful, but the design feature that made it scary for Muley was the metal fence and gate. It had a triangular transom across the top with straight spikes in the design. Gas lamps framed it on each side and the interior of the gate top was filled with iron spikes in a circular pattern that flowed from its center. The enclosure itself had even larger spikes arranged in a windmill design across the top along its entire front perimeter. The bars were an inch thick and all the metal was painted black.

Muley remembered how scary it was to bring shrimp to this place during the Union occupation in the Civil War. In those days, blue-coated soldiers covered Charleston. He shook his head and looked at the fence that lined the property's front, ending in a high redbrick wall on each side of the house.

"'Cause ob Denmark Vesey, fancy white folks, duh high buckruhs, done all dis for keeping Negroes out." He grunted, "And colored folks already in." He shook his head and stepped to the rear of his cart. He semicircled back to his original northward path on King Street.

8

RICH FLAVORS AND EVIL THOUGHTS

Queen Esther placed a plate of food in front of Claude Crenshaw. It contained a healthy portion of shrimp and grits. Bentley Angeltree had prepared them using a cream-based recipe, his usual practice for breakfast; pieces of thin-sliced bacon were in the mixture with plenty of shrimp amongst the thick-ground grits. Orange-colored grated cheddar cheese was on top and the entire earthen-pottery bowl had been browned in the oven.

She smiled while she served the men. Queen Esther stepped around the table to where Charles Crenshaw sat. "Reverend, here're yo' shrimp and grits with fried green tomatoes!" She placed the platter with generous helpings in front of the Episcopal priest. He nodded his head for a silent but quick blessing of his meal. "Thank you, Queen Esthe'."

Charles scooped up a healthy fork of shrimp and grits. He blew on it a few seconds before easing it into his mouth. He reached for the bread basket in the middle of the table and moved the cloth covering to discover a stack of fluffy, golden-brown biscuits. "My, my, what have we here?" He placed two biscuits in the gravy on his plate. "This is the perfect combination!"

Queen Esther said, "Mister Claude, I'll be right back with yo' omelet."

Charles never looked up from his meal. Claude said, "Thanks, Queen Esthe'."

She walked from the middle of the restaurant to check on the Baldwins at their table by a front window.

Charles said, "Claude, you spoke to Queen Esther yet about acquiring her gal's land on the south end of Edisto?"

Claude shook his head and smiled. Charles placed a perfect bite of shrimp and grits, gravy and fried green tomatoes into his mouth and began to chew.

Charles said, "Why do you want June Hale's property?"

Claude said, "Do you know how much Ashley River Fertilizer could make on the phosphate rock underneath her forty acres?"

Charles just shook his head. "Bubba, you care about anything besides making money?"

Claude picked up his glass, smiled, and said, "Salute."

Charles said, "Claude, are you going to build some resort homes on Edisto next year?"

"Yes, we should break ground on four more in July, if things go as planned. Those and the three I'm building are already sold."

Charles said, "Does that colored gal know how valuable that phosphate rock beneath her ground is?"

Claude shook his head.

Charles said, "All right, but my real concern's that man she got."

Claude said, "Gullah John Cotton?"

Charles said, "A member of my parish saw him in a fight in the war once. He fought like a wild man."

Claude said, "Probably got it from his maternal grand-daddy."

Charles shook his head and frowned.

Claude leaned in to the table. "Vesey," hissed from his lips.

Charles said, "What're you going to do 'bout that?"

Claude put his left index finger to his lips and sopped brown gravy with the large biscuit fragment in his right hand. "I got Gunther Mueller working on Gullah John Cotton. There's money to be made with that ground and June Hale's out there growing turnip greens, goobers, black-eyed peas and sweet taters."

Charles enjoyed another bite of his breakfast behind a peaceful smile. His rounded cheeks resembled those of a chipmunk on a run back to his burrow with a mouth full of gathered food.

Claude said, "My other investors are concerned about us running out of phosphate rock." A scowl crossed his brow. "We must have the product to fill our fertilizer orders for next spring. June Hale and most of the Negroes on Edisto haven't paid property taxes for yea's. We might obtain all that Edisto land for the tax money." He started coughing and grabbed his napkin from his lap. He covered his mouth with the white cotton cloth and bent at the waist while the spell intensified. Several patrons around the restaurant noticed his plight and stopped eating.

"You all right, Bubba?" Charles said.

Claude's coughs continued and then ceased with a series of wheezes and whines. He tried, but could not speak. He held up his left hand and pushed the bundled napkin into his face with his right. The fluid in his lungs made bubbling sounds clearly audible to Charles.

Charles sat his fork down and stared across the table at Claude.

Claude wiped his eyes and mouth with his napkin. He said, "Charles, I'm fine." His voice was weak but his scowl strong.

At the front of the restaurant, Queen Esther paused to look back at Claude Crenshaw. When his coughing spell subsided, she turned back to the Baldwins and said, "Captain and Mrs. Baldwin, can I get you anything else?"

"Nothing else for me, my dear," Captain Baldwin replied. "Millicent, how about you?"

She wiped her tiny mouth with a white napkin made from fine Sea Island cotton and smiled past the sides of the triangle of cloth she held to her face. Millicent Baldwin shook her head and said, "Thank you no, Queen Esthe'. The shrimp grits were simply divine this morning. Please tell Uncle Bentley I said so."

"Queen Esther," the Captain said, "at your convenience, please ask him to step out here. I'd like to tell him myself."

Queen Esther smiled and said, "I'll do it now." She turned to walk toward the swinging kitchen doors at the rear of the restaurant, greeting other patrons while moving through the all-white crowd. She promised another customer to return with coffee. Claude Crenshaw made eye contact with her as she walked past his table. She did not smile; neither did he.

At 7:30 p.m., Gillam and Joseph walked eastward along the south side of Broad Street. Gillam said, "Charleston seems to be off to a slow start."

"Papa, dese folks ain't early risers."

A few carriages moved along; a white man stared at them from atop his black saddle horse. They passed a beautiful building with an ornate metal gate.

"Papa, you miss blacksmithing?"

Gillam's brow furrowed. A single nod was his only reply.

"Why didn't you do smithy work in Lucy?"

"Simple. A white man was already doing that trade. It'd a been trouble if I had." He looked at Joseph. "White folks brought us to America to help 'em do things, but now they fight and kill to keep Negro folks from doing much of what we could."

Joseph nodded. "Let's ask somebody directions to where Mauma lives now."

Gillam did not comment. He'd been grumpier than normal the last few days. Twenty-five years of waiting seemed to be eating him up. They met a horse-pulled streetcar filled with men, women and children, black and white, headed west on Broad Street. Gillam looked at the sights, including the large buildings and towering church steeples in the distance.

"Papa, I can't wait to see the look on Mauma's face when we find her."

Gillam remained silent and Joseph chattered on. They crossed Orange Street and looked southward. Gillam gazed ahead and across the street at the front entrance of a large beautiful church. The sign read St. Michael's Episcopal Church. They stopped at the corner and looked up at the white frame building. Its huge steeple tower rose almost two hundred feet into the air. There were large clocks on each of the sides visible to them. The hands showed 9:10.

"Lawd, that's a pretty church," Gillam said.

A song came to their ears. Joseph looked up the block. "Papa," Joseph said, "that's Muley! He'll know where to find Mauma and Cuppie. We grew up at Pine Glen together."

Muley sang, "Charleston, swimps in duh morning makes oona move! I say, Charleston, swimps for dinner gets oona somet'ing smooth. And, swimps, swimps, swimps for de evening meal put oona at ease fuh the night moves. Charleston, yeah Charleston, it's swimps dat makes oona gotta move."

Muley's song warmed the twenty-five year winter in Gillam's heart. Gillam never heard Joseph's last sentence; he had already started toward Muley. They angled across Meeting Street to intercept Muley directly in front of St. Michael's.

Gillam said, "Good morning, I sure like yo' song."

Muley grinned ear to ear. "T'ank you kindly, t'ank you bery much." He stopped his cart on its rear base along the curb and walked around to greet Gillam, but his eyes stuck on Joseph instead.

Joseph's broad smile matched Muley's; Gillam stepped back, grinning. He wanted to witness this reunion and anticipated another he would have soon, very soon.

Muley pointed at Joseph and said, "I know oona. I do. Been a long time, but where I see oona befo'?" He looked at Joseph's neatly trimmed beard. Gray hair was mixed throughout it and into the strands on his head. "You look different now."

"Muley," Joseph said, "we knew one'nuddah as bredduhs when we was boys." His voice took on a cadence Gillam had not heard in the months they had spent in Lucy. Joseph held his arms open wide. "But, we men today and, Muley, bredduhs we be."

"Joseph, Joseph, my friend! I nebber t'ink me see oona no more!" The two grabbed each other, first by the arms and then in a tight embrace.

Gillam Hale smiled wide. The young men swayed before him and Muley pulled away from Joseph to look at Gillam, then back at his long-lost friend.

"Joseph, boy, oona found him! Like oona always said! Dis man yo' papa; dis—" He nodded. "—dis Gillam Hale." Muley released Joseph and grabbed Gillam in a locked hug. Laughter and back-slapping filled the street. Gillam and Muley swayed and Joseph stepped to their sides with his hands on each man's shoulder. They pulled away and the threesome laughed aloud.

Each placed his hands on a shoulder of the other two, forming a triangle. Their noise attracted the stares of passersby, black and white, young and old, walking and on horseback. Even the passengers of a passing streetcar noticed the glee of the three Negroes. Charleston came alive the moment they met.

A woman drove an ox-drawn cart toward them. Muley whispered, "Mistuh Gillam, dat Miss Grozalia Geechee. She a root doctor. I only say good morning, Miss Grozalia, ask how she doing, and keep on pushing my cart."

Joseph said, "Muley, boy you still crazy. You ought to quit speaking 'bout her like dat."

Joseph and Gillam laughed, but they looked serious when Miss Grozalia's cart reached them.

She nodded a greeting and Muley removed his hat. "Good morning, Miss Grozalia. How do today, ma'am?" His voice was laced with fear. She pulled her ox to a halt and bobbed her head up and down.

Joseph said, "Good morning, Miss Grozalia, how do?"

She eyed Muley and Gillam, then stared at Joseph. She spit from the cart into the middle of the street. "Boy, mek me know where I see'd oona befo'?"

Joseph said, "Miss Grozalia, it's Joseph Hale, Queen Esther's boy."

"Lawd have mercy! Boy, oona all growed up with gray hair on yo' head and hair on yo' face. Joseph, I'd a never knowed dat was oona."

Gillam Hale cleared his throat and took a deep breath. "Miss Grozalia, how do? My name Gillam Hale." He asked her the question on his mind for twenty-five years. "Where is she, ma'am? Where's my Queen Esther?"

9

CLOSE QUARTERS

Breakfast was served at Queen Esther's only on Friday and Saturday. This Friday the thirty white folks crammed into her tiny dining room had arrived hungry, and the food was cooking and smelling good. Miss Queen Esther moved from table to table serving hot Charleston tea. She smiled at her customers and the folks of color moved with a quickness to feed each white customer of the segregated establishment whatever they wanted.

In the restaurant's back kitchen, the aroma of the butter mixed with the other foods at various preparation stages—bacon, eggs, pork sausage, shrimp and grits, coffee, a fine English variety of tea, smoked and fresh salmon and beefsteak.

March and Dora Crenshaw were usually not needed to handle that meal. The two young adults entered the restaurant kitchen and walked into a tempest fueled by the restaurant's reputation and a recent Charleston economic upswing.

"Hey, Uncle Bentley," Dora said.

Uncle Bentley raised his girth from the open oven of the

large wood-burning cookstove. He turned to look at her and removed his hat, revealing a bald head with only a band of closely cropped hair on the sides and back of his head. He pulled his spectacles from his eyes and smiled at Dora the way he had since the first time he'd laid eyes on her, moments after her birth. "Hey, baby. U'm glad to see you. We got a big crowd today."

She walked over and kissed him on one of his heavy cheeks. "Is Cuppie in serving with Mauma?"

Uncle Bentley said, "Yeah, she out dere. Me, Cuppie, and Queen Esther been hopping all morning." He looked past her and smiled at March. "Hey, March," Uncle Bentley said.

The young man's brow joined in the middle. He returned Uncle Bentley's smile with a scowl. March nodded and leaned on the cupboard centered between the rear entrance and the swinging door to the dining hall.

Cuppie stepped inside the kitchen from the dining room. She paused for a moment and unfolded a letter. She read a few lines before folding it again and putting it into her apron pocket. She was a pretty, dark-skinned woman, just over thirty. Short and heavy, she had an enviable hour-glass figure.

Dora said, "Hey, Miss Geechee, good morning. How're you today?"

"Dora, I'm doing mighty fine."

Dora said, "You still reading the latest letter from Joseph?"

Cuppie grinned and deep dimples appeared in her cheeks.

As usual, a bandana covered Cuppie's head, but underneath her jet-black hair was as long and straight as any white woman's, a result of her paternal ancestry mixing with the remnants of the few Native Americans left on the Sea Islands. Long hair on a Negro woman made her especially desirable among male suitors, black and white. Cuppie hid her lengthy locks until the day Joseph returned.

Over his shoulder, Uncle Bentley said, "Got some biscuits almost ready." He brushed butter on the tops of his golden-brown creations. He removed the bread from a large pan, blackened from use, and placed them into four straw Gullah baskets. The biscuits, nestled in the white linen napkins lining the dark-brown and light-tan baskets of pine straw, bullrush and sweet grass combined to paint a stunning picture.

"Cuppie, get dese out," Uncle Bentley said. He handed two of the four baskets to her.

Cuppie said, "Dora, take these to yo' Daddy's table and to the Baldwins." She handed the baskets to the young woman who exited through the swinging door.

Dora turned and walked past March with a nod and a smile. Uncle Bentley shifted to making an omelet by pouring two already scrambled eggs into a small copper skillet that was oiled, hot and ready. His large hands flew from bowl to bowl, adding ingredients atop the sizzling mixture.

"March," Uncle Bentley said, "get me some mo' wood."

March did not budge.

At first, Uncle Bentley continued his work. He stopped cooking and turned around when March did not move.

He walked to the young man and put his arm around March's shoulders.

He said, "Boy, don't let dis frustrate oona. 'Member what oona is and dis how we libin'. Never forget dat it gonna be all right and oona gonna be duh high buckruh in yo' dreams." Childless and always gentle Uncle Bentley whispered, "Get us dat wood."

March nodded, smiled, and moved out the back door. Uncle Bentley walked back to his skillet. He pulled a bottle from his apron pocket, opened the top, and added two drops of a milky liquid to the food. He smiled wide and recapped the bottle. The grease sizzled when Uncle Bentley folded the omelet by shaking the small pan.

He whispered, "A couple of drops of sea rose tea with a little croton oil's jus' what he gettin' fuh how he treat his son and daa'tuh."

Cuppie entered the room and walked over to the chef. "Uncle Bentley, Mr. Claude calling for his omelet."

"Dis it," he said and slid the hot food onto a plate. He handed the steaming golden-brown omelet to Cuppie. "Make sho' oona gib it jus' tuh him." He looked over his glasses at her. "Hear me now, gal?"

Cuppie's smile widened. "Yessuh, I do."

Queen Esther entered the room. "Uncle Bentley, that English tea ready?"

"Yeah, baby," he said. "Right ober dere on the divan." He nodded to the large white porcelain teapot with a curved spout of English design, adorned by two Rhode Island red roosters in a cockfight, typical for South Carolina lore.

Queen Esther moved past Cuppie, touching the young woman gently when she did. They exchanged smiles. Queen Esther picked up the teapot, kissed Uncle Bentley on the cheek, and headed back to the dining room just after Dora reentered the kitchen. March opened the door to the room and stepped inside with an armload of wood. Cuppie sped past March and Dora. She stepped into the dining room. Queen Esther stood to the left of the door with her back toward the crowd and the restaurant front tending to the tea.

Cuppie walked over to a table in the middle of the restaurant where Claude and Charles Crenshaw sat. She said, "Mr. Claude, here's yo' omelet."

Greetings for the star of the show filled the room when Uncle Bentley, the engine of the enterprise, eased his girth through the crowd toward the front. He watched Claude Crenshaw cut into his omelet with a fork, blow on it, and wolf down his first bite.

Claude Crenshaw said, "Uncle Bentley, this is just what I ordered."

Uncle Bentley smiled and when the white man looked away, he said under his breath, "And jus' what you deserve."

Miss Grozalia eyed Gillam, then looked at Joseph. "Mistuh Gillam, Queen Esther'd hear ya if oona holla'ed. Huh place down de block on Broad, just past this chu'ch." She thumbed her right hand at St. Michael's grand white building.

Gillam walked up Meeting Street and, in a few seconds,

turned to his right to move down Broad in a rush. Joseph hesitated before following his father. Muley turned back toward his cart. He grabbed the handles and said, "Joseph!"

Joseph looked back at Muley.

Muley said, "Mr. Claude Crenshaw's in dere for breakfast. You tol' yo' papa 'bout that?"

Joseph didn't answer. Instead, he ran behind his father toward Queen Esther's.

10

SWEET HONEY WITH BITTER TEA

Uncle Bentley said, "Miss Millicent, Captain Baldwin, how you dis fine morning?"

"Bentley, my dear sir!" Captain Baldwin said. "Thank you for your work on our behalf today. The food was exquisite, indeed. Wasn't it, dear?" Captain Baldwin placed a few coins in the man's hand.

Miss Millicent forked the last perfect spoonful of shrimp grits and brown gravy with a tiny piece of cured bacon into her tiny mouth. Her smile widened and she laid her utensil on the small table. She raised her napkin to wipe her lips. She jerked after a Negro man appeared in the window next to her table.

He had dark-brown skin and was of average height, older and thin. He wore brown pants, a soiled white shirt, and a worn dark-gray dress coat. He peered in the window and removed his hat. Uncle Bentley, Miss Millicent and Captain Baldwin heard someone say, "Wait, Papa!" The man moved to the restaurant door behind Captain Baldwin's chair and opened it just as a younger male Negro appeared in the window.

Miss Millicent jumped when the second man appeared. The first one opened the door and stepped inside the restaurant.

Uncle Bentley stood still. Captain Baldwin turned in his chair with his back to the window and pushed his wire-framed glasses onto the bridge of his nose. The younger black man stepped into the doorway behind the elder. Every voice in the restaurant ceased. A few forks clanged onto the plates. The two Negroes scanned the room before the older moved through the crowd toward the back and the younger one followed.

Captain Baldwin turned to his wife. "My God, Millicent," he said, "that's Gillam Hale! Bentley, that's Joseph with him."

Claude Crenshaw's eyebrows met when the men walked past. He never stopped chewing his food, in fact, he placed a new bite in his mouth.

The older Negro walked to within three feet of the old china cabinet where Queen Esther stood with her back toward the front of the room. Total silence descended on the full dining room. Gillam examined every lock on her head and how she filled her tan-and-brown dress. She looked the same as she always had.

"Queen Esther," Gillam Hale said. He spoke her name loud and clear.

She turned around. Queen Esther held the rooster-adorned teapot in her right hand; local-area honey harvested this season was in a clear vase in her left. She looked at the man standing before her and the hot tea and honey crashed to the floor, the liquids splashed all over her long skirt. The odors of tea and honey blended with the other smells in the tiny room. Murmurs from the patrons filled the air.

Every person in the room heard her say, "Gillam."

Joseph stepped to his father's side. He looked in his mother's face. "Mauma," he said, "I found him. Tol' you I'd do it. I brought Papa."

The door from the kitchen swung open. Cuppie, with Dora and March on her heels, stepped into the room. Cuppie looked at the mess. White china, clear glass, honey and tea were all over the floor. Her eyes stopped on the feet of the two men. When her vision rose to their faces, she screamed! "Joseph! Joseph! Joseph Hale!" Cuppie rushed into his arms and grabbed her long-lost sweetheart. Her whimpers and cries mixed with noisy voices from all over the room.

Gillam Hale stepped toward Queen Esther, just as Dora and March did. The broken glass crunched under the feet of the three. Gillam looked at Queen Esther. He then stared at Dora and March. Dora was clearly Queen Esther's daughter and obviously biracial.

Gillam turned his head and looked into Joseph's face. His silent son shrugged, despite the now-screaming and wiggling Cuppie hanging off his neck. Claude Crenshaw stepped to Gillam's side, between Gillam and Queen Esther. He was still chewing his breakfast. He glowered at the two Negro men.

Queen Esther said, "Mr. Claude, this is my hus—" The word froze in her throat. She tried again. "This is Joseph's father, Gillam. And you remember Joseph."

Gillam rocked back on his heels. He looked into the white man's face and then back at March. Other than March's kinky hair and thicker lips, his facial features showed he was Claude Crenshaw's boy.

Gillam looked into Joseph's face and the only sounds in the room were Cuppie's moans and the footsteps of Uncle Bentley and Captain Baldwin. The two men squeezed in amongst the tables just behind Joseph and Gillam.

A frown crossed Claude's reddened face. He opened his mouth to speak, but Captain Baldwin caught his eye and shook his head. Claude then jerked involuntarily and covered his mouth. He moved toward the front door, ripped it open and ran outside. The crowd gasped when all heard Claude retching out front on Broad Street.

Uncle Bentley laughed aloud. "Gillam Hale," he said. "Welcome to Charleston and the Low Country!"

Muley peeped through the window at the proceedings from outside. He looked back at a kneeling Claude Crenshaw and his breakfast, now in the gutter behind Muley's cart.

"Marse Claude," in private Muley sometimes broke the unwritten code to not call a white man by the old master term. "If a ain't know'd better, I'd b'lieve somebody done put their mouth on you." Muley nodded over and over. "Uh-huh, that sho' what a t'ink. You been fixed good for sho'!"

A cow mooed and then snorted. It was Miss Grozalia's ox, Rosebud, pulling her high-wheeled cart past Queen

Esther's. She pulled the beast to a stop. Claude yanked out a large white handkerchief and wiped his face. He opened his eyes to look up at Miss Grozalia. She moved her eyes to him, away from the palmetto rose she crafted in her lap.

"Morning, Grozalia!" Claude said.

She smiled down at him. "Claude Crenshaw, bent knees straighten crooked deeds!" she said to the man who had inherited her and all of the Crenshaw holdings when his father had killed himself in 1858. Her crooked right index finger pointed directly at her former master.

Miss Grozalia smiled at him. She said, "Some day soon oona gone hea' what I say." She nodded several times and popped the reins across Rosebud's back.

A sweaty Claude Crenshaw lurched to his feet and stumbled over to his horse, as if nothing had occurred. He removed the reins from the hitching post and walked to the animal's left side, grabbed a handful of its mane, put his foot in the stirrup and raised himself into the large military-style saddle by its horn. His horse backed away, the animal turned westward and Claude rode toward his office at Ashley River Fertilizer on the Charleston Neck. He rose in the stirrups several times to adjust his seat and groin in the saddle while he moved away.

Muley said, "Dat Miss Grozalia done fixed him jus' like she done his daddy."

11

SHE-CRAB SOUP

"Morning, gentlemen, me name's John. 'Round here they calls me Gullah John. How do dis day?"

Gillam said, "Morning. We mighty fine."

Joseph did not speak; his eyes found the grayish-pink tabby oven that sat in back of the wooden porch.

Gillam said, "What's in your sack and crate?"

Gullah John waved his hand in a sweeping move toward his body. "Come, sir. You must see dis befo' oona hear."

Gillam stood from the small table on the piazza where Uncle Bentley had fed them a fine breakfast at Queen Esther's, but Joseph did not budge. He stretched as he moved down the two steps to the ground where the man stood.

Gullah John laughed and gave a smile peppered with brown stains. His right upper front tooth was missing. Gillam's brow furrowed. He looked back at Joseph, who now studied his empty plate. He moved closer to Gullah John. Gullah John opened his burlap sack and Gillam peered inside.

Gullah John said, "Gonna be she-crab soup for lunch and the evening meal!"

Gillam looked up at Gullah John, a tall man of six foot two. He was lanky and light-brown-skinned. He had large ears and a big white man's nose—that facial feature, along with his nappy, reddish-brown hair and freckles spoke volumes about his ancestry. His unshaven beard did not grow on the sides of his face, covering only the area beneath his chin. His mustache was wiry, untrimmed and sparse across his narrow face and above his thick upper lip.

Gullah John said, "There's three dozen blue crabs in dere." He shook the bag to show Gillam the writhing mass inside. "There's two males for each female. That just right for she-crab soup. Eh?"

Word traveled fast in Charleston.

"Uncle Bentley'll add de she-crab roe to duh soup—that makes it rich and better for oona! Heh?"

His voice held the Cajun mixture and cadence of a person from the Caribbean. He threw his head back and laughed. Gullah John removed his hat and used it to strike his right leg. A little dust flew from tattered gray pants that ended at his shins, showing his cracked, unfinished high-top leather shoes. His thick brown hair matted to his skull in the shape of his old hat.

The rear door opened and Queen Esther stepped outside. A large round Gullah basket hung from her right arm by its broad handle.

"Cuppie, Uncle Bentley, Gullah John's here with the

crabs for the soup." Cuppie and Uncle Bentley stepped to the door.

"Morning, Mother-in-law," Gullah John said.

Joseph and Gillam gazed at Queen Esther and then at Gullah John.

Queen Esther ignored Gullah John. She said, "Uncle Bentley, I'm headed to the market for those other items we need to prepare the chicken sandwiches for tonight." She walked past Joseph and from the porch. Joseph's eyes followed her down the steps.

"Gillam," Queen Esther said without facing him as she walked past, "you want a walk with me to the market?"

He stood still, provided a stoic nod.

"Good morning, Gullah John." Queen Esther pointed at Joseph. "You remember my son Joseph. He left Charleston as a boy just before the end of the war."

"Joseph, boy, dat you? You ain't said a word," Gullah John said. "Hab you now?"

Joseph raised his eyes from his empty plate to glance at Gullah John. He shook his head, but did not speak.

Gillam shuffled over to stand next to Queen Esther. It was the closest he had been to her in twenty-five years. His nostrils flared while he took in her smell and he looked at her. She was just a bit heavier, no more than one hundred and forty pounds. A few lines were in the corners of her eyes and across her forehead. Otherwise, the years had not changed her features.

"And," Queen Esther said, "this's his father…"

Gullah John said, "Man, June done tol' me all 'bout her

life wit' oona, her mama and brudduhs. Dis man's Mistuh Gillam Hale."

Gullah John, Gillam and Queen Esther exchanged stares. Gullah John picked up the burlap bag and shook the opening of his sack of crabs. "One female for two males...roe for yo' soup make it rich, heh?" He smiled and chuckled.

A scowl crossed Queen Esther's face; she handed Gullah John a few coins. He received them in his opened right palm, shuffled the silver with his thumb, counted it and nodded.

Gillam put his hat on his head and glared at John before following Queen Esther onto Broad Street. Gullah John and Joseph watched them move out of sight and walk eastward on Broad Street.

PART TWO—

CHERISHED PEARL IN AN EASTERN OYSTER

12

GOOSE AND GANDER

Marjorie Crenshaw stood and pulled the blue dress over her shoulders on each side. She looked into the mirror on the black mahogany armoire. She admired her emerald-green eyes and pink, pouty lips.

Except for her husband's, she won the beauty pageants all men waged in their visually oriented minds when they met her. Claude Crenshaw's otherwise sharp eyes had grown more blind to her glowing beauty each day. Where Marjorie was concerned, Claude could not see. As so many gentlemen of his social class did, he had placed his betrothed on an unreachable pedestal before their wedding night and, for him, there she remained.

"Miss Marjorie," Esmerelda said, "why you wearing dis pretty party dress to duh market?" She began the task of fastening the long row of buttons down the back of the dress by moving Marjorie's wavy auburn hair aside.

Marjorie Crenshaw looked in the full-length mirror again. The blue dress with its puffed sleeves and full-skirted bottom was stunning on her. She smiled at her maid. "Esmerelda, I wanted to be pretty today."

"Miss Marjorie, you good-lookin' all de time, no matter what you wearing or what you ain't!"

Marjorie's skin held a slight natural tan. Her lips and cheeks required no lipstick or rouge—they were a natural light-pink. Marjorie wore her hair in a tight ball during the day, the way Esmerelda would style it at any moment. But, at night, when she let it down, it reached her waist. Even at fifty-nine years old, she had not yet grayed and her face did not have many lines. She looked the way a Frenchwoman should, but her sound and manners were Southern—Charleston on-peninsula through and true.

Esmerelda completed closing the back of the dress and Marjorie Crenshaw turned around and sat in a chair next to the armoire. Esmerelda eased down on a stool she had retrieved from near the bed and lifted Marjorie's dress to reveal black stockings held up by garters just above the knee. Marjorie Crenshaw was a small woman, petite in most ways, one hundred and ten pounds of curves on a small five-foot-two-inch frame. Her hands and feet were tiny. But her real jewels were the legs she had danced on since her days at Charleston's French finishing school for the daughters of wealthy planters. Esmerelda slipped a fashionable black high-top on Marjorie's right foot. She pulled the strings snug and began to weave them over the hooks of the shoe.

Marjorie said, "Esmerelda, it seems Queen Esther's long-lost husband has come to Charleston."

"Miss Marjorie, where you hear dat?" Esmerelda's eyes bulged.

"Millicent Baldwin rang me on the telephone earlier.

She wanted to prepare me and not let the gossips catch me unawares."

"Dat Miz Baldwin and Captain Baldwin's duh nicest people anywheres."

Marjorie smiled and raised her other foot for Esmerelda to repeat the process.

Esmerelda said, "I ain't gone nebber understand white men."

Miss Marjorie said, "What you mean?"

"Yo' husband pay no 'tention to you and runs after Queen Esther like the sun hide up her skirts in the ebening."

"Well, that's where the stray dog wants to lay."

"He might lay wit' her, but he ain't doing not'ing but spending money and time ober ther'."

"Esmerelda," Miss Marjorie laughed as she spoke, "how would you know that?"

"I know 'cause that's what I heard."

"What?"

"Just leave it at dat and trust me." Esmerelda raised her right hand and said, "Mr. Claude might wanna, but he can't. He ain't doing not'ing ober ther' wit' Miss Queen Esther!" Esmerelda reared back. "Besides, look at you, Miss Marjorie." Esmerelda waved her hands at the sculptured leg attached to the shoe-covered foot she laced. "You the prettiest goose in the Low Country! And Mistuh Claude better pay you some 'tention 'cause, 'cause what's good for the gander is for the goose, too." She finished the shoe and placed Marjorie's foot on the floor, covering the beauty beneath her clothes.

Marjorie Crenshaw stood up. She turned to walk away.

Esmerelda said, "Miss Marjorie, you know dat young wife Congressman Sneed done brought wit' him dis time?"

Marjorie stopped and nodded her head.

"Now, Miss Marjorie, don't you ask me how I knows."

Marjorie said, "That's fine Esmerelda." She looked at the clock and calculated her appointment. "Just tell me."

"Dat gal got colored blood!" The revelation gushed from Esmerelda's lips, birthed like a child born of long hard labor and an illicit union.

Marjorie turned back to her servant. Esmerelda had been with her since Marjorie was a new bride at Pine Glen. She said nothing for a while before opening her mouth to speak.

Esmerelda stood and placed her fingers to her mistress's lips. "Ain't I always tol' you straight and true?"

Marjorie nodded.

"Oona hear me now. T'ain't much, but some Negro in dat new gal."

Marjorie said, "He sure is crazy for her. She gets anything she wants."

Esmerelda's face twisted and then she smiled. "Dat tell oona somet'ing right dere! Miss Marjorie, look like they can't help it, but dem white men's crazy fuh a near-white colored gal."

Marjorie shook her head. "Well, I've witnessed that."

Esmerelda said, "I thought you'd like tuh know."

"Thank you," Marjorie Crenshaw said and looked into

Esmerelda's eyes. "Have the driver bring the carriage around. I'm ready to leave."

Esmerelda said, "Yessum," over her shoulder after she started downstairs to relay her boss's wishes.

Queen Esther stepped from the alley and onto the sidewalk. Gillam followed, falling in stride next to her.

Gillam said, "Why'd he call you mother-in-law? He married to June?"

Queen Esther shook her head but offered no further explanation. They walked forward on Broad Street.

Gillam said, "Been a lot a years. You all right?"

She looked at him. "I made it." She looked forward again.

"I don't know where to start," Gillam said.

Queen Esther said, "Begin with where you been!" She frowned at him and kept walking. Her pace quickened.

He shrugged, struggled to keep up. "Near Memphis in a town called Lucy."

"I tried to find you after the war," she said. "I wrote the Freedmen's Bureau and the county clerk in Memphis, but never heard back. I heard they sent you there when you was sold."

Gillam looked at her and stopped walking; he started back and caught up to her again. "I wrote to the Freedmen's Bureau in Charleston." He grabbed her arm. They stopped and he turned her to face him. "They sent back word there was no Queen Esther Hale in Charleston."

She stared at him.

"I inquired a bunch of times—there...there was never any word," he whispered.

"Gillam," she said, "most folks 'round here call me Queen Esther Crenshaw."

She pulled away and walked on. He came toward her and glared in her face. "Woman, why you change yo' name? You still my wife! Is that the peckerwood's name?"

"Gillam, he bought me just like you did!" The next words exited her lips like spit. "What was I s'posed to do?" They stared at each other. "It took you twenty-five years to come looking for me!"

He opened his mouth, intending to continue his verbal mayhem. Instead an elaborate building at the end of Broad caught his eye. He froze.

Queen Esther said, "Yes, that's the Exchange Building where they auctioned us off!"

She started across and looked back when she neared the other side of the street to ensure he followed. He moved slower than he had earlier and appeared tired when they reached the other side. She waited for him and looked at him good for the first time. Gillam was much older; he was gray at the temples and looked worn.

Gillam said, "Joseph tol' me 'bout what happened to Benjamin. Where's he buried?" Benjamin was their son who was two years older than Joseph and three younger than June.

"On Sullivan's Island north of here in a slave cemetery. He and June were bought by a horrible old Irishman, Sean Cohan. Benjamin died on his Palmetto Place Plantation in the summer of 1859—" she paused "—on June's birthday. They worked him to death." Queen Esther looked so sad and her big eyes filled with tears. "I didn't know it for two months. Joseph and I were on Edisto Island at the time." Several tears trailed from Queen Esther's eyes. "June hasn't celebrated her birthday since."

They could not look at each other. Tears continued to fall from her eyes. Gillam used the back of his left hand to stay his before they fell.

Queen Esther said, "You still blacksmithing?"

"Naw," he reached under his hat and scratched his head, "they took that, too. I ran into so much trouble from the whites 'bout being a smithy in Lucy 'til I just left it."

"I'm sorry. I know how much you loved it."

They both smiled.

"How did you live all these years?" she said.

"I done this and that."

She smiled. "So, you still making whiskey?"

"Gentlemen don't speak of such things to ladies."

She smiled, shifted her basket to her left hand, and extended her right hand toward him to push his left shoulder. "Plenty of the folks 'round here say I ain't a lady." She smiled at him. "You're a gentleman now?"

He issued the laugh of a boy. "Baby girl," he whispered his next words, "you made me that when you was mine." They walked a few steps more and he said, "It's just good to see you." He touched her shoulder for a brief second—he had wanted to feel her for years, and his fingertips lingered for a moment before his hand dropped again to his side—they walked on for a while without speaking.

He looked at her. "But, Lawd, you still look good," he paused, "for yo' age."

She pushed his shoulder again, feigned a pout, and smiled. He stumbled on purpose.

She said, "You bring up my age when we talking for the first time in twenty-five years." She kept smiling. "Man, you still Gillam Hale."

"Will be 'til the day I die and beyond if the good Lawd allow it."

"You got any plans?" she asked.

He shook his head. "Scared to make any. That might wake me up—could be dreaming."

She offered no reply, just pinched his arm, and they moved along in silence again. Her physical touch stirred memories. Gillam smiled and said, "That's how you used to do our children when they acted up in them balcony church pews at Emanuel back home."

"Why didn't you go back to Cumberland after the war?" she asked.

He stopped to look ahead and up at St. Philip's Church. He said, "That church building shaped like a cross, look at how tall it is." The sanctuary's brown-and-tan tower was even higher than the one at St. Michael's. The building protruded into Church Street, which curved in a flat semi-circle around the building front—the early Charlestonians copied the design from England, just as they did many of their habits.

Gargoyle-topped parapets guarded the red roof of the Huguenot Church. Gillam stood directly in front of the heavy wooden doors of the only remaining Huguenot French Calvinists church in Charleston.

Gillam finally replied to her question. "Cumberland wasn't home. You wasn't there. Someone wired me that Gilbert and my papa and momma was dead...so why would I go all the way up there to get killed or something?"

She said, "You came for me the first time I was a slave, Gillam. You took me away." She cried again and took a handkerchief with pink and white flowers from her purse. Her right hand hit her palm with every word. "I kept hoping you'd come after the war! But, but—" she paused "—you never did." She wiped her eyes and blew her nose.

"Queen Esther, baby girl," he whispered, "I didn't know where you was. U'm old now and ain't much count. But, I came here soon as Joseph told me you were here."

A horse-drawn fire engine rushed past, headed south. Its blaring siren and clanging brass bell drowned his voice. Several uniformed men clung atop the wagon in back of the driver. The entire Charleston fire department crew aboard was black, a rarity amidst the area's post-reconstruction Democratic Party domination and the ever-tightening Southern segregation laws.

Gillam watched them roar past and Queen Esther walked several steps ahead. He moved to catch her and alternated between examining Queen Esther and looking back at the two impressive church buildings across Church Street and the multistory business and residential locations on their side of the block.

Queen Esther said, "The first African slaves were

brought to this area in the late seventeenth century. They were like us, kidnap victims, forced laborers. They brought skills, culture, tenacity and endurance. They became an important part of everything that is Charleston and the Low Country during the two hundred years since their arrival."

"This sho a beautiful place," Gillam said.

"Yes," Queen Esther said. She stopped and turned to look at him. "For it to be so treacherous. They had curfews for blacks so many times over the years. Just after the war, there were killings by both blacks and whites. Lately, white men have killed colored people with no repercussions."

Gillam shook his head. He said, "It's been the same in Memphis during the struggle for Negroes to have a better life." They walked on and he said, "Why don't they paint some of these buildings and houses?"

"They too broke to paint," Queen Esther said. "Most of these folks 'round this town haven't had any money since before their glorious war."

"Then they better whitewash these bare boards."

"Charleston covering wood with lime in water? Man, a blueblooded Charlestonian's too proud for that."

They both laughed. It was just like it used to be, except for twenty-five years and a great deal of living.

Queen Esther said, "Gillam, who was she?"

He turned to look at her and they walked ahead together, slower than before. He smiled. "Who you mean?"

"Gillam Hale! You never been without a woman. Now who was she?"

Gillam stepped from the curb and walked into the street. He looked back and smirked. "You jealous?"

She did not answer, but returned his smile.

Gillam waved to a man heading in the opposite direction on Church Street. He was riding a big bay horse at least seventeen hands tall with a black mane and tail and four white stocking feet.

"Whoa, whoa," Gillam said to the rider.

A smartly dressed white man pulled his horse to a stop. "Good morning," the rider tipped his hat to Queen Esther and to Gillam. "How can I be of service to you?"

"Well, sir," Gillam said. "Really, I want to be of a help to you. I been watching you ride toward me. The gait of yo' animal is off in his right front. I b'lieve he 'bout to throw that shoe."

The man stepped down from the animal and walked around to face Gillam. He said, "Have we met?"

Gillam said, "I don't believe so." He paused and looked back at Queen Esther. "Can I take a look at your horse?" Gillam asked.

"I'd be most appreciative if you would." They walked to the edge of the street. The white man pulled his horse behind him.

Gillam moved over to the animal. He touched the horse's neck. "Whoa, big boy," he whispered. "Let's see what wrong with you." Gillam bent down and touched the back of the animal's right front leg. The horse raised it. Gillam grasped and straddled the appendage. He raised it to look at the metal shoe at the bottom of the animal's hoof. "Thought so," Gillam said. He placed the foot on the cobblestone street and turned back to the man to look him directly in his eyes. "Mistuh, that shoe's missing two nails. It's 'bout to wear out. You ought to get that see'd to befo' riding him anywheres else."

The man said, "Queen Esthe', you know this man?"

"Yes, your honor. You remember my daughter June?"

The white man said, "Yes, I just spoke to her. She's right up the street there in her favorite spot at the market sheds."

Gillam looked into the distance past St. Philip's Church.

Queen Esther said, "Mr. Mayor, this is June's father, Gillam Hale. Gillam, this is Captain William Courtenay, the mayor of Charleston."

"Gillam Hale," the mayor said. "I take it you are a smithy mechanic," referring to the blacksmithing trade. He examined Gillam from head to toe, as he had when Gillam was sold at auction in July 1858.

Gillam removed his hat. "I used to be a blacksmith, but I ain't done it in years."

"Is that so?" Mayor Courtenay said. He looked at Queen Esther. "Queen Esthe', was he any good?"

"He was the very, very best!" She smiled, then covered her mouth and her now slightly browned teeth—the way she had as a young girl when Gillam had first bought her in the Virginia countryside near Cumberland, Maryland. "His papa was a free man of color and taught him."

"Is that a fact?" Mayor Courtenay said. "Gillam, you got anywhere to ply your trade?"

"Naw, sir," Gillam replied.

"Where you living?" the mayor asked.

Gillam shrugged and a look of uncertainty crossed his face. "I just got to town this morning." He glanced at Queen Esther. "I ain't made no arrangements."

William Courtenay never forgot a thing. Ever-polite Charlestonians like Mr. Courtenay never spoke of their days of dealing in human capital—they acted as if it had never existed. But, Mayor Courtenay had once considered buying Gillam, as had every white man and a few of the Charleston Negro brown elite that were present at that sale.

The Mayor's whisper was barely audible. In a rare confession he said, "I was there," he paused, "at the auction." He lowered his head, shame crossed his face. He and Gillam looked away. The white man grimaced as if he remembered the cries of each adult and child in the Hale clan. He handed the reins to Gillam.

"His name's Mover. Take him to Holley's Stables just north of the market sheds. Queen Esther, show him the way." The distinctive tones of elite Charleston speech dripped from his every word. "Tell 'em William Courtenay said to hold him for ya." He flipped a silver dollar to Gillam who moved his left hand to catch it in his palm.

Mayor Courtenay said, "Come see me this afternoon 'round three o'clock at City Hall. I got an idea 'bout you, Gillam."

His carefully selected and even more meticulously spoken words caressed the surfaces of everything nearby on Church Street. The next ones rang like music in Gillam's ears.

"I think we can get you to make fires that heat iron

again. Charleston can always use another good blacksmith." He looked at Queen Esther. "Queen Esthe', count me in for breakfast tomorrow. Tell Uncle Bentley I want country ham with brown gravy, biscuits and, of course, shrimp grits!" He stepped closer to the black man. "You still make sippin' whiskey as good as you used to?"

Gillam's shoulders slumped. He shrugged, but he did not reply.

Mayor Courtenay said, "Gillam Hale, see you at three o'clock." Mayor William Courtenay continued on his way.

Gillam put his hat on his head. He looked into her fire-brown eyes. He said, "Baby girl, I've come for you, now."

She looked away and changed the subject. "The mayor ruined my surprise. Let's go see yo' girl June." Queen Esther pointed past St. Philip's Church. "She's up there in that market crowd."

Gillam looked at Queen Esther. "You hear anything from Jerome?"

"No, the whereabouts of our oldest son's still a complete mystery—tried, tried to find him to no avail. Just like wit' you, 'til today."

Gillam pursed his lips, dropped his head and pulled Mover forward by the reins. Queen Esther stepped onto the cobblestoned surface of Church Street and they walked side-by-side toward the Charleston market sheds.

Cuppie turned and kissed Joseph as soon as the solid wood stairwell door closed behind them. He pulled back against the wall and she followed.

"Cuppie," he whispered in a raspy voice. "Why Gullah John call Mauma mother-in-law?"

She clung to him and pressed everything she had into him. "He got a boy by yo' sister June. But, he ain't married her." Cuppie stepped away and climbed the tight stairs of the dependency. She pulled Joseph along.

He said, "Where's June?"

Cuppie stopped walking and looked back at him. She said, "I'll tell you all 'bout it later." She gathered her full skirt with her left hand. That motion pulled it tight against her buttocks, which Joseph looked at when he followed Cuppie up the remaining steps. They moved into the bedroom on the right side of the loft that she, Queen Esther and Dora shared.

Joseph breathed heavily from the exertion and what she had shown him during their climb. She took him to the far side of the room, to her cot. Cuppie sat on the small bed and pulled him down beside her. The cords that supported the feather-tick mattress groaned under their combined weight and they kissed again.

Joseph pulled away a little and said, "Wait, Cuppie, wait. Why'd June have a boy wit' Gullah John?"

Cuppie said, "Joseph, folks get they babies wit' who they wants to." She gave him a peck on his lips, but lingered a second longer. "I been waiting for yea's...you here and I ain't gonna a wait no mo'." Her words came forth in measured breaths. She kissed him full on the lips again.

"But, Cuppie, let's marry first."

She pulled the white rag from her head and mouthed

"no" at him. Thick black hair fell across and beneath the young woman's shoulders.

A silent denial formed on his lips and he moved his face from side to side. Instead, Joseph touched her locks. "Gal, I laid awake many nights…remembering how pretty you was." He leaned back to take in the view. "You look even better now. You ripe, just like a Arkansas peach in July."

She kissed him again. "Joseph, ain't no man nebber touched me and u'm thirty yea's old." She stared at him. "I always been yo's." They kissed again. She pulled away and stood before him. Cuppie unbuttoned her blouse. "I held all dis fuh oona," she whispered and showed him what she had kept for only him. "Been thinking 'bout oona, about dis, since oona went away." Her words hissed from her mouth in a smooth whisper.

"Cuppie, Cuppie, I…I been really sick. I almost died."

She leaned into him and kissed away his last resistance. "Joseph, you ain't gone be sick no mo'. You," she kissed him again. "You, you, you fixin' to get well."

Cuppie fell into Joseph's arms. At first Joseph held her gently like a ripe succulent fruit he'd stolen on a hot mid-summer evening. Just like then, he gripped this prize tightly after understanding she was his own.

13

CHARLESTON EAGLES

Gillam, Queen Esther and the mayor's horse approached the crowd at South Market Street. Gillam looked ahead and saw two women sitting outside the market shed between South and North Market. Gillam turned to Queen Esther and pointed ahead to the full-figured woman on the far side of the doorway. "June?" he said.

Queen Esther nodded and took the horse's reins from him. "That's yo' little girl," she whispered. "Gillam," she touched his left arm, "sometime June ain't quite at herself. She went through a lot on Sullivan's Island and then a free Negro bought and married June in 1858. They found him beat to death shortly after that in a swamp on Edisto. He left her forty-six acres of land on the south end of the island."

Gillam shook his head and stared at Queen Esther. He wrung his hands and kicked at the cobblestones.

"Go to her," Queen Esther said. "We'll see how she is today."

She tied the horse to a hitching post. Gillam moved through the crowd of people. He avoided a carriage that had stopped to unload and stepped inside the shed. He walked over to where June sat. Gillam peered at this full-grown woman, hoping for a glimpse of his little girl. He ignored the boy sitting next to her, but young August stared at the old man from the moment he had given the horse's reins to Queen Esther.

June never looked up and kept weaving the row on her rounded basket. She finally noticed the old man after August nudged his mother with his elbow.

"June," Gillam whispered.

She looked up at him. June cocked her head to the left side, like when she investigated things while still a precocious young girl.

"June, it's Papa," Gillam said. "It's me."

"Ha-a-a-a-h!" June screamed. "Ahhhhhh! Ahhhhh! Ahhhhh! Papa! Papa! Papa! No, Papa! No! No! No! Papa! No, Papa!"

She scooted back up against the wall and dropped the basket. She clutched her hands tight against her breasts. She screamed at the top of her lungs as loud as she could. August jumped to his feet and stepped back against the wall of the market shed. A crowd gathered to witness the commotion.

Gillam walked among her wares and dropped to his knees in front of her. "June," he said peacefully.

She stopped shouting and calmed down, like she always had when her Papa Gillam spoke softly.

"It's all right," he said. "I'm here." They exchanged stares and a crowd of blacks and whites gathered.

"Papa, it really you...you ain't a haint?"

He smiled at her. "Everything's gonna be all right. You can't touch a ghost." He reached out with his hand.

June extended her right arm and touched his hand. She held a few of his fingers, then grabbed for his hand after interlocking her fingers into his. It was a ritual she and her father had practiced each time they met. They looked at their intertwined hands and pulled each other forward into an embrace on their knees.

A white man waded into the crowd. "Break it up! Break it up!" he said. His uniform was police blue with three sergeant's stripes. "What's going on here?" He held a reddish colored nightstick in his right hand and popped his left palm with the club.

Gillam and June broke from their embrace as the crowd parted for the policeman. They looked up at him. It was the man from the train in the blue-flannel suit, Sergeant Mueller.

"What's going on here?" the sergeant asked.

Gillam ignored his question and looked past him through the crowd at Queen Esther. He noticed her and a white woman staring at each other.

Marjorie Crenshaw had just stepped from her carriage when June's screams started. She and Queen Esther held each other's gazes.

Marjorie said, "Queen Esther, how do you do?"

"Miss Marjorie, I'm mighty fine," Queen Esther said. She looked at the large Gullah basket hung across Marjorie's left arm. "You fixin' for a picnic?"

Marjorie frowned. She moved around the crowd and into the market shed.

Queen Esther pushed through the crowd. She said, "Sergeant, let me explain. These two have not seen each other in twenty-five years. She was so surprised that she started shouting. That's what the fuss is."

Gillam whispered into June's ear, "Daughter," he said. "Who was that white wench that was talking to yo' mama?"

June wiped her tears. She pulled back to look into Gillam's face before leaning into his shoulder. She whispered, "Papa, dat Miss Marjorie Crenshaw." June glared at her mother, "Mr. Claude Crenshaw's wife. Dat white ooman runnin' 'round wit' Mista Claude's cousin, Congressman Ethan Sneed, from Virginnie."

"Boy, I asked you, not Queen Esther." Sergeant Mueller said, "You better talk to me, boy. You hea'?"

Queen Esther moved closer, but Sergeant Mueller continued to ignore her. A white woman walked from the market shed directly across Church Street. She was short, about five foot one inch, and heavy. Her eyes were sky-blue. True to her Scots-Irish heritage, she had red hair, visible beneath the front and sides of her headwear.

The young white woman said, "Sergeant Mueller, how are you today? What on earth is the matter?" She gathered her full-length black cape with her hands. It parted in the middle near the neckline and just below her waistline to reveal a black dress. A smart hat of the same color, pointed in the front and rear, was atop her head; the mesh netting covered her face down to just about her pug nose.

The policeman went into his best imitation of a Southern gentleman. He removed his hat to reveal a balding forty-something head. He stepped up to the young woman, an instantaneous red blush washing over his face. He bowed low and rose partially to take her right hand, after she slowly offered it to him.

"Why Miss Sophia, it's just wonderful to see you."

Gillam whispered to June again. "Daughter," he said, "who is that?"

June leaned into her father's chest this time, her favorite position with him as a child, but one she had physically outgrown. "Dat Miz Sophia Cohan Smith. Her daddy bought me—he was a nasty old Scots-Irishman." She shuddered and dropped her voice lower. "He lob young colored gals."

Gillam looked at his child; he knew what she and too many young girls had endured.

Miss Sophia said, "Sergeant Miller, is ev'rything all right?"

The Sergeant stared at Gillam, but spoke to Miss Sophia. "I was just asking Queen Esthe' somethin'." He said, "Queen Esthe', why you in this? What's this man to you?"

June whispered, "Some of duh Low Country high buckruhs die young and leave rich widows. Mos' of de folks said it was the climate. Others say it the plantation worries. But, dere were rumors of curses and poisoning from de slaves."

Gillam swallowed hard.

In a soft tone, Miss Sophia said, "Queen Esthe', hon', how're you and who's this with you and our sweet June?"

Queen Esther said, "I'm so glad to see you, Miss Sophia.

I'm fine." She waved her right hand toward Gillam and June. "This is the father of my son Joseph and June."

Gillam's eyes moved from Miss Sophia to the sergeant and back to June, but his look stopped on Queen Esther when she spoke to the policeman again.

Queen Esther's next words rang throughout the nearby streets and into the market shed. "He's Gillam Hale, my husband." A long-lost pride resounded in her voice.

"Well, bless yo' haart," Miss Sophia said. "I still 'member how much fun we all had when Papa and Momma, God rest their souls, used to bring us to the beach at Edingsville out on Edisto to visit Cousin Marjorie and Claude Crenshaw." She threw her hands back and forth and waved a small black handkerchief with her left. "Gillam, welcome to Chawl'stn. I trust you'll enjoy yo' stay here 'bouts." She turned back to Queen Esther. "Honey, I just got back in town from visits in Addlanna and S'vanna', and, I'm thinkin' a leavin' for Paris, France, early next year."

June whispered to Gillam, "Papa, Benjamin was too young to hol' hoe all day in duh sun...I tol' 'em." She paused and moved her head serpentine like. "But, Sean Cohan and his oberseer worked my lil' brother to death chopping Sea Island cotton." She pointed the middle fingers of her hands at Miss Sophia; they protruded in crook-fingered "double-V's". June rotated them counter-clockwise as if placing a spell on the Southern belle. "Papa," the grief still resounded in her voice, after over two decades, "he, he was just ten years old."

Gillam pulled her hand down and looked at her. He started to speak, but June's next whisper cut him off.

June said, "She look old, but jus' barely in huh thirties. Duh men 'round here chase widows with money and land to get rich. They after Miss Sophia like Brer Fox run Brer Rabbit! She ain't got no offsprings and it gonna be interesting to see who win her hand and fortune."

Sergeant Mueller said, "Miss Sophia, when did you arrive back in town?"

June whispered, "They found her husband dead in front of a harlot's house near East Bay on Queen Street." June smiled.

Gillam whispered, "Hush, gal."

June said, "Mos' of duh whites 'round here broke, but her pappy died befo' he throwed his money 'way on duh war. He gib her plenty in his will. Her uncle, Congressman Sneed, run Miss Sophia's affairs!" She leaned into Gillam again while the two whites continued to speak. June said, "Papa, duh colored folks say dey put a hex on old man Cohan when he died just befo' de war began." June dropped her head and smiled, "But, I bleebe him and his wife got poisoned 'cause they treated colored folks like the Debble hissef."

Gillam said, "Shhh, gal!"

Miss Sophia droned on about her recent trips and some items she needed for Palmetto Place on Sullivan's Island.

June whispered, "Miss Sophia crazy for colored men, 'specially March Crenshaw—got it from her mama."

Gillam said, "Stop, hush, little fool!"

June laughed aloud. Gillam tried not to, but just as she

had as a child, his daughter pierced his gruff exterior. He joined in her merriment.

The sergeant turned back to them. With a frown, he said, "What you two laughing at?"

In the antebellum period after the 1822 slave revolt plot, all free Negroes in South Carolina had to have a registered sponsor. After the war, Miss Sophia had unofficially provided the same function for Queen Esther. Today, she did again.

Miss Sophia said, "Now, Sergeant Gunther Mueller, Gillam just got to the peninsula and hasn't seen his chil' in yea's." She grinned at June. "I think y'all ought to be doing an Irish jig. What a wonderful gift, to be together with yo' pappy and mama for the upcoming season." She looked at the white man and batted her eyes. "Sergeant, it just makes me wanna cry my head off." She produced a black handkerchief faster than a magician in a traveling minstrel show. "Why don't you send these other folks away and come help me finish my shopping?"

Sergeant Mueller spoke to the equally mixed black and white crowd that still hovered around them—this hot gossip would make the rounds in close-knit Charleston by nightfall. He said, "All right folks! This show's over. Now move along." He put his nightstick away, placed his hands on his hips, and looked down at Gillam and June. "Boy, didn't I come into town on the train wit' you last evening?"

Gillam stood to his feet. "Yessuh," he said while he helped June up, "we rode in on the same train."

"Charleston's got laws against vagrants loitering 'round

with nothin' to do." The policeman spoke Southern-style with a German accent.

Gillam opened his mouth to reply, but Queen Esther interrupted. "Sergeant Mueller, he's going to shoe Mayor Courtenay's horse for him this evening."

"Is that a fact," the sergeant replied.

Miss Sophia said, "Queen Esthe', y'all enjoy each other. I'll drop in soon to have a meal. You tell Uncle Bentley I want some of his terrapin soup, with plenty of okra. You hea'?"

"Yessum," Queen Esther said.

"Sergeant, come along now." Miss Sophia walked away.

Sergeant Mueller followed. He had business with a rich young Charleston widow.

June reached for the boy and pulled him in front of her. "Papa, dis my boy, August Jerome Hale. He turned thirteen this year."

Gillam said, "I got a grandson?"

June nodded and the boy smiled.

Gillam removed August's felt hat and rubbed the lad's head. Gillam hugged the boy tight into his embrace with June. Gillam whispered, "June, you named him after your brothers and my papa." Gillam spoke of his second son with Queen Esther, August, who was killed after their abduction during the trip to Charleston when he was just sixteen years old. "He jus' like you." His emotions drove him to shake his head side to side. His heart filled with pride.

June said, "When you find out how bad he is, you'll see a lot of my brother August in him, too!"

The grandson smiled up at his grandfather.

Gillam looked at June's face. There was a bruise on the left side of her forehead and her cheek on the same side. June looked into her daddy's eyes. Neither spoke of it.

August said, "Duh oona know me fada?"

Queen Esther moved closer to August. She scowled at him. "Boy, I told you to never use Gullah off the Island."

"Mauma, dat de way we talk!" June said.

Queen Esther said, "This is Charleston! These folks will think we're not intelligent if we speak in Gullah instead of acceptable English."

June said, "Duh white folks put us out dere on duh Sea Islands and left us to raise duh crops while they went to de fine houses dey got all ober. Me tink e talk like e wan!" The words spilled from her mouth in a flash.

Gillam said, "We got too much to be thankful for to be arguing." He looked at June's bruises again and turned back to the boy. "August, I met yo' father, Gullah John, this morning. I know him. I sho do." Gillam reached for the boy, encircled his shoulders, and pulled the lad tight against him. He smiled and touched the sides of the boy's head. Gillam chuckled. "You sure got his ears." Gillam looked at August, his seed. "Boy," he whispered, "you remind me of Gill."

June said, "Papa, is Uncle Gilbert wit' you?" She looked around the market, confusion in her face.

Gillam said, "No, June." His bottom lip quivered. "I'm talking about my boy in Tennessee." He turned his head and looked at Queen Esther. "He's thirteen, like August. His name's Gill." Gillam Hale pulled August into a bear hug.

Queen Esther said, "I'll do my shopping while y'all get acquainted. June, show yo' papa where the stables are so he can deliver the mayor's horse. Gillam, we'll need to get you to City Hall for your appointment with the mayor later today." Queen Esther moved away before Gillam could speak to her again. Gillam, June and August Jerome Hale looked at each other and watched their matriarch disappear into the crowded butcher shed.

14

THE MUSIC OF DISTINGUISHED GENTLEMEN

An early December 1883 meeting gathered men from diverse groupings and dispositions on a Saturday. Like their predecessors, their goals did not always align as they sang from a different hymnal in the same community meeting house.

Holding productive sessions within this group was a challenge, but they tried anyway. With goals that appeared noble, these powerful conductors, with batons in hand, had gathered inside a local seat of power, a concert place called Charleston City Hall, at the powerful corner of Meeting and Broad.

"Ambassador Walker and Bishop Cain are odd bedfellows," Claude Crenshaw said.

The white men with him were Mayor William Courtenay, Captain Baldwin and Congressman Ethan Taylor Sneed of Virginia. No one responded to Claude's baited hook.

"Mr. Mayor," Claude continued, "that ambassador fella, from Liberia, that George Walker, he makes my flesh crawl. He's a slimy sort, but he may be able to help us with some of our Negro problem, especially on Edisto." The room fell silent. Claude said, "Face it, the AME Church wants to send some of their folks back to mother Africa and I want to do all I can to help them folks get home." The men laughed nervously at Claude's candor.

Mayor Courtenay pursed his lips as if to speak, but the politician never said a word.

Claude Crenshaw said, "I'm very concerned about that Bishop Cain. That's a Negro man with too much influence for my comfort. I still remember how he was elected to congress during the Nigger Rule days after the war."

"Those days of Republican rule are over now for South Carolina forever," Congressman Sneed said. "After the voters get that incompetent Robert Smalls out of Washington, this state will never have Negro representation on the national level again."

Captain Baldwin said, "Say what you want, but Captain Robert Smalls commandeered *The Planter* and sailed it right out of Charleston Harbor under the nose of the Confederates. White Southerners curse the memory of his courageous accomplishment, but he is wildly popular and admired among Northern whites and blacks everywhere."

"Sir," Mayor Courtenay said to Congressman Sneed, "it's good to see you again." Neither man wanted to explore the details to determine which Civil War battlefield intertwined their paths. "How long will you be in Charleston?"

"Two more weeks," Congressman Sneed said. "I've

recently married and my wife, Media, and I plan to spend some time here as part of our travels."

"Wonderful, we must get our wives together." Mayor Courtenay said.

"Thank you, sir. Also, could either of you provide assistance for me to hire a girl to watch my wife's two young brothers?"

Claude Crenshaw said, "Cousin, my Marjorie would love to help Mrs. Sneed with that matter. Aren't you staying at the Charleston Hotel?"

Congressman Sneed replied, "Yes, we are, and, as usual, the accommodations rival anything I experience in Washington. Last night there was a Negro band playing after dinner and their skill and polish astounded us."

Mayor Courtenay said, "I hired that same band for a family celebration last year. Their reputation preceded them and, to my surprise, they lived up to it."

"Gentlemen," Captain Baldwin interrupted the white men's move toward festive conversation, "this Liberian Movement affair concerns me deeply. The proposal Ambassador Walker laid out for us sounds more like a reverse slave voyage than colonial revitalization." His voice rang throughout the City Council Chambers. The truth he spoke signaled a refrain none of the others wanted to hear.

The mare's steel shoes clapped a personal but public tune on the granite stones in Charleston's busiest shopping district—each foot hit in a syncopated pattern, occasionally one patted a different cadence that only added to the richness of the tune. Her feet drummed out while she pulled the sightseers along.

"Brother Gilbert, thanks for all you are doing," Bishop Cain said. "Can't tell you how good it is to see you again after all these years."

The man the bishop spoke to turned in the driver's seat. He looked down at the man most called Big Daddy—it was obvious why. Bishop Cain was a robust mulatto who had been instrumental in establishing many of the African Methodist Episcopal Churches in its Sixth Episcopal District, a district that included South Carolina. He was now the bishop in charge of Louisiana and Texas.

"Bishop Cain, it good just to be here with you and Reverend Frazee and 'tend these Conference meetings. U'm happy to serve." He frowned, "Bishop, why you think the mayor was so intent on me visiting this house at 8 Calhoun Street?" Gilbert popped the reins over the back of the bay mare; she stepped a little harder along King Street as they headed northward toward their next stop.

"There's no telling, Brother Gilbert. A powerful white man like that usually does things with a clear purpose in mind. He said that to you in private, real quiet-like. He was so deliberate in speaking it twice that we'll see what tune Mayor Courtenay's playing when we arrive."

Bishop Cain turned to his left to face his seat mate, but ensured his voice carried to Gilbert's ears. Both men were in his choir and he wanted them in on his sermon so they could include his message in their next tunes.

"Reverend Frazee, this is the first time in Charleston for you and Brother Gilbert." He paused and moved his walnut walking stick back and forth in his left hand. It pivoted on the floor of the covered buggy; he unconsciously waved the gold-tipped instrument in time with the horse's steps. "Whites in this country handled the aftermath of the Civil War in the most backward manner."

Reverend Frazee said, "What do you mean?"

Bishop Cain said, "The conquered never decide how the peace is run. The South lost the war, but the Union leadership allowed the South to decide how we would govern the disputed territory."

Gilbert shook his head and Reverend Frazee did, too.

The two men listened to the bishop's every syllable. "King Street's where a good bit of anything money-wise begins and ends in this town. Most of the stores and the buying and selling happen right here." He sat forward. "Most blacks shop in the stores north of Boundary—that's the old name for Calhoun Street. I refuse to refer to the street by that new name since it refers to John C. Calhoun who was from Charleston. He loved money so much that he had a friend read a speech on the floor of the U.S. Senate house defending slavery and states' rights while Calhoun was dying."

"Bishop Cain," Reverend Frazee said, "didn't he die of consumption?"

"Yes he did—glad to see you didn't sleep through your history courses at college." The three laughed and the carriage moved on. The Bishop said, "The colored folks in Charleston call him John C. Kill-houn. Until his death, Calhoun defended slavery and every form of economic-based race hatred in America." The bishop scowled.

"Don't you forget, my brothers, it's 'bout the cash and who gets to have children with the women. With men, it's always money and females."

He popped his stick on the floor board. He shook his head. "Now, you see these crowds on the streets mixed in black and white." Bishop Richard "Big Daddy" Cain eased forward in his seat and made eye contact with his two parishioners. "They live together, work, walk, struggle, eat and even sleep and have children together right here, in Charleston. But, be not deceived, my brothers. This emerald city is one of the most intense hotbeds of Negro and white separatism in the country."

James Frazee smiled. He touched his perfectly trimmed mustache. Gilbert had shaved the young local preacher earlier in the day to ensure his appearance was perfect. The twenty-four-year-old preacher smiled behind his sculpted African lips and rounded cheeks. He asked a question each of the three already knew he could answer.

James said, "Bishop Cain, why is that? Why are they that way here, in Charleston?" James spoke with a ring of the Caribbean sprinkled into a Cajun sound. He was born and raised in New Orleans and knew full well the issues a former slave market city faced.

The bishop laughed and rocked back in his seat. "Boy, your mama sure would be proud."

The young preacher smiled. "I wrote her a few weeks ago that I was coming here."

Bishop Cain released his stick; its silver head caught the noonday December sun that peeked over his shoulders from the south. The bishop raised both hands chest-high, spread his fingers and continued to instruct the Reverend James Frazee, the soon-to-be pastor of Bethel AME Church on Edisto Island and his right-hand man and mentor, Stewart Gilbert Hale.

"The love of money is the root of all evil." He quoted the book of I Timothy. "That's the answer to your question and here in Charleston, like in all places I been, it's 'bout the dollars and how we men sing its praises instead of those of the Lord."

He coughed and his next words escaped his throat in a raspy fashion. "I lived here in Charleston for some years, helped seed churches all 'round the Low Country." His acquired Southern accent resounded when his excitement grew. "I baptized and blessed babies in age and in faith of older years and tried to get the freedmen moved into the fabric of this society.

"But, it's hard for a white man, men like we just left at City Hall, that sold black folks like us just a while ago, to see we should be included as equals in anything they do."

The milling crowds on King Street stopped to notice Bishop Cain and his entourage move through this part of the Charleston shopping district.

Bishop Cain leaned forward again. He said, "Gentlemen, let's say today was twenty-five years ago." He looked into Gilbert's face and then turned to gaze at young Reverend James Frazee. "Pretend, now, we were in the same businesses of the four white men we just left." He looked at each of his comrades. "The Bible might say peradventure that was the case." He smiled and his two pupils laughed aloud—each knew where Bishop Cain was headed. "Let's say we saw some girls in one of the open slave sales outdoors in one of the dozens of businesses that sold Negroes in this town. What if we bought them today, for business purposes of course?"

Gilbert giggled aloud. He looked forward to check their path, but turned again to look into the face of a master story-teller.

Bishop Cain rubbed his bearded chin. "What chance, my brothers—" they exchanged glances—he could not find their eyes this time "—would we have in reaching the beds of our wives this evening if we controlled some young women, let alone a few dozen more in every shape, hue, size and capability in which women of African origin exist?

"That is a slippery slope where no man can stand. Even Abraham fell there when Sarah offered him Hagar, her African maid from Egypt." He paused. "Thomas Jefferson fell. The white and black men in Charleston and anywhere who don't watch themselves and owned or controlled women, slave or free, fell, too."

Reverend Frazee laughed aloud. His shoulders shook the way they had fifteen years earlier when he'd first heard Bishop Cain preach.

Bishop Cain continued. "Now remember. It's some strange situations on Gullah Island, formally called Edisto. The whites and blacks where you're going can be some of the most backward folks you'll ever meet. They're funny about religion, food, haints and a sundry of things. But, remember, the Gullah people you will serve are the salt of the earth—wonderful people!"

He shook his head. "Now, they'll question your religion if you sit on the porch without socks on. And, you better not go to church and not have something to say if they think you are an important person. I've known 'em to run off preachers that wasn't part of the families in the church."

Brother Gilbert said, "Bishop, how's Reverend Frazee gone get past that?"

Bishop Cain said, "Don't worry, this boy has a hedge around him—he just doesn't know it yet." He poked his young pupil and the three men laughed. "Son," he said, "remember. Get your work here accomplished quickly. That includes finding and training a successor."

The young preacher said, "How long did you say I'd have here?"

Bishop Cain said, "Two years here and then you'll be gone." The bishop laughed. "I just can't wait until you in the pulpit this hot summer with the windows open and some of those Edisto gnats and biting flies go up your nose when you start to get your hoop going."

Laughter erupted from the trio. It was going to be an interesting year making music in the Low Country.

Mrs. Media Coleman Sneed, the new wife of Congressman Ethan Taylor Sneed of Morristown Virginia, sat in their Charleston Hotel suite. She was beautiful with dark-auburn hair and a light olive complexion. She was also less than half her husband's age. She sat on an upholstered sofa overlooking Meeting Street below. She held her younger brother, six-year-old Conrad Coleman, on her lap. The young woman struggled with the laces on his brown high-top shoes. This would be the most difficult physical effort she would make on that day. Life for Media had surely changed since she'd left Lucy, Tennessee, for her father's hometown, Morristown, Virginia, five years earlier in 1878.

Her other brother, redheaded thirteen-year-old Raford Coleman III, sat to Media's right in a chair. The door to the suite opened behind her and she turned to see her husband step over the threshold and close the door behind him.

"Hello, Media, my dear," he said and walked across the wide room towards her. He looked past her at Raford.

"Raford—" the Congressman began his most recent struggle of wills with the teen "—I have tol' you not to slouch in your seat. Sit erect like a person of bearing should."

The boy glowered at the Congressman but offered no reply.

Media turned to look at Raford, before looking to her husband again. She said, "Raford Coleman, if you don't do what the Congressman says, I'll tan your hide for the third time today. Is that what you want?" She rolled her pretty dark eyes.

Rafe sat erect and his expression changed for the better. Media turned back to her husband. "Ethan, do you have any plans for later today?"

Her husband stopped behind her, leaned over and placed his hands, his long arms extended at full length, on the sofa on both sides of her. She leaned back. He tried to kiss her on the lips, but Media offered her left cheek instead. The man frowned.

He said, "Yes," and looked at his watch. "I have to head right back out to meet with Congressman Robert Smalls and a Liberian government official at Morris Brown AME Church. Why don't you and the boys get out for a while?" He patted young Conrad on the head and the boy twisted around to face the man. The Congressman tickled the child's tummy and the boy giggled a youthful laugh that grew louder when the man tickled his neck before mussing the youngster's thick brown hair. Congressman Sneed said, "I've hired a carriage for you and the boys. I insist you go out sightseeing."

Media sighed.

"Darlin', I insist." He kissed her cheek again and glared once more at Raford. The boy squirmed to an even more erect position, but the frown on his face remained.

Congressman Sneed said, "I'll be back here by around six-thirty this evening." He leaned down to kiss her neck, but Media moved aside.

"That tickles," she said.

Congressman Sneed exhaled. "Media, I love you, but you have to begin to be more independent and outgoing."

She pursed her lips.

He patted her shoulders and walked around the sofa. "You'll have fun," Ethan Sneed said. "Besides, it'll do the boys good to get out."

Driver Gilbert issued a hissing snicker and looked forward. Their hired horse knew her way around

Charleston and wove through King Street. Even with its crowds of people, horses, buggies and carts there was no need for him to intervene.

"Preacher," Bishop Cain said, "I have provided for you by talking with several other bishops." He spoke slowly and with intent, like the fine Charlestonians he had learned to imitate. "Remember, you'll only be here in this Episcopal district for two years, that's what I have arranged. Get your work here done. Now, James, my boy, u'm asking you again—" he leaned near the younger man "—in front of yo' prayer partner and the Lawd. What you gone do when one of these Sea Island gals offers to help you, an unmarried pastuh of an AME church in the Low Country on Gullah Island, in any way she possibly can?"

"You said that earlier. Where's Gullah Island?" Reverend Frazee said.

"That's what I call Edisto, where the church is sending you. Most of the Negro peoples out there speak the Gullah language. They do it all over the Low Country. Many of the white folks do too, in situations involving work and interactions with blacks." Bishop Cain had learned the culture well during his years of AME field work in the ripe South Carolina crop rows on and off the peninsula.

"Gullah Island," Reverend Frazee said and swallowed hard. His bright eyes widened and he touched both sides of his chin with the fingers of his right hand.

Bishop Cain retrieved his walking stick and shifted it forward like the control on the saw belt at the lumber mill they'd toured on Friday in the Charleston Neck. His head wagged from side to side as he mocked, "Don't change the subject—what's a smart graduate of Wilberforce Unive'sity in Ohio got to say about what those young women are going to ask?"

Reverend James Frazee swallowed again. "Bishop, I know you want me married, and," the twenty-four-year-old preacher smiled, "I believe God does, too." He shrugged and released a sigh. "He just ain't showed her to me yet." He looked at his feet and the floor and then into the distance of King Street. The young preacher's eyes examined the barber shops, offices and stores of every sort imaginable—dry goods, groceries, linens, jewelry and leather items. He gazed into faces in the crowd, young and old, black and white, male and female and a sad look crossed his face. She was still not yet there, though his heart yearned for the harmony only a woman of his own could bring.

Bishop Cain moved his walking stick to his right hand and placed his heavy arm as a shield around the young preacher he had mentored now for ten years. "Brother Gilbert, turn right just ahead onto Boundary Street."

Throughout any day but Sunday, the Christian Sabbath, several blacksmith mechanics chimed out the music of their forebears at shops near where Calhoun intersected East Bay Street. In December 1883 the songs were played by more Negro men than those of other origins. But, at one time, whites of German, English and Scottish descent had made music with their anvils before Charleston market economics, dominated by low-cost slave labor, forced them out of the metal-working trades. Now, Gillam played a tune familiar to his hands, ears and heart.

"August, don't raise and lower that too fast." He spoke of the large bellows in the rear left corner of the shop. This piece of equipment and the greedy fire that it fed with oxygen was the engine of a working blacksmith. Gillam Hale, for the first time in twenty-five years, was doing one of the things his hands craved. He made music on an anvil six days a week. "Joseph, tell your nephew what'll happen if he does."

"August, your grandpapa wants to jab at me for how I used to blow out his fire in my eagerness at the bellows." Joseph finished his sentences with a series of rasping coughs. He bent over in pain as the last few escaped his chest.

Gillam and Joseph found each other's eyes. "That seems like a lifetime ago," Gillam said. "You coughing again."

Joseph said, "I know Papa, but it'll be all right."

Gillam said, "I think it's working with me every day and inhaling this coal smoke."

"A man's got to work for his living."

Gillam said, "Yeah, but we gone find you some work that keeps you here and not south of the daisies. When you going out to Edisto Island for you and Cuppie's wedding?"

Joseph said, "We going December twenty-nine." He smiled at his companions. "But, we here together. You, me and dis runt of a fellow named August Hale."

Thirteen-year-old August smiled wide. He looked so much like his mother, June, but he had those large ears, freckles and big lips of Gullah John. He raised the bellows up and down.

Gillam said, "Now, boy, that the speed we need you to keep. The piece's jus 'bout ready to join 'em together."

The bellows inhaled and exhaled as if it had a life of its own and the greedy flames hissed and crackled. The coal had changed to coke and it now fueled the fire to reach the temperature required to weld the two pieces of metal. He turned two four-foot-long flat metal rods, the corners of a shipping platform from a warehouse at a wharf near the northern end of East Bay. The warehouse manager and several of his workers had delivered five of the large metal racks to the shop for repairs that included welding this corner together, sealing holes in the bottom of the containers, and repairing metal issues of various sorts. The rods were two inches wide and about a quarter inch thick. They glowed red and Gillam knew it was time.

"My dear boys, we near ready to make some music!" He smiled widely at his two apprentices and looked up through the small smoke trail from the fire. "Never thought this'd be." He looked in the blue flames and turned the red-tipped flat rods again. "Didn't think there was no way to find you, Joseph, and," he raised his eyes to August, "boy, I didn't know you'd even come to be."

The three laughed, and Joseph brought up a sore subject again. "Papa, me and Cuppie want you to stand with us at the ceremony. Will you come to the Island for our wedding?"

"Why can't you marry here in the city?"

"Papa, you and me done spoke 'bout this already. Cuppie was born and raised on Edisto. Her mama an' papa still live dere and we getting' married at Bethel African Methodist Episcopal Church."

Gillam grunted, "Huh."

"Besides," Joseph said, "Edisto Island's duh only place I can call home. Can't you see that, Papa? Once you get out dere, you gone fall in love with it."

Gillam's brow furrowed and his eyes squinted. He turned the rods again and conveniently decided they were ready. "Joseph, take this one and we gone move to the anvil at the same time. I want you to hold it just like I showed you before we put 'em in the fire. You ready?"

Joseph gazed at his father, a puzzled look showed on his face. Gillam kept ignoring his request since the wedding date had been set on the day Joseph and Gillam arrived.

Gillam said, "August, stop the bellows when we take the rods away. Don't waste that coal."

The boy nodded.

Gillam said, "Let's move now, Joseph." They transferred the rods to the anvil and the metal tool jig Gillam had constructed just for this job. Gillam's hands belied his age of sixty-three when he clamped the rods horizontally in place; their ends overlapped.

The smithy mechanic grasped his hammer. "Boys," Gillam said with a smile, "let the music begin again."

The metal on metal sang in the December afternoon breeze and another commission was on its way to being earned.

Gillam played this music in his new neighborhood over and over, six days a week. It was the tune that now fed him and his family and was his contribution to Charleston.

Back on King Street, the three men looked ahead when their steed slowed and stopped on her own to allow two women to cross the path of their buggy. Gilbert examined the two females of African descent when they started past the horse. They were pretty and wore tailored clothing, bearing witness to economic blessings. These ladies were not of typical Negro households.

The one farthest away from the mare was the older. She had light-brown skin. Gilbert looked at their faces when they moved just past the horse to the street's edge. The younger lady was biracial, at least a quadroon, no more than one quarter Negro, and appeared to be the daughter of her companion.

Gilbert watched their carriage and dignified gate. "Queen Esther!" he shouted.

The women stepped up to the granite-framed sidewalk. Its cement-like tabby foundation of sea shells, sand, lime and rock crunched beneath their feet. They turned to face Gilbert and gazed up at him. Queen Esther gasped when she looked into his face from underneath the new hat she had just purchased in a King Street shop. She dropped one of her three packages and put her free right hand to the middle of her breast.

Gilbert yanked the buggy wheel brake into a locked position and tied the horse's reins to it on his left. He began his climb from the vehicle's right side. "Queen

Esther Hale!" He turned to the preachers in the back seat. "Reverend Frazee! Remember my older brother Gillam I told you 'bout. That's his wife Queen Esther!" His voice shrilled to a high pitch, several octaves above his usual rich baritone. Gilbert moved to the ground faster than a sixty-year-old should be capable of and scurried to his sister-in-law. They had not seen or heard from each other since the evening of July 9, 1858, one day before the night riders had taken Gillam and his family.

Queen Esther removed her hat when Gilbert reached her and Dora. Gilbert and Queen Esther laughed with glee; her last two packages fell to the ground. They grabbed each other in a tight embrace. Bishop Cain started his climb from the buggy's right side and Reverend Frazee jumped from the left—he reached Gilbert and Queen Esther as her daughter was beginning to retrieve her mother's hatbox from the ground.

The young preacher beat her to it and when he straightened up, his eyes met those of Dora Crenshaw for the first time. She was two inches shorter than his five foot ten. Her two boxes rolled from her hands to the ground. She and the young preacher exchanged stares and smiles.

Gilbert and Queen Esther said, "Thank you, Lord," over and over.

Bishop Cain reached them and looked for a second at the man and woman locked in a swaying embrace, but his gaze moved and lingered on the Reverend James Frazee, soon to be pastor of the Bethel AME Church on Edisto Island.

Bishop Cain whispered, "Thank you, Lord."

His protégé tore his view from Dora for a split second and, as usual, mimicked his mentor. "Thank you, Lord," James Frazee said aloud. He and Dora moved in unison to gather the packages.

Queen Esther and Gilbert cried aloud. Their joy drew a crowd, and white and black gathered around. The male cadets began their Saturday-afternoon activities across the street in the Marion Square parade grounds at the Citadel, the Military School of South Carolina. Their drums and fifes thumped and whistled amidst the roar of cannon and the cadenced sounds of marching feet.

Amidst the joy and excitement, an exuberant Gilbert Hale asked a question that had been on his heart and passed over his lips for twenty-five years. He pulled away from the ghost he happily held in his arms. "Queen Esther," he said loud enough for all to hear above the music. "Where's my brother?"

She leaned in to whisper her answer in his ear. "He and I saw each other for the first time in twenty-five years last month when he and Joseph came to Charleston. He lives and runs a blacksmith shop at 8 Calhoun Street."

Gilbert Hale took his hat from his head and tossed it into the air. "My brother's alive! That's the same address the Mayor recommended we visit."

Bishop Cain said, "How'd Gillam get into that property?"

"Mayor William Courtenay arranged it."

Bishop Cain said, "Is that a fact?"

She nodded. "He met Gillam the day he arrived in town, took an immediate interest in him."

"So Gillam's got a sponsor?" Bishop Cain said.

Queen Esther said, "Yessuh."

Bishop Cain said, "Come along, children. Let's go see Gillam Hale."

15

ORCHESTRATED REUNION

"Get up, hoss!" Gilbert Hale urged. He popped the reins.

"Gilbert," Queen Esther turned to face him and said, "it's that white one with the red shutters just ahead on the right. Turn into the driveway and pull around back of the house."

Gilbert looked back at her and used the reins to direct his willing steed from the cobbled street onto a graveled lane that cut through the undersized yard. It was built with white-painted long-leaf pine and the traditional red roof that most Charleston houses and buildings carried. The sound of a hammer on metal beckoned them into the backyard.

"That's Gillam," he said. Like a patron listening for his favorite musician, he recognized the cadence and tempo his brother played into his iron-issued songs. He directed the carriage into a forty-five-degree angle on the right side of the wide door to the small shed.

Queen Esther looked back at the house. Smoke poured from the chimney in the middle of the single-wide, two-room-deep dwelling. The wood cookstove in the kitchen shared that flue with the front room. The sustaining smells of life for this family across its generations blended in the air. The aroma of vegetables, corn bread and pork meat escaped the house and mixed with the pungent stench of burning bituminous coal from inside the blacksmith shop.

Queen Esther said, "Gilbert, June's here cooking for her papa and there's Gillam in the smithy shop with Joseph and June's boy, August."

Gilbert pulled the horse to a stop a short distance from the door. He pulled the brake forward and tied the reins to it before pausing to peer into the shop through the open double doors at the three generations of his family inside.

Gilbert stepped from the carriage and Joseph Hale saw his uncle. He pointed over his father's shoulder in the middle of his pounding sonnet. Gillam played one last ringing note and turned. Gillam and Gilbert, his younger brother, saw each other and a few short moments passed for recognition to set in.

In that fifteen-by-fifteen foot building, Gillam Hale played a sweet chiming tune of metal on metal. It was one handed down in the Hale family from African days, when their patriarch had been spirited away from his village in the Congo and transported to the slave markets in Richmond in the colony of Virginia in North America. His purchase had eventually brought him and his progeny to a property adjacent to Mount Vernon. Eventually, that slave family became the property of a contemporary of President George Washington.

There, the great-grandson of that enslaved African metal worker, the father of Gillam and Gilbert Hale, pur-

chased freedom. He accomplished this early in the nineteenth century by saving money from his after-hours work
building the President's home in the new capital city of the
United States of America—Washington, D.C. That man,
Jerome Hale, made nails and he used that simple skill and
his ingenuity to acquire a new life for himself and his wife,
Sally, Gilbert and Gillam's mother.

The horse snorted and dropped her head to graze. The
resounding quiet amplified the animal's bites on the yard
grasses with her bit-filled mouth. In the distance, men un-
loading a ship in the Charleston Harbor shouted. Gillam's
hammer rang a note when he dropped it on the anvil.

Gillam and Gilbert Hale rushed toward each other.
They met beneath the crosspiece beam of the shop door
opening. The two men grabbed each other, hands to
elbows at first, as they'd done since childhood. Each
looked the other over from head to toe. The two old men
locked in an embrace. Instantly, tears filled their eyes and
no one in the shop or the coach spoke.

Gillam said, "They told me you was dead! They wired
it to me twice!"

June Hale stepped from the back door and waddled
down the steps. "Lawd, have mercy! Lawdy, glory be!"
she said. "Dat my uncle, Gilbert Hale. Praise duh Lord!
Glory be to God amighty!"

Reverend James Frazee lifted Dora Crenshaw to the
ground. Inside the shop, young August Hale pulled the remaining smoldering coke from the blue-hot kiln fire. He,
a boy aspiring someday to become an apprentice black-

smith, knew to do that to conserve the fuel in an idle furnace.

Queen Esther Hale stepped to the ground on the right rear side of the buggy. Muley walked forward to join her from the street where he had just stepped from his hitched ride with Miss Grozalia. Queen Esther gave him her motherly embrace. She had always done this whenever she saw him.

Muley Jenkins had been two years old when Claude Crenshaw bought Joseph and Queen Esther and sold Muley's mother south. When Queen Esther and Muley broke their clinch, Queen Esther saw Miss Grozalia drive away toward the harbor in her ox-drawn cart.

June walked over to where her mother and Muley stood. "Mauma, u'm glad to see oona, so happy oona came," June said.

Queen Esther said, "June, I'm glad you getting back to being yourself."

June said, "Mauma, since Papa come back to us, I can see so many t'ings better. U'm gonna be mighty fine."

Bishop Cain whispered, "Thank you God for the bent knees you used to make this happen. Thank you for letting me witness, before I leave this earth, a glimpse of your goodness."

Congressman Ethan Sneed left his third-floor suite in the middle of the building. He did not take the center hotel stairs that led to the lobby. Instead, he headed for the southern end of the floor and went down the single flight of stairs, taking two at a time. He opened the door onto the second floor of the hotel. He peeked into the hallway; it was empty. He walked quickly to the door of the first room on the back side of the building, room 201. He knocked softly. Congressman Sneed looked impatiently up the hallway.

The door to another suite opened halfway up the floor and the Congressman turned his head back to the stairs. The man who came out that door glanced Congressman Sneed's way while he locked the door. He turned to walk away when the door to room 201 opened. Ethan Sneed stepped into the room and the door closed behind him.

Marjorie Crenshaw said, "Hello, Ethan."

"Hello, my dear." He stepped toward her. He looked down on her and took in her beauty with his sky-blue eyes. She gazed up at him. He was six foot two; brown was mixed into his long grayed hair that was totally white at the sides and only slightly thin on top. He combed it to the rear and it was parted on the left. As always, he was clean-shaven with long and thick rectangular sideburns. He had slight bags underneath his eyes.

She reached out to him and he took her tiny hands in his huge fingers and kissed each of them, as he had when he accompanied her to her first ball at Hyperion Hall decades ago when they were in their teens. She reached up and touched his cheeks gently and looked at his wide mouth. She stroked his neatly groomed mustache and touched his full lips.

"I've missed you," she said.

Ethan's voice was eloquent, refined from years of

getting his point across on the floor of the Virginia and U. S. Congresses.

Ethan Sneed said, "Marjorie, I'm so glad you came… so pleasantly surprised each year, that you meet me." He looked at her from head to toe, his knowledge of every inch, line and curve beneath her dress recorded in his mind from years of secret holiday retreats. The Congressman from Virginia knew Marjorie Crenshaw better, even though they only met annually for a few days, than her husband Claude Crenshaw ever had. "You're still stunning in that dress." She had worn it on their first and only public date.

She pointed to a nearby table. "I brought food and wine," she said.

A bottle of Vin Mariani sat in her large brown-and-tan Gullah basket. The wine was surrounded by two crystal glasses, fresh flowers, a loaf of bread, triangles of yellow and white cheese, fruit, and a silver dish filled with shrimp, smoked oysters and thinly sliced ham.

Voices from the next room came through the thin walls and three male Negro dining-room staff members laughed outside the window in an alley below while sharing a hand-rolled cigarette during their after-lunch break.

Ethan and Marjorie ignored those sounds.

He said, "I will enjoy those items later."

He gathered her into his big arms, strong from tobacco field work during his Virginia childhood. She tiptoed upward and he bent down. He kissed her as he had forty years ago on Christmas Eve. She felt the muscles in his arms and chest. They pulled away, looked at each other, and embraced again.

Marjorie said, "I feel like I'm sixteen."

He cleared his throat and kissed her. In a whisper, he said, "You look it, too."

She pulled away. "Ethan, there's a delicate matter about your wife I must share."

He said, "Being here with you makes me feel like a boy all over again. Anything else's going to wait!" The fifty-eight-year-old politician kissed his belle from Charleston again as they melted onto the freshly made bed.

16

A HOUSE DIVIDED

Media Coleman Sneed listened to the clop of the steel shod horse team's feet on the cobblestones of Calhoun Street. They were a beautiful pair of carriage grays. Media had come a long way since the days of riding in rough wagons in west Tennessee along Quito Road. She often reminisced about those trips to and from the town of Lucy. She always thought of her family and the fact that she would never see them again—they were dead to her.

The buggy driver turned in his seat. He looked back at the pretty young woman before moving his gaze to the two boys on the carriage seat next to her. They rode eastward along Calhoun Street.

"Miss Sneed, I need to stop up ahead at a blacksmith shop. Dat left rear wheel of dis carriage meking a noise. I need tuh get the smithy tuh look at it."

He pointed his hand toward the left. "Now, missus, that's Emanuel African Methodist Episcopal Chu'ch. It's one of the largest chu'ches in Charleston for Negroes." He pointed his right thumb into his chest. "I belongst there myself." He looked back at her again. A grill of gold teeth showed across the top and bottom of his mouth when he smiled. His eyes lingered; he did not look away this time.

She looked down at her younger brothers. Young Conrad was asleep. Rafe stared into the distance. She did not bother to reach out to him. He reminded her of his cruel father, Raford Coleman, Jr. Media Coleman Sneed could not yet move beyond that part of her past.

It was a beautiful afternoon in Charleston. She snuggled with Conrad beneath the blanket that covered them from the waist down.

"Gee, horse," the driver called out. The animals responded by turning right into the driveway at 8 Calhoun Street. They proceeded toward the shop in the rear.

Media said, "Will it be long?"

The driver pointed to his left at the house while directing the animals to loop the carriage to the right. "Naw, missus. The man standing right ober der. I'll just get him to take a look. We'll be on our way directly. Whoa, whoa," he called to his charges. He set the brake and climbed from the carriage. The rear of the carriage faced the street; its hood shielded a view of the occupants from the steady flow of Charleston traffic along Calhoun Street.

Rafe Coleman III leaned forward. He pointed across the grass to two dark-skinned men standing nearby behind the porch. "Media!" he said and turned back toward his sister, "Media, that nigger over there lives in Lucy where we from! What's he doing in Charleston?"

Media reached out like an uncoiling snake. She pinched Rafe's biceps hard and slapped his face twice. A red hue showed on his left cheek where both blows landed. "I told you never to say that word!" She glared at him and he returned her stare.

The boy did not cry. He said, "Media, you used to be so nice to me. Now you do me jus' like Daddy did." Rafe's eyes showed anger, not tears.

Conrad awoke. He said, "Where are we?"

She said, "Conrad, we stopped for repairs the carriage needs."

She cast her eyes on Rafe. She said, "Rafe, I'm sorry." He did not look at her.

She looked across the yard at the two men. They walked over the grass to meet the driver in the middle of the narrow lawn. A flock of gulls flew overhead, calling as they passed. It was, in fact, Gillam Hale. Media Coleman Sneed thought of all she had been through and the secrets she held inside. At first, she looked sad before smiling.

Media said, "At least I'll have word from home."

On that same Saturday afternoon in Lucy, Tennessee, Rena Erby prepared to move. She did not have to do so, but she desired a change. She was the mourning widow of a man dead to her and her son. She had not smiled in the month since Gillam Hale had left Lucy and the life they had built together. So much of who she was had come to her life through the knowledge Gillam had shared with her and the people of Lucy and Quito Road.

"Gill," she said to the son she'd born to Gillam. "Stop playing with dem sticks and pack yo' things like I tol' you. My cousin gone be here directly to move us."

Thirteen-year-old Gill Erby turned to his mother and

said, "Mama, Papa used to say he wouldn't live on the Coleman place 'cause it was cursed ground." The boy paused and looked back at the bundle of small sticks he held. "He said you couldn't trust your cousin 'cause…"

"Gill Erby, quit that foolishness. Yo' no-good daddy ain't here, and I don't want a hear nothing 'bout what Gillam said or thought! Do what I tol' you or u'm gone tan yo' hide."

Young Gill rose from the kitchen table. He moved from the room in a slow and sullen fashion, a way foreign to him just a month earlier. But that was before his papa went away. Now the frequency with which he listened to Rena decreased, and the accuracy in which he implemented her instructions waned. He walked from the kitchen with a scowl on his face.

Rena watched him move into the front room and the bundle of letters she held transported her to a time in the late summer of 1870. The long August days had been hot and she was just under eight months pregnant. The child within her kicked strongly beneath Rena's left rib cage; the west Tennessee heat tortured her every move. Gillam had recently taught her to read. She had shown her pride just days earlier when she displayed her new skill for the census worker who recorded the details of their household. That's when the first correspondence had arrived.

She held those letters in her hands now just above the hatbox where she had always hidden them from Gillam. They were in two bundles but bound together. She untied them and looked at the two stacks. The ten in her left hand contained a Cumberland, Maryland, return address. The sender was Gilbert Hale.

She turned her chair toward her wood cookstove and used the ends of those letters to open the firebox door. Rena tossed that group inside onto the hot coals. For a few moments, she watched them burn. Then she examined the others. That stack was smaller, only seven, compared to the ones now engulfed in flames.

She wiggled the first from the cotton string that bound them. The yellowed envelope had a Charleston, South Carolina, address and had been sent to Memphis, Tennessee, to the Shelby County Clerk. It was addressed to Gillam Hale, but he had never received it. Instead, over the years, Rena Erby had read and reread those pleas from Queen Esther to whoever opened her on-paper cry for help in finding her missing husband, their oldest son, Jerome, and their youngest boy Joseph, all casualties of chattel slavery.

Rena Erby threw the second bundle through the open stove door and watched the papers burst into flames. Rena said, "I kept him long as I could. Now, Miss Queen Esther, I hope you and Gillam rot in hell together." She began to cry and the frequency of a smile or pleasant thought coming from Rena Erby would decrease with the passing of each day in the years ahead.

17

OLD COATS

The Baldwins bought the house at 32 Battery upon their return to Charleston after the war. It had two-and-a-half stories and a prominent cupola in the middle of the roof. Sixty-five percent of the assets of the previous owner, a planter with vast holdings on the North Edisto River on Edisto Island, evaporated like a mist when the South lost their efforts to continue their economic way of life, chattel slavery. Claude Crenshaw was that planter. The war took almost everything he owned and valued.

The Captain and Millicent loved to sit on the second floor screened piazza. On good days, he would tell her stories from his seasons at sea, times away from her and their son and daughter. Today had not been a good day and he went to the cupola to gaze at what he knew best, the ocean. The times when he came to this part of his home enabled Captain Baldwin to imagine himself far out on the blue deep, a thousand miles from any shore. He sat on the flat window seat, thumbed through his Bible, and fell asleep in the sun, alone with his regrets.

He was just an old man, sleeping in a home purchased

with illicit earnings and bad money. His eyes twitched beneath their lids; as usual, when he fell asleep in this spot high above his current landlocked world, the nightmare began. These unconscious interludes caused him to relive the smell and the worst parts.

In his memory, the stench drifted to downwind ships miles before they saw the highest sail of his vessel, the *Swan*. He saw them brought out onto the upper deck. The Captain looked into their eyes. As usual, the whimpering preceded their screams. This time he was in line with them, connected to the same rusty chains used on each of the dozens of crossings the *Swan* had made. He screamed, "No, no, no! Don't throw us over! Don't, don't throw me in!" He thrashed about on the cupola seat.

On the front piazza of the Baldwin home, the Reverend Mr. Charles Crenshaw and Millicent Baldwin sat in chairs of flat wooden boards made comfortable by bright blue fowl-feather stuffed cushions. The oil-based white paint glistened on the boards of the backs and bottoms of the traditional seaside furniture. A Negro maid in a starched black-and-white uniform produced a swishing sound with each step she made toward a small rectangular table in front of the pair.

The aroma of fine English tea drifted around the screened open-air room while she filled two cups. The servant began to prepare a cup to the specifications of her mistress, two teaspoons of brown sugar and heavy cream. She served Miss Millicent's tea and said, "Rev'end Crenshaw, you still like yo's with white suga'?"

Charles Crenshaw never removed his eyes from his hostess, but he said, "Yes, thank you, that would be fine."

Millicent Baldwin and the Captain expected and welcomed Charles's visit. He was their priest even though Charles Crenshaw now worked for the diocese and not as pastor of St. Philip's.

Charles accepted the steaming tea from the servant. "How long has he been asleep?" Charles asked.

"His struggles are upon him today," Miss Millicent said. A slight frown replaced her eternal smile. "So he climbed up to his crow's nest around noon. The girl took his dinner up an hour ago and found him fast asleep, surrounded by his old charts, log books and Bible."

"It's in his blood," Charles said.

"I'm not worried about his blood, Charles." Miss Millicent looked away across the harbor toward the sea that had taken her husband away from her again and again. "Can he ever get it out of his spirit?" Her blue eyes watered and she said, "Pastor Crenshaw, will he ever feel fo'given for his past acts?"

"Miss Millicent, it's too difficult to say. I think all of us connected with these things wrestle with it on some level, but salvation is a gift and a choice there for us all." He raised the white saucer to his chest level, lifted the cup to his mouth, and sipped the brew. "This is an English variety."

"Yes," Miss Millicent looked at him and said, "a fine Brit' gentleman like the Captain prefers tea purchased from his homeland to the local varieties." She looked out to sea again. "I know you came to talk about our donation." The physical wisp of a woman looked into his eyes. "We are going to support the school the Episcopal diocese is building for the Gullah people on Edisto. Our donation will be generous."

"Thank you," he said. "I've worked a long time to convince my bishop to expand our work in the Sea Islands."

"We put those people out there," Miss Millicent said, "made it illegal for them to write or even read." She shook her head. "They speak that confounded language that confuses me every time the Captain takes me out there."

Charles Crenshaw mocked her with a short speech in fluent Gullah, "Oona know wa dey say, ainty? Jes a leeleetle bit ob yeast da mek kall de bread dough rise. That's 1 Corinthians 5 verse 6 in The New Testament Gullah."

"I'll never understand how a white person learnt that."

Charles sipped from his tea and then placed the saucer and cup on the table between them. "I spoke that befo' I did English."

Miss Millicent said, "And how do you surmise that?"

He intertwined the fingers of his hands and returned her stare. "Gullah first came to my ears from the lips of the owner of the black breasts I suckled as a babe."

"Grozalia?" she said.

"Yes, Dah Grozalia. I'm white, but Negro culture is natu'al for me on many levels." He paused, this time for his own look out to sea. "Unlike most whites in the South, I just never could forget that."

"Charles, more probably have not forgotten than they let on."

Charles said, "Why do you think Papa never remarried?"

"There was no need." Millicent blushed a little. "He had two sons as potential heirs. And he had a variety of female companionship with no restrictions from Charleston or Low Country society."

"When did he take up with the woman on the peninsula?"

Miss Millicent cleared her throat and frowned. This line of discussion was uncomfortable for a Charleston lady of her sensibilities.

Charles said, "Bear with me, cousin. I really need to know this. What about Dah Grozalia?"

Miss Millicent cleared her throat again. She said, "That started during the time your mother was carrying Claude and you. He had always carried on with the colored women. Most of the well-off planter-class white men did."

Charles laughed.

She said, "In Europe, Asia and Africa, the kings and emperors had at least one wife and their concubines and they still kept time with the servant girls. Even the Native-American tribal chiefs did. Here, the servants happened to be Negro. A wealthy male will unfortunately most often become a greedy one-eyed man where manly indulgences come in."

Charles said, "When did Papa take up with John Cotton's mauma?"

"You mean that vile creature Gullah John?"

Charles nodded his head. "Yes, my half-brother, Gullah John."

"Your father was the only man that colored woman knew up until he sold her off."

"Why did he do that?"

Miss Millicent looked around. She gazed around the porch. Her servants were not near. She said, "Vesey! He was afraid of any trace of Vesey being left in his holdings."

Charles said, "I don't understand."

She said, "Whites here were terrified when the alleged plot on the Negro insurrection surfaced in 1822."

"Why do you say *alleged?*"

Miss Millicent said, "I'm old now and a bit calmer." She paused and frowned again. "Looking back, some of the main accusers of Denmark Vesey were other Negroes with much to gain from his downfall."

"For example?" Charles said.

"The earlier witnesses to the plot were granted their freedom for their role in the discoveries. And another man was a direct competitor of Vesey's carpentry business."

Charles said, "Crabs in a bucket and old coats."

Miss Millicent said, "Yes, whites with slaves learned early in the practice of our peculiar institution to pit Negroes against each other with rewards for spying and reporting on each other. They still destroy each other so often. It saddens me for them." Her paternalistic Southern attitude still showed. "But I think to this day they do not understan' how to work togethe' to accomplish important goals."

They sat in silence for a few moments. Charles pointed to the schooner coming into port with an oceangoing steam vessel in the distance behind it. He said, "There's the old and the new. The proliferation of steam-powered boats has hit the Charleston economy hard."

"How so?" Miss Millicent smiled at the mind break; the Vesey affair still set her on edge, even after sixty years.

Charles said, "The ships from Europe and Africa and the Far East don't have to follow the currents to Charleston anymore. Their engines can take them straight to the northern ports like New York and Boston."

She nodded. "I remember how the area dignitaries wouldn't let anything come into the city for decades that was powered by steam engines because that interfered with our ways."

They shook their heads. Both understood the economic disparities old ideas like that left in their city. They sat still for a while, watching the harbor and White Point Gardens with its mixture of live oaks, palmettos, oleander bushes and other flora. A cool gentle breeze touched their faces; they both shivered in their seats.

"Cousin," he said. She looked into his face. "How did my father come to do these things? Why'd he sell John's mauma and Grozalia's daughters?"

"Your father was young. It's difficult to have wisdom at that age. Marion followed the footprints left by his fore-bears, like most do. His father, grandfather and most of their contemporaries acted in this way." She paused and fanned her face. "We don't talk about these things, but I have colored relatives in the membership at one of the local colored Methodist churches that won't allow Negroes in for worship if their hair isn't straight enough. And there's a dispute right now at the two Negro cemeteries near the Catholic Diocese over burial in the mulatto graveyard versus the parallel all-African plot."

She looked at the preacher. They both laughed at this fact's absurdity, but they both knew it to be true.

Miss Millicent said, "Your grandfather was an attorney and a principal in the inquiry into the slave insurrection. Vesey was captured as a teenager and was supposedly some sort of royalty in Africa." She stared at Charles and at South Battery below as a carriage sped past. Her eyes stayed on the street below when she spoke next. "Denmark Vesey's society believed in having multiple wives. He had several and most were slaves. So even after he purchased his freedom, his children by the bondwomen carried the chattel status of their mothers. This drove Vesey mad, and whites believed it fueled much of what he was accused of plotting."

Charles said, "And, what exactly was that?"

"He and his conspirators were alleged to intend to kill all the whites in the Low Country, take control of the area and sue for their freedom."

"So, that's why nobody white talks about it."

"Yes. That's also why so many houses in Charleston have such beautiful ironwork fences, gates, windows and door guards."

Charles said, "But, what's that have to do with the sale of Gullah John's mother."

"Gullah John's mother, the one your father had an affair with in addition to Grozalia was Vesey's daughter. Your father didn't know it and was furious when he found out. He had some money trouble later and he sold John's mother and the three daughters he had fathered by Grozalia to a plantation in the Mississippi Delta. He sold the girls as partial retribution for Grozalia keeping that secret about Vesey's daughter."

"Why didn't he sell off Grozalia or Gullah John?"

Miss Millicent laughed and then became serious. "That bastard John escaped to the Florida Everglades, not to resurface until he came back to Edisto to guide the damnable Yankees. And Marion was scared of Grozalia. He believed in her 'mystical powers.' His fear drove him mad."

Charles said, "After Daddy died, Grozalia told me I was first-born."

Miss Millicent looked at him. She said, "What did you do with that information?"

Charles said, "I did nothing. I'm no crab or old coat."

Millicent said, "I can't believe you didn't do more."

"I have plenty and wish my brother no ill. Besides, when you net his holdings against his losses and mort-gages, I have more physical wealth than Claude and far less responsibility. If she switched us, it was a blessing to me. Crenshaw holdings were cursed. It's bad money!"

From the third floor, Captain Baldwin screamed, "No! No! No!" Something crashed to the floor above. "Don't! Don't throw us overboard! No-o-o-o!"

Miss Millicent said to Charles Crenshaw, "Go up to him. Confessing it to you will help him today."

18

TROJAN HORSE

Gillam, Gilbert and Media Sneed's driver approached the carriage. Gillam said, "How do, missus?" He looked away and never made eye contact with the young lady or the two boys.

Media Coleman Sneed acted as if she had never seen Gillam. Young Rafe glared at the three Negroes.

Gillam squatted down to examine the wheel. The driver bent over next to him. Gillam felt the hub of the wheel and pulled his hand away because it was hot. He said, "You can't drive this today. Those bearings need to be switched out."

The driver stood up. He removed his hat and looked at his passenger. He said, "Mrs. Sneed, I need to walk over to the livery and hire another carriage. Is it all right if I leave you here tuh go do that?"

Young Conrad said, "Aunt Media, I got to use it!"

Rafe laughed. He said, "I bet you go in your britches again, Conrad."

Media pinched him before she remembered her plan to

treat him better. She said, "Driver, we'll be fine here until you return."

"Yes ma'am," the driver said. He turned and moved across the yard toward Calhoun Street. He headed west toward the market area.

Gillam said, "Ma'am, might we be of service?"

Mrs. Sneed said, "Thank you very much."

Gillam nodded. He said, "Gilbert, will you take these young gentlemen in to June. Ask her to tend them."

Gilbert nodded.

Mrs. Sneed said, "Go ahead, Conrad." Conrad popped up and walked past Rafe. Gillam lifted him from the carriage to the ground. Mrs. Sneed said, "Rafe, you go also."

Rafe said, "I don't want to go with them!"

Media Sneed slapped his face before he could finish. She said, "Raford Smith Coleman III, get moving or I'll get a switch to use on your bare bottom!"

Rafe pouted for a brief second but rose to his feet and jumped from the carriage when Media reached for him. He raced across the lawn.

Gillam whispered, "Gilbert, keep them inside 'til I call for you."

Gilbert frowned, but he took young Conrad's hand. They followed Rafe to the back door. He led them up the steps, opened the door and the three disappeared inside.

Gillam Hale turned back to the carriage. He said, "Hey, Media! My daughter, June, told me you was in town. How's the prettiest girl from Lucy?"

She said, "Mr. Gillam, it's so good to see you."

He said, "Everybody in Shelby County, Tennessee, read the newspaper article about you marrying that rich white man."

She smiled and scooted across the seat. They touched hands.

Media said, "What are you doing in Charleston?"

Gillam said, "My youngest son by my wife found me. I came here last month to find my Queen Esther."

She released his hand. "You left Cousin Rena and young Gill?"

Gillam dropped his head and a sad look crossed his face.

She said, "How's Mama and my brother?"

"She's wonderful and yo' brother is, well, he's yo' brother!"

She laughed. "Mr. Gillam, it's so good to see you. Did you see my cousin before you left?"

"Yeah, I did. She's all right, but she's having a tough time with money." Gillam looked up at her before dropping his head. "You sent her anything?"

She shook her head.

"You need to do that. After her daddy's widow took her inheritance, she's in dire straits, like most of the folks, colored and white."

A look of despair crossed her face.

"It's time to do what you can. Do you handle the household accounts?" he asked.

She nodded.

"Then, hell, slip her a twenty-dollar bill or something like that in a brown envelope with no return address on it. Do it kind a regular like. That'll make her life so much better. Will you do that?"

Media nodded.

Gillam said, "Now, we got to speak 'bout something really important and we don't have much time. Do you think your husband loves you?"

"Why do you ask?"

"Answer me first."

She said, "Yes, I do believe he does."

"That's good." Gillam placed his foot on the step. "There's no time for me to tell you how I know, but I got to tell you two things. How you handle it'll set up the rest of yo' life."

Her eyes widened. "Mr. Gillam, what is it?"

He looked away from her. "'Member this. Congressman Sneed's a man." He looked at her and she nodded. "He's fooling 'round with his cousin's wife, Marjorie Crenshaw."

Media said, "Oh, I know that."

He said, "How?"

"I just do. I was born into a house with a white woman and my mostly white mama having children by one white man."

"Huh, then you gon' be better off with this next piece of information than I thought. Young Conrad was just a baby, so I know he don't know, but has Rafe III figured out anything about who you really are?"

She said, "No sir. He was young when the yellow fever epidemic hit the Memphis area. And, all the death he witnessed at such a young age kept him half-crazy for a while."

Gillam said, "Good. You and your white sister looked so much alike that you couldn't hardly tell you apart except she was a little heavier than you and had longer hair." Gillam laughed. "The fever killed all the adult white folks that coulda told y'all apart in Tennessee."

Media said, "Some days I still can't believe my sister died and I took her place."

"Well, you did. U'm glad we switched you and sent you and them boys away to Morristown, Virginia, before any of the Negroes that knew the difference could see you and tell it."

Media said, "Mr. Gillam, why are you bringing this up now?"

Gillam said, "Simple, the Negroes 'round here done tol' Marjorie Crenshaw you got colored blood!"

She stared at him and blinked. "How could they know?"

"You know colored folks know hidden Negroes when they see 'em!"

Media nodded her head. She whispered, "Mr. Gillam, what am I going to do?"

He said, "You gone take care of yo' business and everything gonna be mighty fine. Let's talk 'bout some real delicate matters. Now, you know why an older man like Congressman Sneed marries a tender young thing like you, don't you?"

She laughed and flushed red. "Of course I do." She smiled and covered her mouth with both hands.

He said, "Now, you taking care of that?"

She just stared at him.

He said, "Don't you go getting shy on me, missy! You the one brought up what was going on in the house where you was born."

She giggled and shook her head.

"We ain't got long, but I'm gonna tell you a few things, real fast. They ain't gone be what dainty high-society ladies like you want to discuss. Let's talk like a dirty old man would to a po' gal. Understand?"

She nodded. "But won't he be furious over this and put me out?"

Gillam said, "He'll be mad as hell and he'll consider that. But, if you do what I tell you, he'll crave you every moment he's away."

She laughed.

He turned serious. "You think you the only woman with some Negro blood that he been in the bedchambers wit'?"

She shook her head.

Gillam said, "You just the first one he married."

She giggled softly.

He said, "Now, remember, he's running for the Senate soon and he don't want no public scandals. Thomas Jefferson had a colored gal having his babies while he was the President!"

She shook her head. "Mr. Gillam, how do you always know what to do?"

He laughed. "I had a smart colored daddy that was a fine African Methodist Episcopal preacher. I didn't listen then, but I remember now. Your rich husband is gonna bring this up soon. When he do, you got to make him feel like he back in the days before the war! Act like he wit' a colored gal that can look like a lady of fine breeding and carriage, but can work wit' him in the bedchambers like a field hand gal with a week off during cotton chopping time!"

Media laughed and Gillam Hale did, too. He leaned in and took her hand again. He began to whisper and his pupil's eyes widened. Her giggles echoed across the yard and made the music this afternoon instead of his anvil.

19

ELLIS ISLAND SOUTH

Later that evening at Queen Esther's restaurant, Charles and Claude enjoyed a hearty conversation over a bottle of wine.

"Why'd you walk here?" Claude Crenshaw asked.

Charles said, "I met with the Rabbi at Beth Elohim this afternoon. His sabbath wasn't over until after five o'clock so I walked to respect that."

Claude said, "You always been so good at following the rules."

They both smiled and sipped at their wine.

Claude said, "I'm leaving for Edisto Island tomorrow with the outgoing tide. I'm going to inspect that Seaside land near Edingsville we talked about with Congressman Sneed earlier today." Claude found Charles's eyes across their favorite table along the wall near the rear of Queen Esther's. "I just need to know if you still in?" He leaned into the table. "You gone help me get my land that damn Yankee Sherman took for the niggers out there?"

Charles shrugged.

Claude said, "That place was in our family for a hundred and twenty-five years. Sherman and his damn field order carved it up and gave it to stupid Negroes that don't even know what they got."

"Edisto land's going to be very valuable someday," Charles said.

"It's valuable cropland right now!" Claude pounded his knuckles into his left palm. "Do you know how much Sea Island cotton that place used to produce? Mos' yea's, we got two to three hundred pounds of cotton an acre!"

Charles said, "That was fine when you had the labor system that was in place, but we can't get Negroes to work like that today. The future will be developing that land like's already being done in some of the other Sea Islands."

Claude shook his head. "You right. Niggers rather go fishing or catch their food in a Low Country marsh with a trap or a snare today."

Charles said, "You need me out there this week?"

Claude said, "You need to come negotiate with June Hale. That gal hates me." He sipped his wine and then bit into one of the small cookies Cuppie had just served. The door to the kitchen opened partially then swung back closed. He whispered, "Let's don't speak on this anymore in this place."

Charles raised his glass to his lips and slurped a large quantity of the Vin Mariani down.

Claude shouted toward the kitchen. "Cuppie, girl come here!"

The young woman stepped halfway through the portal. "Yessuh, Mr. Claude," she said.

"Tell Bentley to prepare our salmon now. I'm faint with hunger for something more than this wine and small biscuits."

* * *

Uncle Bentley walked over to Miss Grozalia's cart, parked behind Queen Esther's. He said, "Don't know wher' Queen Esther at. She and Dora went to the King Street stores dis afternoon and ain't come back." He frowned and looked around. "Ain't like her to stay gone dis long."

"She at 8 Kill-houn Street," Miss Grozalia said, her eyes twinkling in the already full moon that peeked just above the double Charleston house across the street.

"Naw, sis."

"She sho ober der. June cookin'—you could smell it all way to de street. And the Bishop Cain and the new young preacher out for our chu'ch on the island. They dere with another man I don't know."

"Uh-huh," Uncle Bentley said.

"De man, he look like Gillam, and Gillam know him." She paused and flung both hands palm-out and fingers wide. "Dem two hugged like death tore 'em apart and dey wouldn't be severed again."

"Uh-huh." Uncle Bentley looked over his shoulder and said, "Mistuh Claude in there talking 'bout takin' the land back and getting Negroes to move back to Africa wit' that Liberia man."

"When's he leavin' fo' Edisto?" she asked.

"With the tide tomorrow evening."

"I'm meeting Gullah John over at Oyster Point in a while. I'll arrange to leave with him on the morning tide tomorrow."

"How much Gullah John know 'bout all dis?" Uncle Bentley asked.

"Jus' 'nough to keep his thirst for blood at bay, nothin' mo'."

Uncle Bentley looked at her. "Sista, you keep it that way."

"Do not worry, baby brudduh. Another t'ing oona can know. A few black fools gwine back to Africa, but mos' stayin' here. De Lawd brung us to America fuh a reason and whateber it is, we need to get it done." She handed him a small bottle of sea rose tea, the usual dropper container of a few ounces.

Uncle Bentley gave her his empty one and a few coins in return. He said, "I'm outa saltpeter. You got any with you?"

"Didn't our mauma name me Grozalia?" She cackled and Uncle Bentley moved his hands to quiet her. She handed him a small cotton sack and he placed it in his apron pocket.

The rear door of the restaurant kitchen opened. Cuppie stepped over the threshold and closed it behind her. She walked into the moonlight. "Evening, Mauma," she said to the woman who brought her into this world. "Uncle Bentley, Mistuh Claude and Reverend Charles ready for they poached salmon."

"What you holding in that sack, daughter?" Miss Grozalia said.

Cuppie moved from the piazza to stand beside the cart next to her Uncle Bentley. "I fixed somethin' fo' you." She handed the burlap bag to Miss Grozalia. Cuppie rubbed her left eye. She said, "Dis eye been botherin' me all week."

Uncle Bentley said, "Huh."

Miss Grozalia peeked inside and saw two quart jars of stew. "Dat cuzghat?"

Cuppie said, "Yessum, and it made just like you showed me. Y'all, it cold out here!"

Uncle Bentley laughed.

Miss Grozalia said, "Chile, yo' know what I like, but it ain't cold out here. Bentley, give her that saltpeter."

As usual, her brother did what his older sister instructed.

Miss Grozalia said, "Suga, gone in der and fix dey food, just like yo' uncle would. You know how."

Cuppie's dimples showed with her smile. Her several nods signaled her knowledge of their plot.

Miss Grozalia said, "Dat new preacher gone be at church on the island next Tuesday for Christmas. I can't wait 'til you and Joseph come out to jump the broom on New Year's Day. You waited on that boy a long time."

Cuppie said, "We going out next Sunday on the special charter boat."

"Good, now gal, put that saltpeter in that salmon when you add the dill, the rosemary and the saffron." She laughed and her breath produced just a little fog in the chilly evening air. "Don't give him no sea rose tea—we need him strong enough to do what he ought to this week while he at Edisto." She laughed and Uncle Bentley gently warned her again with his hands to lower her volume.

"Mistuh Claude and Miss Marjorie goin' to Edisto?" Uncle Bentley asked.

Miss Grozalia said, "Muley tol' me Mistuh Claude was going, but Miss Marjorie's staying here, like usual."

"Huh," Uncle Bentley said. "Now I know that white man crazy. He leavin' his good-lookin' wife in the town with all these left-ove' scalawags and carpetbaggers."

Cuppie said, "Esmerelda say he ought not be worried 'bout dem, but he better keep watch on his own cousin."

"But that man got a pretty young wife," Uncle Bentley said.

Miss Grozalia laughed, "She might be pretty, but she don't much care for no man putting his hands on her."

"Mauma," Cuppie said with a smile, "now how you know all that?"

"'Cause it my bus'ness to know." She looked around. "I tell you two somet'ing else." Uncle Bentley and Cuppie inched closer. "Dat gal they call Miz Sneed ain't not'ing but a octoroon."

"Na-a-a-w!" Uncle Bentley said. He laughed.

Cuppie shook her head. Her dimples preceded her smile.

Miss Grozalia said, "Look here—I done birthed mo' babies in my years, colored, white and 'twixt in between, than oona togedda done see'd." She cackled. "Negro in her, sho nuff is! It ain't just Scots-Irish like she tol' that high buckruh she mar'ied. It ain't Mexican and she can forget sayin' it any kind a French or Welsh. I know a spade when it stand in front of me, now!"

Cuppie said, "Reckon her husband know?"

"Naw, he don't hab a clue. He from Virginnie. Up

dere dey don't solemnly practice marriage rituals wit' octoroons, like dey does in Charleston and Louisiana."

Uncle Bentley and Cuppie laughed again. Both shook their heads.

Miss Grozalia said, "But, I bet he'll know directly."

Cuppie said, "Mauma, how dat gone happen?"

Miss Grozalia shook her head. "Don't worry yo'self 'bout that none. My name Grozalia and what is planted will be up befo' daybreak tomorrow." She looked toward the restaurant where she knew Charles and Claude Crenshaw plotted. "U'm fixin' to get some of dese white men t'inking 'bout t'ings dat don't include makin' money." She whispered her final thoughts on the matter. "I shoulda smothered Claude Crenshaw when I held him to my titties fuh milk."

Cuppie said, "Ooh, Mauma."

Uncle Bentley just laughed.

Miss Grozalia looked up at the rising moon. "I hopes the Boo Hag suck his breath plum 'way when he on Edisto!" She spoke of the Low Country tale about a night haint. Part of the Boo Hag myth told that it avoided rooms with blue ceilings, thinking it was the daytime sky. The aberration could suck the breath from its sleeping victims. "I been conjuring on Claude Crenshaw and he 'bout ready to grow what I planted in him ober fifty years pas'."

Cuppie smiled, belched and clutched her abdomen.

Uncle Bentley looked at her. "Gal, you gone make a pretty bride next week."

Miss Grozalia said, "Gal, why that vein under you' neck jumpin' so? Dat mean a woman wit' child."

Cuppie said, "Mauma, you ought not speak dat!"

Uncle Bentley said, "Cuppie, if yo' left eye's jumpin' and your flesh begin to crawl, oona can bet your bottom dollar that somet'ing new's kickin' inside duh stall."

A cat meowed from his nearby haunt under the porch. He came forth with a piece of the salmon backbone and tail from the fish Uncle Bentley had filleted earlier.

The excited laughter, fishy smell and the moonlight sight of the feline's prize had an unexpected impact on Cuppie Geechee. She ran to the curbside, bent at the waist and grasped her knees.

Miss Grozalia looked at her daughter bowed over the edge of the street. Loud guttural groans and gasps escaped her throat and echoed in the cool night air.

Uncle Bentley said, "Grozalia, Cuppie and dat boy Joseph Hale been getting' together. She ain't waiting no mo'."

Miss Grozalia turned back to her brother. "Bentley, mos' times two folks lay down, but three git up! Dat boy Joseph say he don't feel good. Huh, he ain't dat sick. Been here jes' a month and my daughter so full wit' his seed 'til she can't keep her dinner down." They laughed.

"Bentley, gone fix the food fo' dem white folks yo'self. I got a go see my Esmerelda."

Uncle Bentley stepped away and Grozalia shook her head as she popped the reins across Rosebud's back. She, the beast and the cart lurched away toward St. Mark's Alley. "Get you some baking soda in water, gal," she said to Cuppie. "Oona be fine," Miss Grozalia cackled, "in 'bout eight months."

20

OYSTERS, PEARLS, AND PLUFF MUD

It had been easy for the early settlers at Charleston to notice the area's rich assets. The warm ocean currents produced a mild winter climate. This made for a longer growing season and provided a year-round opportunity to enjoy the outdoor wealth.

Over time, silt from fresh water estuaries combined with the salt left from the ocean tides to produce a thick, dark mud that the residents call pluff. Charlestonians struggled to rise from their muddy domain and to separate the shimmering jewel that Charleston became from the pluff of its environment.

Fresh and salt-water Low Country streams, rivers, lakes, as well as the Atlantic, offered fish, shrimp and succulent oysters for the taking. Lush woodlands provided game of every sort for hunters.

The settlers recognized what Native Americans already knew. Oysters often attach themselves to structures in the mud along creeks and river banks, where they are fed by the rich currents. The best of the shellfish are small, succulent and salty. Occasionally, an oyster snatched from the mud produced a jewel—a pearl. Treachery often follows if a rival is found in possession of such a treasure.

The Reverend Mister James Frazee felt he had found such a pearl as he had searched for it all through his short life. After an evening at church on his second night in town he took Dora Crenshaw on a stroll through a park.

James dropped the brick attached to the horse's bridle to the ground after he parked the carriage along South Battery. That would hold the animal there while he and Dora strolled through White Point Gardens, as Oyster Point was now called. Helping his date to the ground, he said, "Miss Crenshaw, may I call you Dora?"

"Sure you can. I'd also like to call you James, in private, of course, Reverend." They both laughed.

He offered her his curled right arm and she put her left through his. He turned and they headed along the gravel-and-seashell path toward the lapping call the waters of Charleston Harbor made on the sea wall.

James said, "What do you plan to do next year?"

Dora said, "What do you mean?"

"Will you keep working for your mother or would you like to put your education to better use?"

"I don't understand."

"The AME and Episcopal denominations are starting a school on Edisto. We going to put it in Bethel AME to start."

"Really," she said. "That's wonderful news. The people out there need a great deal of help."

He said, "Would you like to join our efforts as a teacher at the new school?"

She laughed, "Me, teach?" The path's surface crunched beneath their feet. They looked up at an open gazebo and paused on the trail. She said, "Sometimes they have musicals under there."

James said, "Do they allow Negroes to attend?"

"Things are changing so rapidly around here. It's probably not a good idea to come to them. Whites are terribly uncomfortable with former slaves so near during their social times."

"Dora," James said, "you didn't answer my question about teaching."

"I know," she said. "I'm thinking about it."

James said, "What is it that you want to do with the rest of your life?"

She laughed. "You college men move fast, Reverend."

"I thought I was James in private."

Still laughing, she said, "You become Reverend when you ask questions like that."

They walked ahead through the darkness under the live oaks along the pathway. The full moon illuminated the surface of everything under their gaze.

"My dear Miss Crenshaw, please allow me to direct my question into safer waters. What would you like to do this spring and summer?"

She giggled. As usual, it sounded like music to any that heard. Dora said, "You're good on your feet. I better watch you, Wilberforce man."

"How did you know where I went to college?"

"Bishop Cain made sure to mention it and, you should recall, my mother also asked you twice."

It was James's turn to light up the air with laughter. "Evidently she liked my answer."

Dora said, "Why would you think that?"

He smiled and his white teeth glistened in the light from the moon and gas lamps. "She entrusted me with her precious pearl, you."

"You keep this up and I'll start to call you Reverend again." They both laughed.

They reached the sea wall and stood before the rail. James said, "Dora, I don't mean to be forward and I hope you understand that I speak with the utmost respect. You do know that?"

She smiled at him and nodded. Even in the moonlight, it was obvious she blushed.

James looked out to sea and then turned away from her to look at the lights across the harbor on Fort Sumter. The wind picked up. He turned back to her and smiled. James said, "I don't quite know what to make of these things in my life. I can't see what God is doing or allowing."

Dora said, "James, it's not for us to see. We're here to do what we're sent to accomplish. That's what matters."

He turned to her. "I like everything I see and hear this evening. In fact since earlier today, my entire outlook has brightened."

Dora laughed. "Preacher, there you go again. Let's talk about our mothers." They both laughed. She said, "When was the last time you saw your mother?"

He looked at the waves bouncing from the sea wall surface below their feet. "It's been four years, since I went away to college."

Dora said, "I've never been away from my mother. What's your mother's name?"

The sound of multiple pairs of feet crunching the surface materials sounded behind her companion. Dora frowned. James turned around to face three white men; an older one was flanked by two younger contemporaries, one on each side. They were unkempt and looked as if they were the crew members from one of the ships at anchor nearby.

The eldest, the one in the middle said, "Boy, what's that you got wit' you?"

The man to his right said, "You know how long it's been since I see'd a woman?"

James said, "We don't want any trouble!"

The man to the far left laughed. "Hee, hee, hee!"

They spread apart into an attack formation that surrounded James and Dora against the sea wall rail. It seemed they had used this tactic together before. Their previous quarry was unknown, but, on this evening, it was Dora Crenshaw and anyone between them and her. They advanced. The water popped against the tabby-cement wall below just as the one in the middle swung at James Frazee.

The preacher ducked and landed a punch into the man's nose. James shouted, "Help! Somebody, help us! Hel..."

The man on James's left attacked him high while the one to the right tackled him low. The preacher went down into a heap with the flanking assailants.

Dora screamed and tried to run away, but the middle man grabbed a handful of her hair. He yanked her back to him and covered her mouth. The man swung Dora back around to watch the fight. She elbowed him in his right side and fought to get free.

James Frazee rolled onto his back. He threw the man on top of him against the railing. The one to his left hit James on that side. He doubled over in pain. The other thug rose from the railing and kicked James in the head. He fell and, as he did, Dora bit the criminal who held her. She screamed and tried to rip away from him. He tore her cloak and dress at the collar. Her new hat fell to the ground. The man regained control of Dora and pulled her to him.

He said in her ear, "Where you going, missy? Don't you like our company?"

She tried to scream again, but he covered her mouth before much of the sound escaped.

Someone ran quickly into the crowd. The newcomer struck a blow to the rear of the head of the man who held Dora. He fell in a heap. He would never rise again. His blood dripped from the tupelo-wood club of the rescuer.

Dora said, "Gullah John, thank God."

Gullah John stepped on the fallen man's ribs when he moved toward the two who were now kicking James Frazee from both sides. He struck one with a blow to the middle of his back. He fell across the preacher on the ground.

The third turned to run north down the battery walk. Before he could take a step, March Crenshaw hit him in the forehead with a loose brick he had retrieved from the sea wall just after Dora's first scream pierced the night. A sound like a Sea Island melon falling from a wagon onto hard ground echoed across their surroundings.

Gullah John swung his club one last time. That blow was a killing one. The last man collapsed across James Frazee into a heap. Dora Crenshaw screamed.

Gullah John said, "Hush, little gal. No need tuh holler."

She ignored him and opened her mouth to let go again. Dora was startled when Miss Grozalia approached them from behind. Dora shouted, "Dah Grozalia, dey, dey, dey wanted to…"

Miss Grozalia put her hand to Dora's lips. Dora stopped her racket and calmed down. She behaved as she had as a baby when this same old woman had soothed her during the explosions between the opposing armies on Edisto just after Queen Esther birthed Dora.

Miss Grozalia said, "We got oona now, Dora."

Dora settled into her arms. She looked at Gullah John and March.

Miss Grozalia pointed to the rail and said, "Throw this vermin into duh sea from whence dey come. Could be dere's sharks in duh harbor dis ebening."

James Frazee tried to rise, but could not. He moaned beneath the man's dead weight.

March said, "Stupid preacher. I can't believe you brought Dora out here at night."

Miss Grozalia said, "Hush! Oona complain later. Do wha' I say and do it now!" Dora sobbed again and Miss Grozalia said, "Hush, chile." She pointed to the rail and looked to Gullah John and March. "Ober wit' 'em now."

The two moved like Negro longshoremen. In a few

seconds, three splashes sounded and the assailants sank beneath the murky waters. Their remains would sink to below the tidal line where past Charlestonians had buried marauding pirates of a similar spirit. They would be out of sight for at least a few days.

"March, oona know where Bishop Cain staying?"

March nodded.

"Take duh preacher to the bishop and tell him in private 'bout dis." She pointed at Gullah John and then to March. "Don't speak on dis again."

They both nodded.

Gullah John moved toward March and tried to touch his shoulder.

March said, "Don't you touch me! I was a child, but I remember what you did to my brothe'." He moved over and snatched James Frazee from the ground. He said, "Come on, Reverend." March headed toward the carriage with his charge.

Miss Grozalia said, "Gullah, let's get 'way from here to my cart and take Dora to Queen Esther's." Miss Grozalia and Gullah John stood to each side of Dora. They moved across the lawn toward her cart at the end of White Point Gardens.

21

OVERDUE FREEDOM

About the same time during Saturday evening, a man used his key to open the front door of Queen Esther's restaurant. As usual, he came and went from the place as he pleased; he owned her building. He stepped inside, closed and locked the door behind him. He was a fertilizer business executive, a planter and former factor, the term used for those speculating in marketplace commodities and finance. He adjusted his clothes and walked to the rear of the restaurant. A single candle on a table lit his way. He picked up the holder he did not need; he knew every inch of this place by heart. The eyes in his head and his perfect vision did not supply the sight that led him here on this or any other evening.

Claude Crenshaw raised the candle to illuminate a narrow stairway with shorter than normal steps to the second floor and another closed door. When he reached this point, he was anxious, even after twenty-five years. He took the steps and was winded when he reached to open the upper entrance. What awaited him took his complete sight.

He stepped into a small room with a seven-foot ceiling. He lowered his head and the candle. The spartan space had a cot on the wall to his right and the smooth plaster walls were off-white with a blue ceiling—no Boo Hag worries here. Unfinished pine boards provided the flooring. A small washstand with a yellow pitcher and matching basin stood next to the end of the bed away from the door. At the far end of the six-by-ten-foot room was a quilting frame.

That's where Queen Esther sat now, with her back to him. She never moved when he opened the door and did not speak or vary her motions when he approached and stood at her side. That is what they always did.

"Evenin', Queen Esthe'," Claude Crenshaw said.

She never looked away from the multicolored quilt tightened across the wooden frame that took up almost the entire width of the upstairs nook. Two oil lamps sat atop rough wooden tables on each end of the rack and cast shadows of her and Claude along the wall and onto the bed.

After a delay, she replied, "How you?" She glanced at him and nodded to a chair, slightly behind her at the end of the bed. "Have a seat."

He said, "I been sitting down all day and my injury's bothe'ing me, so I'll just stand a while." He removed his hat and coat and, in a motion of familiarity with his surroundings, tossed them on the chair. Claude paced behind Queen Esther to her left and leaned his back against the wall.

She looked away from her needlework to him. Their

eyes met before she turned back to the maple leaf design she stitched from above and below. She said, "Claude, why aren't you home with your wife?"

"That woman's hated me since our first two young'uns died of a fever. You know she blames me 'cause I was away on a hunt when they died." He paused. "Then I was away at war when young Marion drowned on Edisto."

She said, "What were you hunting?"

Claude dropped his head, but he never answered her question. It did not matter. They both knew. He took a step toward her, but paused when the flooring creaked beneath his weight.

"Queen Esthe', I noticed something about the quilts you make," he said. He paused for her to reply and continued when she did not accept his invitation to converse. "That shape, those maple leaves...you use that same design in all yo' work." He paused and moved closer to her. "Why you use them all the time?"

Queen Esther carefully pushed the needle through the top of the quilt. She found it below with her thimble-covered left index finger and returned the needle through the multiple cloth layers before speaking. She paused for another perfect stitch like the ones that surrounded the multicolored leaf designs on the white cotton backing. "The maple was one of my favorite trees near my home."

She never looked at him, but his eyes roved over every inch of her. His visual review was completed with a mental one which took him underneath her white blouse and gray skirt. Claude walked over to her and put his hands on her shoulders. He removed two long hairpins from her hair. He reached around Queen Esther to her right and stuck them into the quilting while releasing her auburn-brown locks from the ball behind her head. Her hair was thick and wavy; it fell below her shoulders to the middle of her back.

He stroked her locks with both hands and moved it over her right shoulder. Claude bent down to kiss her neck. She shuddered and shrank from his touch. It was the first time in her twenty-five years under his control that her true feelings showed. She stood up and moved to her left, her breathing increased. She stood near the wall facing the rear of the room and her breasts rose and fell.

"Since yo' nigger back you won't let me get close!"

Her glare met his when she turned to face him. "You better let me go!" She blurted it out with the energy of a hurricane moving inland.

They both froze in the small space. Many of their private moments had been spent here since the war and emancipation. Her new slavery began here, still under a white man's beck and call.

"What you talking 'bout, Queen Esthe'?"

"I am ready to move on with my life and you won't release me. I'm free! You don't own me no mo'!"

He stepped toward her and reached for her with his right hand. She stepped away toward the doorway and he grabbed at her twice with his left hand before grasping the woman. He pulled her to him and pushed her against the wall. There was a cruel look on his face when he leaned into her. He kissed her cheeks, eyes, neck and then her lips.

Like a wayward schoolboy hounding a young girl at

recess, he groped her body. Nothing happened between his legs, and Claude's sneer morphed into an empty look.

Queen Esther struggled against him. He would not release his hold, even though holding her there could serve no purpose. He was not capable; had not been for years…they both knew it. Her look told him how she felt and, since he could no longer use her or any woman, it gave Queen Esther a power foreign to them both.

One word at a time, she said, "Let me go!"

His grip slackened and she ripped free. She adjusted her clothes. He looked at all he had enjoyed over the years, but could take pleasure in no more. His torture was at hand. Victory was now in her grasp.

Her shadow moved across the wall when she bundled her tresses behind her head again. She put her hairpins back in place and made eye contact with him. His scowl deepened. She would have used the long straight pins she had pulled from the quilt on him if he had not freed her. She walked toward the door and reached for the knob.

"Queen Esthe'." Claude Crenshaw now spoke her name as if it were a dirty word. "Don't forget I own this place."

She opened the door and moved onto the first step. She paused without looking at him. "Nothing better happen to Gillam."

"What you say?" he said.

She looked down the stairs. "You heard me and you know why I spoke it." She glared right at him. "Don't you?"

She stood there for a time. "You and yo' red-shirted rifle

club killed black men in the early evenings before you would come here to me. How did you think I felt with you doing those things before putting your blood-stained hands on me?"

"We was just protecting our property, trying to regain our heritage."

"What are you going to do with it now? Who will inherit what you leave, my nigger children?"

He opened his mouth to speak, but could only cough in her direction.

She said, "You despise Negroes, but soon the only part of you left on this earth will have colored blood! And you will not even leave them a part of the money you have left!"

She stopped talking; he said nothing. He stared at her for a few moments and coughed several more times before looking at the floor between them.

Queen Esther said, "I remember when the Confederate order came to evacuate Edisto. You insisted March, Dora and I come to Charleston with you and Marjorie. I wish you had left us on the island. It was hell living in that house with your wife. We were all living right there in the townhouse at 32 South Battery."

Claude said, "I had no idea."

"I was in her home with your offspring just after two of her children had died and it never occurred to you how she'd feel?"

He did not answer and refused to look at her.

"You are a stupid, cruel, and now an impotent man, Claude Crenshaw."

He stepped toward her. Anger was etched into his every facial feature.

She raised her right hand toward him. Her fingers and palm opened like a blossoming flower. He froze.

She said, "Don't you ever touch me again. I know you're the reason I'm in Charleston."

He spread his arms wide. A puzzled expression washed across his face.

Queen Esther said, "I'm moving out of this building by the end of January." She turned to stare at him. "Put the lamps out before you leave." Queen Esther turned back to the stairs, walked down the steps, opened the door at the bottom, and crossed the dining room to exit the restaurant.

That day, she freed herself as she had helped many others escape from oppressors in the South. She had been an Underground Railroad conductor in Cumberland, Maryland, at the end of the Chesapeake and Ohio Canal. Her maple-leafed quilts had hung from the fencerows of her home to point the way to freedom. Her road markers in cloth told those runaways that midnight must find them at the gate of an open-topped tunnel at the base of the steep hillside just across Wills Creek. Their last conductor had told them the building overlooked the junction of that stream and the Potomac River. That passageway led to a small cavern at the top of the hill beneath Emanuel Episcopal Church.

That grand worship building of brown and tan stone stood on a steep knoll and used the historic defensive battlements of Fort Cumberland as its foundation. Ironically, the British, who dug those trenches, also started slavery in America in the late seventeenth century by following in the footsteps of the Spanish and Portuguese. But, by the early nineteenth century, free persons, black and white, helped enslaved Negroes northward to freedom in Pennsylvania, Ohio and Canada via these same passageways.

Each Negro that stepped into the eastern end of the caverns beneath Emanuel felt a wind. It was the breeze of freedom blowing across their cheeks from the exit tunnel beneath the church parsonage on the western side of the great hill beneath that Maryland church.

Queen Esther Hale felt a similar stirring breeze in Charleston when she stepped from the kitchen door that December evening. It was crisp, cool, soothing to her soft skin.

She walked across the piazza, down the steps and across the courtyard to her residence. She was working the latch to open the door when the steps of an ox on the street surface caused her to stop. She looked up to see Miss Grozalia's ox-drawn cart pull up to the dependency. Gullah John sat on the left and held the reins. Dora was in the middle and was slumped into Miss Grozalia's arms.

22

TIGHT COBBLESTONE

For centuries, boats bearing wares of all sorts came and went from Charleston. They brought the world's best spices, Caribbean rum, sugar, tea, coffee, fine milled cloth and food items. The cargos they unloaded at the dozens of wharfs in the harbor and along the Cooper and Ashley rivers often weighed less than the staples of tobacco, cotton, rice, indigo and lumber exported from the Low Country. The tall sailing ships needed ballast to even out the equation and much of that weight came in the form of bricks and cobblestones.

These were left behind and now lined many of the streets in the city. During any examination of the mixed surfaces of the town's thoroughfares, it was important to remember that these same vessels brought most of the people whose descendants now inhabited this cosmopolitan city. This was true for both black and white inhabitants who crowded all the spaces on the peninsula.

"Papa," Joseph Hale said, "when are you and Mauma going to sit down and talk?"

Gillam Hale smiled. He shook his head and walked a

few more steps along the pathway toward the Battery along East Bay. Gravel and seashells crunched beneath his feet. "Joseph, you asking the wrong person. Yo' mama is slipperier than a freshwater trout when it comes to talking to me. She's avoided me since we got to town last month."

"Papa, anyt'ing I can do to help?"

Gillam looked into the street and then his stare returned to the harbor and the hundreds of tall sailing ships anchored there. "Boy, you done enough. You almost gave up your life to find me."

Joseph kept pace with his father; Gillam always walked fast and the younger man's lung function had continued to improve, despite the recent cold weather.

Gillam paused and looked at a heavily loaded freight wagon that sped past. Two black men sat on the front seat and a third atop the load. The wheels produced a rumbling sound when they rolled over the street stones. He looked at Joseph. "Whether she speaks to me or not, I'll be nearby somewhere in this area."

"Do you think Mauma's coming back to you?"

Gillam stared at Joseph. A frown swept across his face. "Remember, yo' mama never left me." He grunted and spat onto the walkway. "White folks took her away."

They walked along in silence. "Papa, dat just means you got to convince her to come back."

"Huh," Gillam grunted. "I still wish you'd a tol' me 'bout Queen Esther and that damnable Claude Crenshaw before you brought me here. I still don't think it's straight in my head."

"What you mean?"

"Hell, my wife had children by another man, a white one at that!" The anger over it all stayed just below the surface in Gillam—it bubbled over now. "She belonged to me and not to him." His hands balled into fists.

"Papa, dat jus' might be the reason Mama doesn't talk to you."

Gillam's frown deepened and he stared at his son.

Joseph said. "I believe Mauma don't want to belong to nobody—most women don't. You aren't around when he's there, but she doesn't talk to Mistuh Claude either."

Gillam's fingers released into the chilly breeze. "Who tol' you that?"

"Cuppie did. She keeps me up on it all."

Gillam laughed. "I bet that Cuppie does keep you up on it."

"Papa!" Joseph said.

Gillam issued a twisted laugh. "You deserve that and more for not telling me what I faced befo' we left Lucy."

"You sure you would've come if I'd told you?"

Gillam paused. "Sure, I'd a come. I love yo' mama."

Joseph said, "If you want her back, stop trying to own her and, instead, let her become a part of you. After all that's happened to us, that's what Mauma needs." He looked at Gillam. "It's what the two of you deserve."

Gillam smiled and then laughed aloud. "Boy, you just got a whole heap of sense." He put his left arm around Joseph's shoulders.

"Yessuh, I do. My daddy's smart—most times—and his papa before him was, too. That's what I been told."

"Is that a fact?" Gillam said.

"Sho' is." Joseph smiled. He showed his teeth. "Papa, there's something else you need to know."

"What's that?"

"Stop for a minute." They turned to the walkway railing toward the harbor. Joseph opened an old leather case he carried in his left hand—he'd acquired it in Charleston to replace the bundles he and Peter Johnson used to carry. He pulled a document from inside and sat the case on the ground. With a single tug, he loosened a string that held the roll closed. The paper uncoiled. "Papa, this is a deed to twenty-five acres of land on Edisto Island. Captain Baldwin gave it to Cuppie and me for a wedding present."

"Is that a fact?" Gillam smirked. "White folks jus' full of surprises. Where is it?"

"It's next to Mauma's place," Joseph said. "Why do you think Captain Baldwin did this?"

"I got my ideas," Gillam said, "but the important thing is what you think."

"I know why he did it."

Gillam said, "Did he tell you his intent?"

"No, sir. He didn't say and I could tell he didn't want me to ask or say myself."

"But, you think you know why?" Gillam turned to him and put his hands on Joseph's right arm. "Boy, you putting some weight back on? What that Geechee gal givin' you?"

Joseph laughed and shook his head. He looked into the harbor waters a few feet below. Then, he raised his eyes to the numerous three-masted ships anchored nearby, just as he used to as a boy walking along the Battery. Their sails were tied to the crosspieces.

"Papa, don't be changing the subject." He looked into his father's face. "Reverend Peter Johnson told me all about it after we left Charleston." He looked at his father. "I was ready to give up and come home to Charleston and Cuppie, but Pete wanted to go on."

He looked at Joseph. "Is that a fact?"

Joseph nodded.

"That's what I still don't understand."

"What?" Joseph asked.

"Queen Esther never tried to get help from Pete to go from Charleston back to Cumberland!"

"Papa, you didn't even travel back there." Joseph put his right hand on Gillam's left shoulder, "Besides, the war had just ended. You don't want to hear it, but Mauma had two young children by one of the richest and craziest planters in the Low Country." Joseph shook his head. He said, "The Yankees put Pine Glen up for auction for back taxes after the war. The first two carpetbaggers that bought it came up dead before they could pay the auctioneer."

"Damn!" Gillam said.

"Yes, sirree! After that wouldn't nobody 'round here even bid on that plantation. Claude Crenshaw got the money together and paid dem taxes."

They stared at each other for a while.

"Papa, March and Dora are his only living children! That's a whole lot for a colored woman to carry across from here to Cumberland by herself against a rich white man's will."

For a few moments, silence fell on the two men, except for the tidal waves that lapped at the concrete-and-brick landing where they stood. In the distance, a group of Negro longshoremen struggled with a load, and two black lovers stole a kiss in the morning sunshine further down the Battery walk.

Joseph said, "You and Mauma need to be talking 'bout this. I want to make sure you know about this land and the small houses that're on it." He paused and tears formed in his eyes. "Papa, I want you to come stay with Cuppie and me. We got room and, and…" Joseph dropped his head.

Gillam finished his thoughts. "Don't worry, son. I ain't going away again."

Joseph looked at him.

Gillam said, "I thank you for your offer, but I figure to work out some other way to stay nearby you on Edisto."

Joseph said, "Papa, do you know why Captain Baldwin did this?"

"Of course I know. He yo' mama's pappy. Everybody in Cumberland knew it."

"Really?" Joseph said.

"Yeah, they sure did," Gillam said. "There wasn't a soul around that didn't."

Joseph stared at Gillam. "Then, why didn't you and Mauma ever tell us 'bout it?"

Gillam shrugged and said, "Some things you just don't like to tell. That's one." He looked into Joseph's face.

"The folks 'round you always know yo' dirt...they just talk behind yo' back and never in your face." Gillam shook his head. "These fine folks in Charleston, the black and the white, know a whole lot mo' they ain't tol' yet about all that's happened to us."

Bishop Cain looked at his young protégé. "My boy, I'll be parting from you this day. I'm taking the train from here to Savannah and on to Atlanta from there. Eventually, I'll get back to New Orleans." He looked around the room of the host home where he and Reverend James Frazee stayed during their time in Charleston. Bishop Cain said, "I don't know when or if I'll see you again."

Reverend Frazee said, "Bishop, why do you always talk like that?"

The bishop laughed. "Son, it's simple. I'm a smart, old, fat, controversial Negro preacher." He chuckled again. "Any of those five can get you dead, especially in these United States."

23

CYPRESS, OAK, PALMETTO AND PINE

The steamer *Osprey* was a small vessel with a single smokestack in the middle and a single paddle wheel in the rear. Thick coal smoke poured from the large pipe into the air. The southeastern wind swirled the black exhaust and dispersed it across the stern of the boat. The crowd of Negroes and whites covered their faces.

The ship's captain shouted, "Cast that line onto the dock!"

A crew member, already poised to do what he had done countless times before, launched the thick coiled rope into the air. A black man on the long narrow dock caught it and wrapped it around a metal mooring. The process was repeated at the back of the *Osprey* and the ship was pulled against the long, T-shaped wooden pier. Another crewman unleashed the ties to drop the gangplank. It slowly lowered to the dock and a throng of people, black and white, began to pour from the special pre-Christmas 1883 charter. It was the Sunday before the Tuesday holy day and residents had come home to the island they loved from their current homes off Edisto.

From the side of the boat away from the dock, Gillam Hale scanned the horizon. It was flat land with not one hill in sight. Water was everywhere and in the distance flocks of ducks, geese, cormorants, egrets and sea birds of varied sorts flew westward. They moved toward the now-harvested rice fields further inland, away from the salinity of the Edisto River waterways near the coast. A group of brown pelicans flew eastward toward the sea— Gillam quickly counted the seven birds and smiled in amazement at their six-foot wingspans.

The landscape was dotted with palmetto palms, straight and tall. Large groves of trees, dominated by live oaks, cypress, tupelo and pine, mixed with other varieties, stood on both sides of the creek. All were draped with Spanish moss. In the distance, several gunshots sounded.

Gillam turned to Joseph on his right. "Hunters?"

Joseph said, "Yes, Papa, probably after ducks and geese. Might be Gullah John. He hunts these woods 'round here. You know he lives with June on her place on the south end of Edisto."

Gillam pursed his lips and cocked his head to his left side. "How'd June get that place?"

Joseph said, "Her husband bought it after emancipation."

Gilbert said, "June was married?"

Joseph said, "Yeah, she was just before I left here."

Gillam said, "What happened to the man she married?"

Joseph said, "Cuppie said they found him dead on the island. His head was bashed in."

Gillam said, "I bet they never found out who done it, did they?"

Joseph shook his head and the three men eyed each other.

Gillam said, "So Gullah John took up with her and had a place to live."

"I guess so," Joseph said. He pointed into the distance about a half mile down the winding waterway. "That's Pine Glen Plantation. Mr. Claude Crenshaw owns it. All this land around here belonged to him 'til the Yankees deeded this part to the Negroes." He waved his hand to the east. "A bunch of these colored folks was already here, but some of 'em came into the area with Sherman from the Sea Islands to the south."

Young August leaned out from behind Joseph. "Grandpa, are you going to move out here or stay in Charleston?"

Gillam looked at the boy and began to open his mouth, but before he could speak, Queen Esther, Dora and June joined them from the ship's stern. Gillam froze and never answered the boy. He said, "Ladies, was your voyage pleasant?" He removed his hat and bowed his head.

Dora said, "Mr. Gillam, you sound like a Low Country gentleman."

Queen Esther said, "Child, let me talk with you this evening about his genteel traits before you give him all that credit."

The men and women of this family gathered their bundles and laughed.

Gillam looked at Dora and said, "Baby, we gotta figure

what you gonna call me." He paused to look at Queen Esther. "I want you to know I hope it ain't Mistuh."

Dora surprised everyone. She said, "My sister and brother call you Papa Gillam. That's mighty fine for me," she paused and continued, "if it is with you."

He smiled widely at her, showing his big front-gapped teeth. He nodded his head. Queen Esther laughed at his loss for words.

The group of Hales and one Crenshaw turned to cross the deck and leave the ship. They joined the rear of the crowd in line to walk down the gangway.

In the elevated steering house, Claude Crenshaw stood to the right of the small enclosure. He sweated profusely even though the weather was cold. He looked down on the assembly and pulled at his unkempt facial hairs. His eyes narrowed, but never left Queen Esther. A cough erupted from his throat. He hacked again and looked for somewhere to spit. The ship's captain stood at the wheel. He reached for a small tin cup in the window and handed it to Claude whose coughing spell worsened.

"Mr. Crenshaw, you all right?" the man asked Claude.

Claude took the cup, wheezed again, spat into the half-full container, and frowned from the tobacco smell along with his discomfort. The spittle contained blood. He started to shake his head, but stopped when Queen Esther glanced at him from the deck below. He walked to the exit door on his left, opened the door and motioned to Dora as she moved past. She crossed the fifteen feet from her place in line to stand just below the platform around the cabin where Claude stood. He reached in his pocket, extracted a purse, and bent down to hand it to Dora. "Happy birthday and Merry Christmas, sweet Dora," he said.

She smiled at him, as only she ever had. "Thank you, Father. I'll be by to see you tonight."

Claude Crenshaw coughed several times again. He said to the captain on his right, "Soon as this mob disembarks, take me to Pine Glen."

"Yes, sir," the man said.

The side-wheeler *Pelican* was an elegant and fast steamship. She had an open upper deck and an enclosed lower-level passenger compartment. The boat backed away from her mooring on the Ashley River on the south side of the peninsula—she could make the trip between Sullivan's Island and Charleston in just under an hour. March Crenshaw watched the crew during the trimming-out process with fascination, as he always had. He stood at the rear of the ship and looked out to sea, wondering what the rest of the world was like and thinking how much he disliked this part of it.

Though black blood ran through his veins, March felt as white in thought and action as any Charlestonian male of European origin. His olive-colored skin and negroid features signaled his origins to all he met. And nothing he thought, did or said would ever change that in Charleston or anywhere else in the United States.

Only a few people milled about the upper deck of the *Pelican*. The weather on this late December Sunday afternoon had turned chilly and windy. Choppy waves whipped up by the changing tidal currents and those generated by the convergence of the Ashley River to the south and the Cooper River to the north produced eddies and miniature white caps across the harbor surface. Locals often said the two rivers came together here at Charleston to form the Atlantic Ocean.

March pulled his old coat closer around his shoulders, leaned into the waist-high rail, and thought of how he would spend a first Christmas away from his mother and sister Dora. As did many a young man's, those holiday plans included a lady.

He thought of her, and while he did, heard a throat being cleared behind him. He straightened up and turned to his right. There she was, Sophia Cohan Smith. The young widow's thin lips and cheeks had turned a slight shade of scarlet due to the brisk breeze and dropping temperature.

"Would you like any company?" she said.

March shifted his weight from one foot to the other. He looked to his left and right at the other passengers atop the boat. "Do you think that's a good idea?"

"March Crenshaw, when we were young, we used to ride the ferry and stand at this rail to watch the ships race across the harbor."

"Sophia," he looked over her shoulders again. Several of the more than ten locals watched their interaction, "What will the fine Charlestonians think?"

She smiled up at him. He stood about six feet high, tall by local standards, especially for a French-descended Crenshaw, but March also had Ethiopian genes from Queen Esther. Sophia stepped toward him and pushed her gloved hands from beneath the cape through the slits in both sides. She touched first his shoulder with her right arm. He moved his weight to his right foot, then back to his left. She placed her left hand on his right forearm.

"Sophia Cohan Smith!" March whispered with insistence.

"March, you better get used to being seen with me or this will never work." She looked out to sea and the *Pelican* jerked forward. The boat's new movement nudged Sophia toward March; she steadied herself by digging her fingers through the open-ended ebony gloves she wore into his arm.

"This has nothing to do with being seen with you. It's about who sees us." He shook his head and looked out over the choppy waters. "When folks ask, what will you say?" he said.

She rolled her eyes, smiled and shook her head. "It doesn't matter to me, but I'll tell them you're my overseer, as we agreed."

He said, "They'll never believe that."

"People will think what they want." She looked away to her right across the harbor toward Fort Sumter. The boat swayed and the sweeping wind pressed her veil against her upper face. She blinked her eyes and said, "Let's go downstairs. It's cold up here."

He looked around. "Sophia, there's one thing you must understand. We aren't children anymore and these folks 'round Charleston will see me dead if they get wind I'm more than a person that manages your plantation on

Sullivan's Island." He looked back toward the Battery and then to her again. "Do you understand that?"

She paused, removed her hands from him, and grabbed the rail with both hands. Looking back to the south, first to the peninsula then across the harbor to Fort Sumter and the Sea Islands to the south, she said, "I'm from the up-country where tobacco is king. I picked up a newspaper last year and saw a picture of a Negro man who had been lynched on Sassafras Mountain in the northwestern edge of the state. It was the most gruesome thing I ever saw."

"Sophia, do you realize that can happen to me for what we are doing right now?"

They had played together as children on Edisto Island at her family's summer home in the Edingsville resort community near Edings Beach. But now, for the first time, Sophia shrank away from March.

March said, "Now, hear this good. We'll keep this quiet when we get to Sullivan's Island and to your plantation at Palmetto Place. Things can work, but we must be discreet. The Negroes'll talk, but, as you know, there are no white people at your place."

The boat's twin wheels turned faster and grew louder. She looked down at the churning water trails they produced on each side of the vessel. Sophia nodded her head. "I'll see you when we land. My plantation foreman will be there to drive us to the Palmetto." When she turned to walk away, she looked sad.

March said, "Remember to come to the overseer's quarters after dinner tonight for our first business meeting."

Sophia smiled and whispered to him, "If I come to dinner, I'm staying for breakfast."

March Crenshaw smiled at her and turned to the rear railing again, whistling as he did. He laughed out over the water. He was his father's son.

A heavy-set black man stood next to a white mule that was hitched to a weatherworn green-and-red wagon with two seats. He was a handsome man, with dark-brown skin and high cheek bones. He held an old straw hat in his hands, along with a crooked walking stick—the straight three-foot staff had swirls along its length from a vine that had encircled the cypress tree from which it was harvested. The man's white shirt, yellow braces and blue pants cut quite an image.

Queen Esther said, "It's Mr. Geechee."

Dora moved past her mother and the group. "Mr. Geechee!" She ran to him, set her suitcase down, and jumped into his arms, their routine since her Edisto childhood.

"Hey der li'l gal! Ain seen oona since duh last time." He boomed a laugh at his play on words. Mr. Geechee smiled wide and showed a mouth full of large teeth behind his thick lips.

Queen Esther said, "Daa'tuh, get off Mr. Geechee. Mr. Geechee put dat gal on de groun' befo' yo' back gib out." Queen Esther switched to her Sea Island vernacular. This was Edisto, Gullah Island, and she was home, as best she could know one.

Mr. Geechee squeezed Dora in his stovepipe arms and

swung her before placing her feet back on the ground. She kissed him on his right jaw first and then on the short, wavy hair on his head. Deep dimples formed in both cheeks with each smile he gave—Esmerelda and Cuppie looked just like him. He was their daddy.

Dora said, "Mr. Geechee, my brother's come home." She placed her left arm around him and stepped to his side.

Joseph moved forward to greet his soon-to-be father-in-law. "Mr. Geechee, it's good to see you, sir." He reached out his hand to the old man, but Mr. Geechee engulfed him in a tight embrace.

"Boy, I done prayed and called yo' name befo' Jesus many days and nights!" He squeezed Joseph hard. "U'm so glad, so glad you done come home. Don't eber go way ag'in." He held Joseph at arm's length. "Hear me now?"

Joseph nodded his head and swallowed a lump in his throat. They hugged again. Joseph said, "Mr. Geechee, look what the Lord done." He pulled away from the man and said, "You tol' me I'd fin' 'em and I done it. Dis man me papa. He Gillam Hale." Joseph was home and he conversed in Gullah, too.

Mr. Geechee waved Gillam to him. He provided the same treatment to Gillam that he had for Dora and Joseph. "What a gift, to live and witness dis dey. A present from God fuh Christmas, dat what oona is!" He released Gillam and they shook hands. "Welcome to Edisto Island. Anyt'ing oona wan', jus' ask Geechee." He swung his hands wide toward the south and the flat farmland dotted with groves of trees. A cluster of identical small wooden houses stood in the distance, arranged in a circle. They were obviously former slave quarters, now inhabited by freedmen.

Gillam Hale smiled. Mr. Geechee's outlook infected even him.

"Queen Esthe' gal, we celebrate today. Tomorrow night at watch meeting, we gonna join in the ring shout and we dance and praise duh Lawd. The women been cooking and we done killed the fatted calf. Y'all home and here oona bet'er stay."

Queen Esther opened her mouth to speak, but Mr. Geechee stepped over to her and said, "Hear me, now! Dat bet'er do!"

June moved to him. "Hey, dere, Mack Geechee."

"Cousin June! Come to me gal and gib us a kiss." They pecked on the lips first and then each cheek, an obvious ritual for them as well. Mr. Geechee hugged her and they leaned into each other cheek to cheek, despite their combined girth. At five foot ten, June was taller than Mr. Geechee and the same height as Gillam. Mr. Geechee looked past her at August. "Come here, boy." The lad stepped to the two and Mr. Geechee pulled him into a three-way embrace.

August smiled, but struggled for air. He said, "Mr. Geechee, this's my grandpa's brother, Uncle Gilbert."

Mr. Geechee released June and August. He moved toward Gilbert Hale and grabbed the man by both arms. "Welcome!" he said. "Tonight, I gonna serve you fried shrimp fritters. Dat make you strong, like me, heh?"

Mr. Geechee picked up the suitcase and bundle nearest him. "We go to Queen Esther's place now and then I take

Gillam and Gilbert home with me to Seaside." He wound through the group. "Gillam Hale, you stay with Grozalia and me dis time. Dat fine?"

Gillam Hale smiled. "Mighty fine wit' me."

As usual, Mr. Geechee's unique experiences helped him know how to solve delicate problems caused by cross-race plantation relations. He knew the Hales would need time to adjust to a house where Queen Esther had lived with Claude Crenshaw.

They moved past the white mule. Joseph dropped the wagon's rear gate and they piled their belongings and bodies inside. The men helped the women climb into the rear of the wagon. After that, August Hale bounced up on the front seat and Mr. Geechee climbed aboard next to him. Gillam, Joseph, and Gilbert Hale sat next to each other in the second seat in the middle of the wagon.

It was good to be on Edisto. They felt at home.

The *Osprey*'s horn sounded in the distance. Aboard the ship in the wheelhouse, Claude Crenshaw witnessed the reunion ashore. A coughing and wheezing spell hit him when Mr. Geechee popped the reins on the mule's back and the Negroes rode away. Claude shook from physical and emotional pain and anger.

"Damn," he said. "Damn, damn, damn!" Another wheeze escaped his lips. He wiped the sweat from his brow and noticed his skin was warm with fever. Claude Crenshaw was sick and for the first time in twenty-five years, Queen Esther would not be there to soothe his pain. No other Negro would be either.

24

NEW YEAR'S RESOLUTION

Early on New Year's Eve day Gullah John sat near the front porch of the house he shared with June, a two-room former slave cabin with unpainted, weather-worn wood. The dwelling stood on brick piers, was two feet off the ground, and its rear was just in front of an unnamed creek. John's fourteen-foot, flat-bottom boat was tied up at a short pier to the back of the house.

Gullah John looked up from his work of cleaning his shotgun and peered through the trees to see Mr. Geechee and Gilbert and Gillam Hale approaching. He stood to his feet and placed his shotgun across the arms of his native-wood chair. The ramrod he used to clean the old gun was still in place inside the barrel.

"Gentlemen," Gullah John said to his guests. "Good you come my way today."

Mr. Geechee said, "Morning to you, John! We come for duh ducks me wife say oona hab fuh de wedding feast tomorrow."

Gullah John thumbed his left hand toward a Gullah basket on the other end of the porch of his dilapidated dwelling. "Thirty birds in dat basket, a few doves and quails, some little black coots and woodys, with mallards, even some loons and two small turkeys I caught on the roost."

A flock of black birds that had noisily rested in a grove of trees at the cabin's rear took flight; they called loudly and moved as one in a circular then straight pattern.

Gullah John said, "I got dem birds to the west on a side creek just befo' the Edisto split into the South and North rivers." He looked at Gillam and smiled. "Father-in-law, u'm heading back up der for more Thursday, two days after New Year's. Why don't you come wit' me?"

Mr. Geechee moved over to the basket. He removed the lids and peeked inside. "John, hear me now! Generous of you to gib em tuh us and eben better dat you cleaned dem birds. How much we owe you?"

Gullah John laughed, "Just a thanks 'til de good Lawd gib me better pay." He grinned wide, showing his browned front teeth; those on the top and bottom of the right front of his mouth were missing. "We all in de same family and u'm looking forward to seeing how good a job Grozalia and Bentley do wit' 'em." He giggled like a child. "Wild ducks roasted with Carolina Gold rice, homemade bread, collard greens and sea chowder." He removed his hat from his head and hit his left thigh. His reddish gray hair was matted and had not known comb or brush for quite a while. "Now, that's gone be good to my insides." He looked into Gillam's eyes. "Even better to my soul to see Cuppie and yo' boy jump dat broom tomorrow."

"Uh-huh," Gillam replied.

Mr. Geechee picked up the basket by its two handles woven into the sides near the top and stood still for a moment.

Gullah John said, "June told me Joseph weaved that basket before he went away. They used to keep rice in it." He looked at Gillam again. "You know your son can do dat?"

Gillam admired the traditional mixed tan and brown patterns of the baskets. He shook his head.

"Maybe, oona get to sit down with your children soon, and learn de whole of the story. That just might surprise oona."

Gillam Hale nodded. Gullah John's words forced him to think on what he knew and possibly did not.

Mr. Geechee said, "T'ank you kindly, John." Gilbert moved over and took hold of one of the handles. Together the two men walked toward the path that brought them.

Gillam Hale said, "What time we going hunting Thursday?"

"Meet me at the dock where the steamship left you at five o'clock in the morning so we can catch the tide heading inland. I'll be in my boat ober der. You got a scatter gun?"

Mr. Geechee and Gilbert reached the clearing edge. Mr. Geechee said over his shoulder, "I'll see to it Gillam have a gun wit' cartridges." He and Gilbert turned single file with the basket between them and Mr. Geechee led the way into the thicket.

"Thank you, John," Gillam said.

Gullah John said, "June tell me oona know how to mek

whiskey real good. Oona see what I got under duh corner of me porch?"

Gillam looked. It was several sheets of flat copper about four foot square in dimensions.

Gullah John said, "I bet a smithy like you could beat dem sheets into a fine cooker fuh moonshining right here on duh island. We could sell it in Charleston for a good penny."

Gillam said, "I don't do work like that no more." He paused and looked from Gullah John to the copper and back again. Gillam turned and followed his comrades across the clearing and into the thick woods for the ride to Mr. Geechee and Miss Grozalia's home.

25

WATCH MEETING FREEDOM

On December 31, 1862, early in the day, a squadron of Union soldiers had come by Bethel AME Church on Edisto Island. Their job was to ensure the community was safe, and, more importantly, that each member of this congregation received word that President Abraham Lincoln had issued a proclamation declaring slaves to be free.

That night, just before midnight, there were well over one hundred Negroes crammed into the fourteen-by-thirty-five-foot-long building. Another two hundred stood outside on the lawn in groups around fires. They listened and waited. The people watched each other; the congregants outdoors gazed at the stars and peered through the open front door and windows. They understood that life for them was changing in ways no one could comprehend.

Inside the white clapboard church, Mr. Geechee led the congregation in a ring shout. His sweaty brown skin glistened under the lamplight as he stomped his feet. He grinned and, clapping his hands, set the time for the other worshippers to follow. He bent over and twisted from side to side as he moved about the circle. His rhythm was perfect and the crowd's stomping sounded like the instrument of its origin, an African drum.

Mr. Geechee boomed, "I wish I could serve in dis army, oh in dis army. I wish I could serve oh in dis army of my Lord. Army, oh in dis army, I gib up my life in duh service of my Lord. Army, oh in dis army, reckon I will die in dis army of my God. Army, oh in dis army, good to be born fuh dis army of my God."

He moved about the inner circle of the throng of men, women and children. They clapped and shouted, joined in community to celebrate, as they always had in worship and witness, sometimes in secret.

In this African Methodist Episcopal sect of the protestant church formed by that former Episcopal preacher from England, Mack Geechee led the ring dance with more fervor than even he ever had. On that evening, they celebrated the Emancipation Proclamation and their freedom from slavery. It was a new beginning.

Twenty-one years later, the crowd kept on clapping and stomping their feet on the rough cypress boards. Cuppie, less than twenty-four hours from being a married woman, said, "Sing it ag'in, Daddy! Lead that one mo' time." She swayed next to her seventy-five-year-old father, Mr. Geechee. He moved as he had twenty-one years earlier.

Another female worshipper shouted, "Sing it, Mr. Geechee! Sing it!" After the war, Mack had taken the surname of Geechee to represent his heritage from the Georgia Sea Islands where his folks had been purchased by the Crenshaw family. Mr. Geechee refused to bear the slave name of those who had owned him. Many of his other relatives and peers joined him under that new surname.

Now, he faced the church's small pulpit and looked around the room as he danced. There was much to celebrate. Cuppie, was home on Edisto to marry Joseph Hale. Joseph stood in the front right corner of the room. Next to him was the Reverend Mister James Frazee who, as King David of Old Testament lore had done, danced before the Lord with all his might. To Mr. Geechee's left, Queen Esther Hale moved, celebrating her emancipation after years of waiting.

Just behind her, Dora swayed. The girl was barely African at all, a quadroon, but that one quarter Negro of her ancestry came through in the ring shout. Dora's eyes turned to the young preacher in the midst of her praise—James Frazee returned her stare—he, too, had much cause to celebrate.

Mr. Geechee turned around and looked in the face of his wife, Miss Grozalia. Normally, the eighty-five-year-old matriarch of black and white alike did not dance, but this evening she danced like she did twenty-one years earlier when she had understood for the first time how it felt to be free.

Miss Grozalia kept pace with the crowd, clapping her hands and stomping her feet. Muley stood next to her, in his new black leather Christmas shoes. He swayed like a willow in the wind before an August Low Country storm. His long arms flailed and the skinny legs beneath him launched his narrow frame into the air. Mr. Geechee smiled; behind Muley stood Esmerelda. He understood who Muley and Esmerelda were to each other.

"Army, oh in dis army, I'd give up my life in duh service of my Lord. Army, oh in dis army, I reckon I might die in dis army of my God. Army, oh in dis army, good to be born fuh dis army of my God."

Outside, Gillam Hale held his hands to the fire. He listened and he shivered a bit in the swirling Sea Island breeze. Cold air had rolled from the upstate Blue Mountains and hilly piedmont to meet southeasterly winds from the ever-warm ocean driven by the northbound Atlantic Gulf Stream. The falling temperatures squeezed a fog from the atmosphere. It now shrouded the coastal plain giving every bush, tree and building a spooky appearance. Gillam looked into the church through the open front door and shook his head at the rejoicing crowd. He did not join; there was no movement in his hands, feet, limbs or soul.

Gilbert said, "Gillam, these folks sho' know how to praise the Lawd!" He clapped in the cadence set by Mr. Geechee. Gilbert added a double clap to his hand-made music. "Gillam, it remind me of when we learned to make steel sing in Papa's shop."

Gillam nodded, but he never moved in their worship. Instead, he stood frozen and he watched the crowd, inside and out.

Inside the small chapel, Mr. Geechee prayed aloud in corporate worship. He always began this same way. "De Lawd me shephud, a hab ebryt'ing wa a need." This quote from the opening of the Twenty-Third Psalm signaled Miss Grozalia to begin her leadership of a song.

"The Lord is my shepherd-d-d-d," she shrilled in perfect English, an echo of her husband's Gullah prayer. "I shall not want-t-t!" The congregation joined her as she repeated in a slower cadence, "The Lord is my Shepherd, I shall not want."

Beneath the din of their singing, Mr. Geechee's Gullah call to God continued, audible to their ears, but discernable only to their maker.

To the west, across several miles of dense woodlands, watery marshes, dormant crop acreage and open pastures, Claude Crenshaw shivered in his upstairs bedroom. His house at Pine Glen was cold. The servant he'd hired as caretaker had received the message about the pending arrival of the estate's owner, but he had ignored the instructions to lay in a fire in his hurry to reach the watch meeting. There was no food, also opposite to Claude's instructions.

The white man made a fire for himself. He started with some resin-filled fatwood strips from an old longleaf pine stump he had dug up years ago. The resin collected so thoroughly in the taproots over the life of an old tree that this wood would not rot. It was often sold in the Charleston markets for the same purpose he now used it. He said, "I remember when I used to dig these up." He corrected himself, "I should say my blacks done it." He frowned and then laughed at the irony.

The flames in the old parlor fireplace grew and consumed the kindling. He sat in the same old chair his father, Marion Crenshaw, had used—somehow it had survived the Union occupation—and he listened to his former slaves celebrate their freedom, life and the opening of 1884.

Gunshots filled the air when his mantel clock struck midnight. Claude Crenshaw pulled an old quilt around him. The small fire provided little help against the darkness, but he could still see the gold, green and rust-colored maple leaf patterns across the white background of the quilted handiwork. Still, he shivered in the plantation house though its physical characteristics warmed his soul. His anger, frustration and illness fueled him. He sweated beneath the covers as though it was August in the marshlands and in spite of his chills.

Claude leaned back in the chair and looked at the white ceiling. "Damn!" he said, "that Boo Hag gone ride me tonight." He issued a giggle, twisted by his own belief of the Negro mysticism that governed much of the Sea Island culture. Claude Crenshaw thought of Queen Esther again and he frowned.

He coughed hard and wheezed to get air into his mucus-filled lungs. The congestion bubbled inside him like a slow-boiling pan of thick shrimp grits.

He raised a near-empty bottle of Vin Mariani to his lips, took several gulps, and swallowed each. He reached down and picked up a thick ledger that lay on the floor next to his chair. The bound book was faded gray with red corners. He opened it and the top two rows on the first page read Slave Record Book, Pine Glen Plantation, Edisto Island, South Carolina.

He fanned the pages, remembering the years, purchases

and sales of people of color, the way a dealer does equipment. Claude found the entries he sought. He had memorized them and did not need the records he, his father and his grandfather had prepared. He strained in the darkness to read aloud his writing on several lines dated July 1858. "Purchased for $850 mulatto seamstress, age 33 and child, 7." He smiled thinking of his memories. "Queen Esthe's mine!" Claude said of his property. "And he ain't takin' her that damn easy."

He raised the source of his cocaine addiction to his mouth again. Claude did not know it, like most that consumed Vin Mariani, but the acids in the wine stripped something very destructive from the plant and left it in the completed concoction—cocaine was in every ounce of the wine. Claude Crenshaw had come to rely on the substance every day in his struggle with tuberculosis, like he had depended on opium for his injury in the years after the Civil War. Claude threw his head back and sucked the remaining drops from the container. He wheezed hard, gasped for air, and suffered another coughing spell. Some of the wine sputtered from his lips and ran down his chin and onto his white shirt. He dropped the now-empty glass container to the long-leaf pine floor. Its shattered fragments dispersed across the wide boards.

The current master of this Gullah Island dominion tried to stand. Instead, he slid unconscious from his seat onto bent knees before falling face-first to the glass-covered floorboards with his arms at his sides. The maple leaf patterns in his quilted cocoon danced in the fire light shadows.

* * *

In the Charleston Hotel on Meeting Street, Ethan Sneed sat alone in the living room of the suite he always rented for his annual pilgrimage to Charleston. He was an old man and the activity of the past few days had left his muscles sore. However, his male pride made him smile when he relived each moment in his mind. He thought of his first wife. He had married her after Marjorie broke his heart. He had returned to Edingsville the summer after that first dance to find her betrothed to his cousin Claude. Ethan's match with his wife of thirty-five years had been strong, but had produced no children as they'd both known it would not.

He lifted his glass of Kentucky bourbon and drank heavily from it. It was midnight, a new year. Outside, revelers, black and white, moved about the streets. Policemen blew their whistles in failing attempts at crowd control. Nearby, perhaps in the ballroom of the building a few floors below, a band played. It was a time of celebration, but Ethan Sneed, a wealthy Virginian, with accounts full of tobacco money, did not celebrate.

A padded step on the carpet caused him to turn around. He looked back at his wife, a new bride whose body he still had not seen or explored. Earlier in the week, he had completed the sale of his and his niece's tobacco crop to a Charleston-area cigar manufacturer. He used that and the need to manage his niece Sophia's trust as an excuse to visit Charleston each year.

Anger welled up inside him when his bride Media walked around the end of the sofa upon which he reclined.

When Media sat down, Ethan's words burst from his lips like a large puff of acrid Charleston-made cigar smoke. The congressman from Virginia said, "When were you going to tell me you're a niggah?"

PART THREE—

SEA ISLAND SALVATION WITH
LOW COUNTRY GOLD

26

SHROUDED HISTORY

On New Year's Day morning, 1884, the wind remained still on Edisto, unusual for a Low Country Sea Island. Warm ocean currents elevated the temperature above its normal range. By nine o'clock, when Gillam and Gilbert Hale arrived at Queen Esther's house in a wagon borrowed from a neighbor, it was in the upper forties.

A thick fog remained from the previous evening. The mist hung in the air and hid the details of the water-filled flat terrain with its thick forestation from view.

Mr. Geechee and Cuppie set out to make sure her soon-to-be uncle and father-in-law could navigate the sandy road over the forty-two acres owned by Mr. Geechee and Miss Grozalia. The Hale brothers arrived with no issues, and Gillam pulled the mule to a stop in Queen Esther's front yard near a small palmetto tree. He pointed to a wooden walkway in the front of the house that led into the dense woods and marshlands.

Gillam said, "Wonder where that leads?"

Gilbert said, "We'll see when the fog burns off."

They stepped from the wagon. Gillam set the brake and

tied the reins to the front left wheel. He moved onto the porch and knocked on the front door. Gilbert followed him up the steps and through the door after a voice bade them enter. They stepped into the small front parlor of the five-room cottage. Gillam said, "Morning, Joseph. Where's Queen Esthe'?"

"Mauma and Dora went over to duh church early to clean up from last night and make sure everything's all right."

Gilbert Hale said, "Gillam, this fog reminds me of the morning we found August's body."

Gillam and Joseph looked at each other and then back at Gilbert.

Gilbert said, "We buried him in Cumberland. Papa and Mama right next to him. Gillam, yo' mark was on them shackles I cut from August's body."

The room filled with a silence that only guilt can generate. Joseph walked to a chair near the potbellied stove on the far wall and sat down. Gillam leaned back against the front door. The white curtains billowed around him like an angelic veil.

Gillam said, "Papa Jerome was against it, but I sold shackles for white folks to put on slaves they was sending to the deep South. They put my chains on me and my wife and children." Gillam's lips quivered.

No one spoke for a while. In the distance, a crow called.

Finally, Gilbert said, "How did August get killed?"

Gillam whispered, "It happened just outside of Cumberland on the Chesapeake and Ohio Canal." He clasped his hands together in a tight grip and looked at the floor.

Gilbert said, "So, they took y'all out by canal boat?"

Gillam nodded. He said, "They split us up, so they could handle us. Me, Queen Esther, August and Joseph was in the back of the boat with the mules and milk goats. They held June, Jerome and Benjamin in another room at the middle of the ship with some other runaways." Gillam shook his head from side to side. "They brought us down from Cumberland through Georgetown. From there, they put us on a clipper ship for Charleston."

Gilbert said, "Damn, no wonder we couldn't find y'all!" He frowned like there was bright sunshine in his eyes. He shook his head, too.

Gillam turned. He pulled aside the white curtains made from soft and luxuriant long-fiber Sea Island cotton and looked at the front door. Gillam looked back. "Did your mama make these?"

Joseph nodded. He stared at his daddy.

Gillam said, "I jumped the big, red-headed slave catcher, a fellow named Rafe Coleman...almost got the best of him." Gillam smiled. "August was a big boy for sixteen. He tried to help me, but we had shackles on our hands, feet and 'round our necks." Gillam exhaled through pursed lips. He whispered, "My irons that I made. Coleman was a big man. The bastard knocked me down and then dragged August up on the deck. He threw him over the side."

Gillam and Joseph began to cry. Gillam stared out the front window, and Joseph walked over and patted his back. Tears ran down Gilbert's cheeks also.

Joseph said, "I had nightmares for years...I could still—"

he paused "—hear my brother hollering just before he hit the water. After that big splash, the mule that pulled the canal boat brayed ober and ober. There was nothing else after dat but my mama crying." He looked back at his Uncle Gilbert. "Rafe Coleman laughed about it. Then, he came back downstairs and beat Papa senseless before him and that other peckerwood...they took Mauma."

The men did not speak.

Gillam said, "Rafe arranged for a fellow to buy me in Charleston so he could have me make whiskey for him for free!"

Joseph shook his head.

Gillam continued in a hoarse whisper. "He tricked a white man in Lucy, Tennessee, to come in wit' him. They bought me, even though Rafe Coleman knew I was free. I made one big batch of whiskey and aged it for 'em in some white oak barrels for 'bout a year."

Gilbert said, "Gillam, whatever happened to Rafe Coleman?"

Gillam turned his head away from the door. His lips curled into a sneer. He said, "I drowned him and his hoss in the muddy Mississippi!" He spat it out as though something nasty was in his mouth.

Gilbert laughed. "Damn, wish I coulda helped, brother."

The room fell silent again, and outside the birds began to sing. For a time, the three men listened to the natural concert.

Gilbert laughed aloud. Joseph and Gillam showed puzzled looks.

Gilbert said, "Gillam, I know that was some good whiskey if you made it! Probably better than anything our pappy used to make."

Gillam said, "Gilbert, what you talkin' 'bout?"

"Yo' pappy, the Reverend Mistuh Jerome Hale used to make whiskey!"

"Quit lying on Papa Jerome," Gillam said.

Gilbert laughed and Joseph did too. Gillam's brow deepened into a frown.

Gilbert said, "He learned whiskey makin' at Mount Vernon. Gillam, did you know a friend of George Washington owned Papa and Mama?"

"President George Washington?" Gillam asked.

Gilbert said, "Yeah, the one and only general and near king of these United States, if he'd a wanted it. Papa Jerome was rented out to build the capital city. He made nails and whiskey to get the money to buy him and Mama."

Gillam said, "Gilbert, Papa hated whiskey! I know he ain't made no damn spirits!" He shook his head. "Not as much as he fussed at me 'bout doing it." Gillam moved toward Gilbert, shaking his head as he went. He stopped in the middle of the room, turned back to Joseph, and spread his arms wide before dropping them to his side.

Gilbert said, "Every man, slave and free, that worked building Washington, D. C., got a half pint of whiskey ev'ry day in his rations." Gilbert's light-colored eyes danced in his head. "Papa said he took his chances on the bad water and saved his whiskey to sell on Saturday—that was three and a half pints a week for several years. He made the rest of their freedom money from cooking whiskey for himself."

"Is that a fact?" Joseph asked.

Gilbert said, "Uh-huh, it is! But Papa quit after he moved to Philadelphia and he met up with a Negro Methodist preacher there, Richard Allen."

"Bishop Richard Allen, the founder of the AME Church?" Joseph asked.

Gilbert nodded. "He stopped Papa from making whiskey and tol' him it was bad money that was causing his troubles."

"What was wrong?" Joseph asked.

"Him and Mama couldn't get a baby to live 'til they moved to Cumberland and had Gillam. Bishop Allen said Papa bought Mama and fed his household on whiskey makings. It was bad money."

Gillam lowered his head and peeked outside. He said, "Joseph, where does that walkway out there lead?"

Joseph did not answer.

Gillam paused in thought, then said, "The fog's lifting now, outside…and, in here for me." He looked at Joseph. "That the same type dollars I used to buy my Queen Esther and to feed y'all." He turned back toward Gilbert and said, "Gilbert, when did Papa and Mama bring all this up?"

He and Joseph looked at Gilbert.

Gilbert said, "They told me when him and Mama got real sick, just after they took y'all." He dropped his head and then looked past Joseph directly at Gillam. "Papa repeated it all to me again on his deathbed, a few weeks after we buried Mama in the fall of 1860."

"Damn!" Gillam said.

Gilbert said, "Gillam, how did you get away wit' killing a white man in the deep South?"

Gillam smiled. "I tol' the old white man who owned half of me what Rafe done to us...when I spoke 'bout what they did to Queen Esther, that white man went wild—he was crazy for colored women."

Gilbert said, "Naw, boy!"

Gillam replied, "Hell, he loved 'em! You ever met a rich white Southern man that didn't?"

Joseph broke into the conversation. "Papa, in my years of traveling, I saw red and half-white colored folks in every place I stopped to look for you. Most of them born was from a white man who owned colored women." He laughed. "Now, every now and then, a white ooman had some of the fun."

A loud smack resounded when Gillam pounded the back of his left hand into his right palm. "Boy, you sho' is right."

The three men laughed.

Gilbert said, "Still can't figure out why them white folks took y'all." He scratched his head and squinted into the bright sunshine that now came through the front door and parlor window. It was ten o'clock in the morning, the sun had risen to well above the horizon, and the fog was lifting from the Low Country. "You reckon it was just the money from selling you they was after?"

Gillam shook his head. He said, "I don't know—ain't sure—wit' angry white folks, you just can't figure it."

Joseph said, "Papa, Reverend Pete Johnson told me why they took us. It was his fault. He and Pastor Buehl recruited Mauma to help runaway slaves escape through Cumberland. The slave catchers whipped Pete real bad and he told 'em about what Mauma was doing. That's why he helped me look for you."

Gillam looked out the window again. He said, "Joseph, I understand so much now. That walkway across the marsh heads to the back of a big white mansion over there." He turned to look at his son. "That's Claude Crenshaw's house, ain't it?"

Joseph nodded his head.

"That bastard built that so he could get over here to Queen Esther, didn't he?"

Joseph said, "Papa, his daddy built it for the colored women he used to keep over here in this same house."

The three men heard the front door swing open. Queen Esther stepped inside; she said, "Y'all ready to celebrate a bright day in this family?"

27

SEA ISLAND QUARANTINE

The only doctor on Edisto said, "Grozalia, he's God-awful sick. Not much else I can do now. He's so far gone and his lungs are full of fluid."

Grozalia said, "I rubbed him down with pine liniment. He be fine with res' and care." The turpentine-like smell filled the room.

The doctor shook his head. He said, "I'll try to get word to his wife tomorrow when the special charter boat heads back to Charleston after the holiday."

"Dat white ooman yent gwine Edisto. Miss Marjorie ain't been here since de wah." Miss Grozalia looked at Claude.

The doctor said, "Their boy drowned in that tidal creek out back, didn't he?"

Miss Grozalia nodded.

"Oona daa'tuh getting married today?" the doctor spoke in flowing Gullah.

"Yessuh," she said.

"Can you get a gal to stay with him?" he asked.

"U'm stayin'. He might get wassuh."

"Grozalia, what about the nuptials?" the doctor questioned.

She looked at him. "His mama hab chile fus dark and I tended huh 'til she died. I brought this buckruh and his bubba into the world."

"Grozalia, you birthed this white man and his brothe'?"

Grozalia nodded. "Yessuh, dat why it need to be me here wit' him right now." She patted her chest. "I nursed 'em like they was mine."

The doctor said, "You loved 'em, didn't you?"

Grozalia nodded. "I knew they wouldn't neber be sol' like duh chil'un I birthed. Still lob duh Crenshaw twins. Even dis one dat done so much ebil."

He said, "Grozalia, how do you help folks that have done such terrible things to you?"

Grozalia stared at him. She said, "U'm Gullah and that's who I am. We here to be a help tuh folks. Besides, ain't dat what duh Lawd want us tuh do?"

The doctor stood there and let her statements soak into his psyche. Finally, he said, "All right. Give him that laudanum to keep his pain down and let me know if anything changes." He turned to walk away, and then stopped. "Grozalia, wash your hands with warm water and soap a lot and don't handle food or drink for yourself around him. I read an article that said consumption is caused by a thing called a bacterium. It's so small you can't see it and the only way to kill it is washing with hot soapy water." He looked at her face. "You understand, Maum Grozalia?"

"Yessuh, but u'm gone stay to help him. I been trying to mek him do right."

The doctor said, "Is that why I hear you been giving him sea rose tea?"

Grozalia smiled, but she did not speak.

The doctor said, "I have eyes and ears in the Low Country just like you do."

They both laughed.

The doctor said, "I noticed he cut himself on a broken Vin Mariani wine bottle. I was over at Bailey's General Store the other day. They have an American version of it, Pemberton's Coca Wine. Why don't you send a boy 'round to get him a few bottles? He's used to having it. Claude Crenshaw'll get downright ornery if he's without it."

She nodded and the doctor left. The stairs creaked beneath his weight as he exited.

Claude moaned and thrashed about his bed. "Dah Grozalia," he said. He tried to sit up, but was too weak and fell back down. His eyes remained closed.

"Li'l buckruh," she said, "quit yo' struggles. Do what I say now."

He moaned and continued to thrash about.

"Ya hear?" She shook him again. "Wake up, Marse Claude! I know oona hear me and it time fuh oona to open up yo' eyes." He did not respond. She repeated her command in Gullah. "Marse Claude, yah don hurded what a wah say. Oona know hit time fuh to wake up!"

That language, the first he had ever heard and learned, pulled him from his sleep back to this world. She had whispered it to the twin Crenshaw babes. The Gullah had resonated in their souls. Miss Grozalia would hold one child across her lap, patting his little back, while clutching the other in the crook of a single arm to her ebony breasts. There, that boy's pink lips suckled the only mother's milk Claude and Charles ever received.

She said, "Buckruh, oona ain't a boy no mo', and it time fuh oona to waken to dat fact."

Her comments startled him and the realization of who he and she were roused him to consciousness. He tried to pull away when he saw himself very close to a face he used to love, but now feared. He jerked to free himself from her grasp, but Claude Crenshaw could not move. Three large cloth sheets wrapped around him in mummy fashion held his arms fast at his side.

Claude Crenshaw screamed, "Ahhh! Ahhh! Ahhh!"

In a calm voice, and in command, as always, Miss Grozalia said, "Lay still. Oona can't move."

Miss Grozalia shouted over her shoulder toward the open door. "Esmerelda!"

In a few moments, her daughter's voice replied "Yessum," from the base of the stairwell below.

"Oona got wha' a tol oona tuh mek?"

"Yessum," Esmerelda replied.

"Bring me the tray fuh Marse Claude and dat med'cine I brung wit' us." She stood and retrieved two feather-filled pillows from the floor and placed them beside him on the bed. Miss Grozalia smiled at Claude Crenshaw and placed both hands underneath his back. She raised him in the bed and placed the pillows behind him. His eyes bulged when she moved onto the bed next to him. Like a concerned mother would, she pulled his head to her shoulder. She had done so when he was sick as a boy.

He struggled to pull away, but she held her emaciated patient fast. He thrashed about a bit at first, then relaxed, only to tighten his muscles again before succumbing to her will with an exhausted gasp followed by weak wheezes and coughs.

"I picked oona to he'p us." She leaned in and whispered into his ear. "You wa'n't born first. Mr. Charles came first, but I swapped him to second-born 'cause I just knowed you gone do bett'r by colored folks." She pulled away from him and touched his hair on the left. He jerked and she stroked his right temple.

"You still gone take me and June's prop'ty?"

Claude's chin dropped to his chest. He shook his head. Claude Crenshaw trembled.

"Negroes made all yo' crops while oona visited duh fine houses de Lawd gib oona at Edings Beach, in Charleston or up north." She shook her head. "The wind shot in our cabins." Miss Grozalia drew close again to his left ear. "Counting Pine Glen, oona had fou' places tuh lay yo' head. Now, oona wan' tek de little piece ob land we got fuh our labor and all dem yea's."

The bottom step popped when Esmerelda began her climb to the second floor. When she entered the room, she held a tray with a long-handled wooden spoon and two mugs; one was gray and the other blue. She set it on a table across the room and moved the small piece of furniture next to the bed.

"T'ank oona," Miss Grozalia said.

Esmerelda did not reply. She looked at her former master and smiled widely. She covered her face with her right hand—it seemed she was in on a secret.

"Claude Crenshaw," Miss Grozalia said—it sounded as though a snake had entered the room, "one of these bitter, duh other sweet. Which oona want?"

He shook his head.

"Oona gone drink one," Miss Grozalia said. "Pick one or I decide fuh oona."

He shook his head, refusing his medicine like a wilful child.

She laughed the way she'd done when he disobeyed her as a child. Miss Grozalia said, "Ain' not'ing but catnip and Spanish moss tea with some damiani. High buckruh, oona do wha' Grozalia say, right?"

Esmerelda laughed.

Miss Grozalia said, "Oona wanna do better or wussuh?"

"Better, better," he whispered.

Miss Grozalia said, "Pick duh cup oona want."

He shook his head again and Miss Grozalia used her right arm to grab him in a headlock. She pinched his nose shut with her left.

Claude thrashed about on the bed; he and Miss Grozalia were locked in a struggle for a short time before his weakened condition helped the old woman win. Esmerelda laughed, but did not speak.

Miss Grozalia said, "Gib de Yankee blue!"

Esmerelda grabbed the cup in her left hand and the wooden spoon in her right. Their captive sucked in air through his teeth. He kicked and thrashed about but gave way again in a few seconds. Miss Grozalia held him fast. She nodded to Esmerelda. Her daughter inched closer.

He opened his mouth to gulp in air and scream.

Miss Grozalia said, "Now!"

Esmerelda forced the pine fatwood between Claude's teeth and immediately poured the tea into his mouth.

Claude tried to spit it out, but he couldn't because of the stick between his teeth. He gulped instead to take in more air. His horror sounded out, "Ahhh!"

A few ounces of the tea poured down his throat before he regained his bearing and gagged on it. The greenish-brown liquid ran from his mouth, down his chin, and stained the white sheets.

Esmerelda placed the blue cup against his lips and poured the liquid into him. He gave up and stopped struggling against them. Claude Crenshaw drank the remaining tea without spilling another drop.

Miss Grozalia said, "Tank oona, daa'tuh. He get betta now." She stroked her captive patient's hair. "Oona know sweet tea good, Marse Claude."

Tears ran from Claude's eyes. "Dah Grozalia, forgib me! Please, Dah, u'm sorry." He cried like a baby.

"Oona now know what it feel like to be under the control of another poson. A few minutes done mek oona holler. Tink how long colored folks been under the power of duh high buckruhs en dis country," Miss Grozalia said.

Claude Crenshaw sobbed. He dropped his head onto his right shoulder.

Miss Grozalia said, "Now, I know you wants to get up

and find yo' foul wine." She leaned in and dabbed at the drool coming from the left corner of his mouth. "I ain't gone gib you none. Oona get betta now." She brushed his cheek. "Yo' bubba was born first, but I picked oona," she said.

He moaned. "No, no, I was the heir. I was…"

She put the fingers of her hands to his face. She said, "Oona been chasin' money an caught up in all kind a snares. I switched the birth order fuh sho' 'cause I reckoned I seen somet'ing in oona."

Claude moaned. "No, Dah," he said. "You didn't do that."

Grozalia said, "'A got plenty mo fa tell oona, but that mo den oona kin stan jes now.' Dat be from John 16:12, from de Nyew Testament, Marse Claude."

Marse Claude Crenshaw fell asleep in his Maum Grozalia's arms.

28

THE SEARCH FOR CAROLINA GOLD

Joseph and his bride knelt before the altar at Bethel AME Church on Edisto Island. As the couple finally stood, they alternated between looking at each other and at their loved ones while the crowd cheered.

Queen Esther had properly dressed the handsome couple. She'd sewed both outfits herself from patterns and materials she'd purchased at her favorite King Street dry goods store in Charleston.

Joseph, her baby boy, had on a starched white shirt, a red bow tie, and a black suit. Proper rest and Cuppie's regular attention had continued putting weight back on his frame. His handsome smile cast no doubt that Joseph Hale was a happy man.

Cuppie wore a long-sleeved white dress that reached to just above the floor; it was high-waisted and gathered beneath her bustline to show off her hour-glass figure. The sleeves and bodice were finished in fine lace work and a white sheer veil covered her face. Esmerelda had loaned her sister the petticoats Miss Marjorie had given her for

Christmas a few years earlier. Miss Grozalia had provided white stockings with blue silk garters to complete the wedding ensemble.

Cuppie held a beautiful bouquet fashioned from an open horn with a handle woven by June from the same materials she used in her Gullah baskets. It was filled with palmetto roses and fronds adorned with the silvery Spanish moss.

Reverend Frazee looked around the beautiful setting. Queen Esther, Dora and young August had tacked and tied palmetto fronds and roses in clusters on the altar and the windows of the chapel. The preacher said, "I thank the Lord for the privilege to present to some and introduce to others, Mr. and Mrs. Joseph Hale."

Reverend Frazee wore a simple white cotton robe with a red cross embroidered into the collar. He smiled widely and held his hands up.

"Brother Gillam Hale now has charge."

Gillam walked up behind the couple. Gillam unrolled the long green burlap fabric bundle he had carried with him from Charleston to Edisto earlier in the week. Inside was a thick and elaborate broom. He said, "Folks, the straw for this came from broom corn grown on my daughter June's plot near Peter's Point. I selected this sycamore sapling in a thicket just on the Cooper River." It was white and brown, five feet long and two inches thick. The straw was eighteen inches long and curved at the ends. Gillam said, "A wild grape vine twisted and shaped the tree trunk. I removed it to reveal the beauty that struggle left behind." He dropped his head. "My family—" he looked around the room "—we all been through so many difficult times, but there's still such wonder beneath. I used my God-given talent to weld the wire to hold the straw in place."

He fingered the two double rows that formed the broom head. Gillam faltered when he tried to speak. He shook his head.

Someone in the crowd shouted, "Dat all right!"

Gillam took a deep breath. "When I married this boy's mama in Virginnie, my daddy made something like this for us to jump into matrimony. I know Papa's here, in spirit." Gillam laid the broom down and stepped away to the front of the standing crowd. "Mr. and Mrs. Joseph Hale, I invite you to jump the broom into a new life as one. God bless you!"

Joseph and Cuppie exchanged bright smiles and jumped high over into better days. It was considered bad luck to touch it and they made sure neither did.

Choruses of shouting erupted from the crowd. Mr. Geechee held up his hand. "Folks, dinner served at me and Grozalia's humble abode. Come, enjoy each other, and celebrate 'til de food run out!"

The crowd opened and Mr. Geechee led the couple from the church. The people celebrated by throwing grain at them when they approached Mr. Geechee's colorful wagon. They threw the same rice used in the traditional New Year's Day dish, Hoppin' John, Carolina Gold. Along with the other area-grown staples, it had fueled a two-hundred-year insatiable demand for black slaves from the West African rice coast.

On January 1, 1884, that grain signaled the beginning of a new life for this deserving couple.

The afternoon light came into the sitting room of the suite at the Charleston Hotel. Their argument had continued all night and throughout the day.

Ethan Sneed said, "Do you realize this marriage is illegal in Virginia and most other states in the South?"

Media shook her head. A sad look covered her face.

He said, "When were you going to tell me?"

She said, "I wasn't."

"Media, your candor astounds me. How do you think this was going to work—" he stopped speaking.

"Ethan, this was not my idea. I was happy as a young colored girl in Lucy, Tennessee. My cousin came up with all this when she saw I was able to pass for white."

He said, "How did you do that?"

"Most of the white folks died, including my daddy, his wife, and their white daughter—she and I bore a very close resemblance. My brothers were so young that it was easy to fool them. My daddy's family left Morristown, Virginia, before any of us were born so I moved back there to seal the secret." She began to laugh and rubbed her now-dry bloodshot eyes—her tears had run out around midnight.

"How can you sit there?" He rose to his feet and began pacing back and forth again.

She looked at him; he sat on the sofa next to her. "I'm

not scared anymore now that the worst has happened. Ethan, I'll make arrangements to return to Tennessee."

"Like hell you will! I'm running for the Senate next year! This scandal would ruin my public and private life."

She said, "You men are all the same. Your ambitions and money are all that concerns you. Y'all play with colored women, but have a fit when you find out you married one!"

He walked to the window and looked out. He stood there shaking. For a few minutes, neither moved nor spoke.

She said, "I better go check on my brothers." She rose to leave the room.

He turned and said, "Wait, Media, I can't lose a wife again!" They exchanged uncomfortable stares. "What...what...what should I call you?"

"Ethan, call me what you will. Nigger's fine, if that suits you—I've been called that before. For as long as we'll be together, it won't matter!" She turned toward the door.

He said, "Sweetheart, don't go. Come here and let me speak to you. The boys're all right with the maid I hired last night."

She turned to face her husband of two years. She said, "Your Charleston mistress was right. My mother was one-quarter white and my daddy, Raford Coleman, Sr., was white. I'm an octoroon."

He dropped his head at her knowledge of his secret.

She laughed. "You didn't think I knew about you and Marjorie Crenshaw?"

He shook his head.

"I grew up in a house where my mother had a baby every time the white woman that lived on the other side of the breezeway did. You don't think I understand when a man and a woman're carryin' on?"

Ethan Sneed looked at her. The frown across her pretty face morphed into a beautiful smile.

He asked, "How'd you know?"

"You two look at each other like y'all been slipping in the bushes all yo' days."

He dropped his head and looked sad.

She smiled at him. "Considering my background, it's not the end of the world. How long have you been doing this with your cousin's wife?"

He said, "Ten years ago, my wife became ill, she was dying. We knew it. That year, I came to Charleston by myself to settle up my tobacco crop and check on Sophia's trust."

She said, "Your sister was her mother?"

He nodded. "My sister married that horrible Irishman against my family's wishes." He paused. "I was so lonely."

Media said, "And so was Miss Marjorie Crenshaw, whose husband is just crazy for Queen Esther, but indifferent about their two quadroon children."

He looked at her. "What did your family call you?"

"Eula Mae when I was in trouble." She laughed. "And that was usually for being mousy and crying. Most times, they called me Baby Sister."

He walked over to her. "Baby Sister," he said when he stood three feet away. "You lit a fire in me the minute I saw you. I'm sorry for what I've done and said, but I'm not going to let you go." He paused and his shoulders rounded into a slumping posture. A humbled man held out his arms and said, "You're worth more gold than I could ever have. I'll give up anything, but not you."

"Ethan, what do you want me to do?"

"Just be my wife. Why are you afraid of me?"

"It's not you." She paused and said no more.

He edged closer and wrapped his big arms around her. She cuddled into them the way he had wanted her to since they'd first met. He said, "Well, what is it?"

"Ethan, I'm of child-bearing age."

He waited for her to continue and leaned back when she did not. He placed his right hand gently underneath her chin and looked into her dark-brown eyes. "What's the problem with that?"

She leaned into his barrel chest. "What if we had a child and it had some Negro features?"

He started to laugh—soft at first before the sounds boomed into her ears. He shook from the enjoyment of his private thoughts.

"That's not funny," she said.

Ethan said, "You don't understand. I visited Charleston when I was thirteen for the summer. My cousin Charles and I caught the mumps. They went down on us and our testicles became swollen. The Crenshaws' favorite slave, Dah Grozalia, said neither Charles nor I would ever have children. We didn't believe her, but neither of us have had."

"What!" she said.

"Yes, my dear young beautiful wife. I couldn't impregnate you if my life or anything else depended on it."

"Really?"

He said, "Do you want children?"

"Not if you don't."

He said, "I have other things on my mind."

"Your career?" she said and pulled him down. She kissed his lips, cheeks, eyebrows and forehead. She found his mouth again and he moaned when she pulled away. Gillam Hale had schooled her well. She said, "I need to ask you something."

He held her close.

She wiggled free and walked over to lock the suite door. She swayed while walking back to him. She said, "Do you want to keep your mistress?" She pulled his face down and kissed him again, harder this time; his knees almost buckled.

He said, "What mistress?" This time, he initiated the kiss.

When he stood up straight, she asked him, "You sure this is what you want?"

He held her close. "I am as sure as I have ever been on anything in my life. I want you to give me all you have to offer. What do you want?"

She found a way to get even closer to her husband. "I want this life we have together."

"Are you sure?"

"Yes, you are the only man I have ever known and I do love you." She laughed. "You better do two things."

"What's that?"

"Hire that girl for overnight to keep the boys." She pulled away and headed toward their sleeping chambers. She reached the door, stopped and looked back after she opened it. "We'll need her." She walked into the bedroom with a sway and looked back at him. "And you better let that room on the second floor go. You won't require it anymore." She released her hair and it fell to just above her waistline.

Ethan Sneed's mouth dropped open.

Baby Sister said, "It's amazing what a colored bellman shares after a small tip from a helpless white woman who bats her eyes." Her Southern belle act drove the satire home.

He started laughing and moved through the door behind her.

Sergeant Gunther Mueller continued his prospecting business on the afternoon of New Year's Day. Like most at the start of their missions, he was certain of his success. He dressed up in his best uniform and hired a small boat to ferry him across the swirling waters of Charleston Harbor.

Then, he walked several miles along the muddy road from the lighthouse near the southern end of Sullivan's Island until he reached Palmetto Place. He was sure Miss Sophia, a young widow with more wealth than he could spend in his remaining years, would be happy for his company. He could see the smoke from the manor house fire in the twilight when he arrived just after four-thirty in the afternoon. He did a double take when he walked past the open windows at the back of the overseer's quarters on his way to the big house. Inside, he saw Miss Sophia Cohan Smith in the arms of young March Crenshaw.

"Damn it!" He removed his crab apple switch knife from his pocket. He popped the long blade open with a wave of his right hand. He blew his breath out like an angry stallion. It fogged in the cold air and he threw the knife into the ground. The entire blade was buried up to the handle. "You can buy me with a plug nickel! She done took up with Claude Crenshaw's nigger son!"

He watched Sophia and March cavort for over ten minutes until he sickened and shivered from the sight and the forty-degree cold. He picked up his knife and crept onto the porch. Sergeant Mueller pulled his nightstick and kicked the door open. He rushed into the room with murder and mayhem on his mind. His nightstick beat on the head of March Crenshaw over and over while Sophia Cohan Smith screamed.

29

LOVES ME SOME YOU

The wedding feast at the four-room home of Miss Grozalia and Mr. Geechee drew near its close. Most of the guests had left, but a few were busy helping Esmerelda clean up inside the home. Queen Esther and Gillam Hale moved outside to the back porch for a brief time of quiet discussion.

Gillam looked at her. In the distance, an owl hooted and a group of small nighthawks screeched when they flew overhead. Gillam turned away to look into the night sky for the birds and then lowered his vision into the thick woods behind the Seaside Edisto Island house.

Gillam said, "Queen Esther, Joseph told me 'bout yo' Underground Rairoad work." He turned to look at her.

She said, "How did he know?"

"Reverend Peter Johnson."

"Ah," Queen Esther said, "a debt never repaid."

"He helped put us back together."

"Gillam," she said—he turned to look at her. "We're not together."

Gillam said, "Why can't we be?"

"Gillam, you always acted like you owned me and expected me to do everything just like I was your li'l ole gal. I won't go back to that again!"

He came over to the native cypress-wood chair she sat in. Gillam pulled a chair next to her and dropped into it. He said, "Is that why you never told me about the runaways?"

She looked into the darkness and the dense forest behind the house. "I knew you'd put a stop to it and that work had to be done." She stared at him. "Gillam, you had never been a slave and you didn't understand how it affected a person."

He said, "I sho' know now."

She sighed.

Gillam said, "I'm sorry, Queen Esther. Was I that bad?"

She smiled. "Naw, you wasn't bad. You just did some bad things. You cooked whiskey and drank what you made. You and your buddies at your lodge liked to act like white men and enjoyed your women and cigars."

He said, "Queen Esthe', I'm sorry and I'll never do that again."

"Really, Gillam?" She looked at him. "You ain't never gone kick one off again or run after all these hungry colored women in the Low Country?"

"Baby girl—" A whine echoed in his voice. "U'm old. I ain't interested in no parts of what them other women got."

"Is that a fact?" she asked.

"It is for the ones other than you."

She giggled. "What 'bout the whiskey and cigars?"

Gillam interlocked his fingers. He inverted and flexed them away from his body; they cracked. He twisted his face. "You could let a man take a drink and have a cigar every now and then, right?" He tilted his head to the side and pursed his lips.

"You can be so silly sometimes."

"Gilbert tol' me that my Papa used to make whiskey."

"I knew that," Queen Esther said.

"How?" he asked.

"Your mother."

Gillam shook his head.

Queen Esther said, "She told me how much trouble it caused them and that she worried it would do the same to us. Are you still going to make whiskey?"

He shook his head. "Not after what I know now... wish I'd known then." He looked at her. "I regret I taught my boy in Tennessee how to cook whiskey before I left there." Gillam shook his head. "I done him a disservice."

The back door opened and Mr. Geechee said, "Esmerelda, I'm going to the cistern for some mo' water." He stepped outside and was surprised to find Gillam and Queen Esther Hale sitting next to each other. Each had an earthenware plate on their laps. Mr. Geechee said, "It cold out here, but y'all got duh right idea. It was so crowded in there that we ate in shifts."

He laughed and they joined him. The owl hooted from its nearby perch. The three stared into the darkness for some sign of the great bird in a nearby grove of long-leaf pines and palmetto palms. In the distance, the sounds of waves breaking on the nearby white-sand beaches reached their ears.

Gillam said, "How far away is the ocean? I can hear it."

Mr. Geechee said, "Less than a half mile."

Gillam grinned. "It's wonderful here. I never had roasted oysters befo' today." Gillam spoke to Mr. Geechee, but his eyes were where his mind usually was, on Queen Esther.

"Man, you ain't libbed 'til you eat the eastern oyster. I lub 'em wit' grits."

Gillam said, "Y'all like ever'thing with grits. I ain't never seen folks that liked boiled ground corn so much."

The three laughed. They had already formed a bond that would rear grandchildren for years to come.

Mr. Geechee said, "The Indians showed the white folks 'bout hominy, uh, you know, cracked corn, when they got to America." He laughed, holding his girth with his free right hand. "In the South, we probably make mo' bread from corn meal than wheat flour."

Gillam said, "Sho' you right."

Mr. Geechee said, "I been out in the cold after ebry tide fuh weeks to get dem oysters." He smiled. "How you like that fried chicken and boiled cabbage?"

Gillam said, "That was mighty fine, but my favorite was the Hoppin' John with that smoked ham, followed closely by Bentley's shrimp and grits."

"Swimp grits is good food! But, conch, that my fav'rite shellfish. Make a man strong in the way oona need to be!" His eyes twinkled and the Gullah hint rang in his speech. He smiled and stared at Queen Esther. "Right, gal?"

She said, "Mr. Geechee, didn't you say you needed to get more water?"

The three laughed together.

Mr. Geechee dropped his head. He looked up and said, "Gillam, that was Sea Island black-eyed peas and Carolina Gold rice grown right here on Edisto in that Hoppin' John. You eber growed any rice?"

"Whoo, Lawdy, naw!" Gillam exclaimed. "They didn't grow no rice in Maryland or Tennessee. I heard they growing it now in Louisiana."

Mr. Geechee said, "They got to, 'cause these colored folks 'round here don't wan' work in no rice field no mo'. Growing rice the way they did it here will kill a man." His voice shrilled. He looked around to ensure their privacy. "Folks, Claude Crenshaw dead sick. Me and my friend Gilbert gone hitch up my mule again and ride ober to Pine Glen to help Grozalia after the rest of the folks leave. Bentley a'ready caught a ride ober tuh dere." He cleared his throat.

Gillam coughed. He squirmed in his seat and placed his plate on the floor. The fork clanged when he dropped it the last few inches. A frown formed on his face. He looked into the distance. He said, "Let him die."

"Naw, Gillam, don't let his ebil get in oona." Mr. Geechee smiled at them and moved from the porch. " 'Specially when a pretty ooman like dat sitting next to oona." He walked toward the cistern near the rear corner of the house.

Queen Esther picked up Gillam's plate and raked the remaining scraps onto hers. She said, "Gillam, when I first came here, Claude Crenshaw had Muley and the other children eating from a trough."

Gillam frowned and shook his head; she nodded. He opened his mouth to speak, but she interrupted him.

"He was bankrupt. His father had put all the family money in bonds for the Charleston Railroad—it went under and he was about to lose everything. His two youngest children, a girl and a boy, had just died of a fever. His wife wouldn't speak to him."

"Then he bought you," Gillam spat. "Johndaddit!"

She showed him the bottom of the glazed earthen dish. Dave was etched into its underside. She said, "I ordered these from a place in the South Carolina hill country. The slave that made 'em always signed his work." She stacked the plate beneath hers and placed them on her lap. Her eyes started to fill with water as she gathered the two forks with her right hand. "I told Claude what happened to me on the canal boat. He didn't touch me for a year. I needed that time. I got pregnant with March the first time he did."

Gillam looked at her, but did not speak. In the background, the cistern pulley creaked when Mr. Geechee dropped the long rope of the well bucket. A splash resounded in the cool winter air when it hit the water below.

Queen Esther pulled her dark cloak closer around her. She said, "Gillam, I never wanted to be here." She looked at him. "I don't want the life I've lived. I didn't ask for it or him." The tears in her big eyes flowed down her cheeks. "I can't explain it, but there was a reason for this, for me to have been here." She wiped her face.

Mr. Geechee returned with his bucket full. He paused next to them to say, "Y'all got any plans?"

Gillam looked at Queen Esther. He said, "I don't know what I'm gone do, where u'm going or where I'll live."

Mr. Geechee laughed. He said, "Gillam Hale, man, u'm talkin' 'bout tonight, New Year's ebening, not next year." Mr. Geechee laughed again. "Hab some fun. Yo' son married me daa'tuh today."

Queen Esther giggled and wiped her face with both hands.

Gillam said, "Aww! That sounds mighty fine!"

Mr. Geechee said, "Now, June and August gone over to Gullah John's for the evening and I done already took the newlyweds over to Queen Esther's." He ducked his head lower and from side to side. "Dat Muley and Esmerelda going fuh a visit wit' folks on the Island. Dey ain't coming back 'til over in the night, if dey do den."

Queen Esther said, "Mr. Geechee, would you take Dora with you?"

Mr. Geechee said, "Ooman, Dora and de pastuh lef' fuh Pine Glen a'ready."

Queen Esther said, "De gal know dat ain' proper!" She smiled, "Out wit' de man alone again!"

Gillam issued a booming laugh from his gut and slapped his thigh.

Queen Esther and Mr. Geechee chuckled. She said, "Man, what's so funny?"

Gillam said, "Two t'ings, as y'all say. Won't be long 'til Queen Esthe' ain' need ta worry 'bout Dora." He laughed again. "And uh beginning tuh know what oona say 'round her." He laughed again.

Queen Esther and Mr. Geechee joined in. She placed her hand on Gillam's right forearm. Both Gillam and Mr. Geechee looked at her. She did not remove it and her small fingers stroked his flesh through his shirt.

Mr. Geechee said, "So, Gillam, Queen Esthe', after we finish washin' dem plates and pots, ain't nobody gone be here but y'all."

Queen Esther smiled; Gillam did, too. Mr. Geechee nodded and carried his bucket inside to Esmerelda and the dishes.

Gillam said, "Oona been doing that a lot more lately."

"What?"

"Smilin'," he said.

She did again, wider this time. She turned to him and said, "Gillam, what you want?"

"Baby girl, today it's the same thing since the moment I saw you the first time." He paused. In the partially lighted back porch, his emotions showed in his eyes and on his face. In a raspy voice, Gillam Hale said, "Oona all I wan'. Oona all I eber needed."

She leaned into him. The forks clanged onto the top plate. She steadied them, touched his arm and kissed him, softly at first, and then with an insistent need from twenty-five years of waiting. Gillam moved to the edge of his chair and put his arms around her. She pulled back and looked at him before kissing him again. Queen Esther placed her left cheek next to his—they exhaled, as if both had just emerged from the depths of a Sea Island tidal pool.

He said, "I got something for you." He removed his arms from her and pulled away. Gillam produced a round roll of U.S. greenbacks from his pocket.

"Gillam, what's this?"

"Cash."

"I know, but—but where'd you get it?"

His eyes looked into the darkness and his breath frosted from the suddenly cold air. "I took it from a white man who bought me even though he knew I was issue-free."

"How?" she asked.

"Long story, I'll tell you later." His breath quickened. "I kept it for years to give it to you 'cause it was my fault this happened to us." He placed the roll in her hands.

She shook her head and moved the cash from her right into her left hand and back again before squeezing it in both. "It wasn't your fault. Gillam, I caused us to be in trouble—"

Gillam put his left index finger to her lips. He said, "Shhhh."

"Gillam, I was a conductor on the Underground Railroad. That's why they took us."

He looked into her eyes and took her face into his hands. "It's five hundred dollars and it's for you."

She said, "Gillam, I won't be bought again."

His eyes bulged and he shook his head and dropped his hands into his lap. "Queen Esther, what you mean?"

"I won't live my whole life a slave. You bought me when I was thirteen, and you never freed me." She looked at him. "Claude Crenshaw bought me when I was thirty-three years old. I'm just getting free."

Gillam said, "Queen Esther, I didn't treat you like a slave."

"Naw, but many times you done me like the white men did their wives and that wasn't right."

"I'm sorry for the pain I caused you, for the other women. I can't take none of that back. This money's for you. Do what you will with it."

"Gillam, I can't decide what to do with my life right now…or, about you or us."

He said, "Baby girl, Mr. Geechee say you ain't gotta do that tonight. Let's just you and me be here together this evening."

She smiled at him, reached inside her blouse and tucked the greenbacks away.

Gillam said, "Good, they safe in there."

She playfully hit his arm and they kissed again; this time for a few minutes. She pulled back and fanned her face with both hands. "It's getting hot out here," she said. They both laughed.

Gillam said, "I been wanting you for twenty-five years."

"A man ain't touched me, in the way men and women do, since before the war."

"How's that?" Gillam said. His face scowled.

"Since Claude got hurt in the fighting," Queen Esther laughed, "he ain't been able to please a woman."

"Shit, gal!" Gillam laughed loud enough to startle the nearby owl. It hooted and its large wings rustled in the pine-needle-filled limbs when it flurried away. Gillam said, "There's some justice in this life."

She looked into his eyes, "Gillam, I need to tell you something else."

He nodded.

"I had the Yankees put your name on the deed to my place along with mine."

Gillam said, "The acreage and the house here on Edisto?"

She nodded. They sat there for a while and he said nothing. The owl hooted in three short blasts followed by a fourth lengthy call.

Gillam said, "I don't know what to say. Why?"

She said, "Me t'ink oona coming fuh me someday."

He nodded and smiled. They paused and the owl called out again from farther away. In the distance inland to the west, another like him answered his cry.

Queen Esther said, "I might open another restaurant in Charleston or I might want to stay out here and just work our land."

Gillam said, "We can do whichever you would like. If you do the restaurant, let me make you a beautiful gate for the fencing and some ironwork to put on the windows."

Queen Esther said, "That would be mighty fine." She looked at him. "Gillam Hale, you a fine man to have around. I just want to have a say in what happens to me."

He nodded and swallowed. He said, "You mind if we get rid of that walkway that heads over to Pine Glen?"

Queen Esther leaned into him. "I've wished it gone since the first night I slept in that house."

Gillam said, "Queen Esther, tell me what yo' wishes are and I'll work on 'em every day."

She nuzzled against his left cheek and whispered in his ear. "Oona's what I want. Gillam Hale, I been praying for oona tuh come and burn that t'ing down fuh twenty-five yea's. When you ready, I'll hand you the torch."

Gillam said, "Whooo, Lawdy!"

They kissed again.

She said, "You still my husband so I guess it all right for me to—" she looked around "—spend a little time wit' you this evening."

"You always been my wife," Gillam said.

Queen Esther said, "Let's help—"

Gillam put his left index finger to her mouth and completed her sentence "—with the dishes."

He took the plates from her lap. They both stood and Gillam followed Queen Esther inside. He watched her sway through the door. Gillam Hale felt as he had the first night he'd bought Queen Esther in Cumberland, Maryland. All he could see was what he had wanted for so long.

30

THE COLOR OF MONEY

Claude Crenshaw lay in bed. He said, "Dah Grozalia, you woke?"

Miss Grozalia said, "You know u'm up ebery day befo' daybreak."

He laughed. "Yeah, I know. Those birds sure are singing their heads off."

She said, "Duh birds got enough sense to be happy to see 'nother day and dey show it first thing in the morning. Dat one of the reasons I neber sleep late. I don' wanta miss dem worshipping the Lawd in dey way."

He laughed. "Dah," he said. He looked in her direction, but could not see her face in the darkness. "How long I been asleep? What day is it?"

She sat up on the single cot she'd had Mr. Geechee place underneath the window across from Claude's bed and next to the old wardrobe. She said, "It Thursday. Oona sleep through Wednesday."

Claude said, "I need to get up."

The ropes of the old wooden bed creaked when she rose. A flock of seagulls in flight toward the beach to begin foraging on the nearby coast called out. The quacking of ducks resounded throughout the house when a large group flew past Pine Glen from a nearby marsh where they had spent the night.

Claude said, "I remember the time I would've been at that old rice field to get some of those ducks before they ever took flight this morning."

The floor did not make a sound until she reached his bedside. It creaked slightly just before she chuckled.

He said, "Nothing's better than blue-winged teals this time of the year."

"You bet," she said. "I like the woodys myself. Dey my fav'rite."

"Listen at 'em," he said. "I could get at least seventy-five with a single discharge of a double-barreled gun." He rose up on his left elbow. "Those summer ducks—" he used the other name for wood ducks "—are some of the most beautiful waterfowls I ever seen."

Miss Grozalia said, "Geechee and Esmerelda cooked some ducks for the wedding feast on New Year's Day. He say dey so nice and fat." She laughed. Her rich Gullah cadence and tone filled the room like a fairy tale each time she spoke.

"Dah," he said, "I forgot how much I love just to hear you talk."

"U'm jes a Gullah Geechee gal from duh islands." She looked at him. "Oona papa lobed to hear me speak in Gullah."

He smiled. Discomfort showed on his face. He said, "You missed Cuppie's wedding to stay with me?"

She nodded.

He paused and looked into her face. "Dah, I need to look for something in my downstairs office."

"Marse Claude, you need yo' rest. Can't dat wait?"

He looked at her, but his mind was already in different places, on other things. "I just might have been putting some things off too long already. I need to get some records from my safe downstairs."

Miss Grozalia returned his stare. "What you want?"

He paused for a while. Finally he answered. "Dah, I need my slave record ledger. I'm so glad you saved it from the Yankees."

The outside light was beginning to filter into the room and he looked up at her. Her expression was blank, without emotion. She nodded. He said, "Those records hold where Papa sold Mae, Omega and Seven."

He tried to rise. Miss Grozalia pulled his covers back. She reached down and helped him sit up. He was naked, but clean. Claude smelled of the pine resins she had rubbed on him. Miss Grozalia had cared for his every need during the thirty-six hours he had slept—he knew it. He turned in the bed and placed his feet on the heart-of-pine floor.

"Dah, I'm sorry Papa sold yo' children away." He paused and then looked up at her. "He didn't write down who bought your four oldest or where they were sent."

She walked to the old wardrobe at the foot of the bed. She opened it and removed a long white cotton nightshirt and dark-brown robe. "Marse Claude, I had dem first four by a Gullah man. Yo' daddy didn't track my oldest when he sol' 'em 'cause dey wasn't his." She moved to his bedside. "Yo' daddy fathered my next three named in yo' ledger, Mae, Omega and Seven. They was born a few years before you and Marse Charles. He let me lone after dat and took up wit' another Negro woman. Dat how Gullah John come into the world. Later, I jumped de broom wit' Geechee. He Esmerelda and Cuppie's papa."

"Why'd he get rid of Gullah John's mother?"

"Vesey!" she said. "He was some kind of hot when he found out she was Vesey's daa'tuh."

"So he sold her off."

She laughed. "Yeah, y'all white folks scared of anyt'ing to do with Denmark Vesey. Yo' pappy was in on duh trial of Vesey. He got rid of ebery Negro he thought had anyt'ing tuh do with the Vesey situation!"

Claude said, "Why'd Daddy sell your first four?"

"Money—Sea Island cotton prices dropped 'cause too much got made." She stared at him. "I knew Marion Crenshaw was gonna sell my last three someday, like he done my first four. Eben if dey was his. So, I named my last gal Seven. Negroes not'ing but numbers to a high buckruh."

Claude shook his head. He said, "So my half brother Gullah John ran off before he could sell him."

"Yassuh, and helped guide duh Yankees into the Low Country during the war." She put the nightshirt over his head, helped him feed his arms into the sleeves. She grasped him under his arms and helped him stand. Miss Grozalia pulled the long garment down around his knees. She put on his housecoat and reached under the bed for a pair of leather slippers.

He looked down at her and raised each leg while she placed the shoes on each foot. "Dah, you sho' are good to me."

She looked up at him and stood to his side. She smiled and waited on his next order.

"Help me downstairs to my office. Let's see where Marion Crenshaw sent our lucky Seven."

Gillam Hale arrived at the wooden pier at the same time Miss Grozalia was helping Claude Crenshaw descend the stairs at Pine Glen. He looked into the distance at the manor home and saw that the lamplights were already shining bright through the upstairs and downstairs windows. Gullah John waved a lantern from the end of the boat dock and Gillam proceeded toward him.

Gullah John interrupted his private thoughts with one of his own. "Mistuh Gillam, duh man in dat house ober dere bought and sold our flesh like it was beef at Charleston Market."

Gillam said, "Good morning, John. How you today?"

Gullah John said, "Tolerable well. Anyt'ing special been keeping you up at night so you couldn't rise on time dis morning?" Gullah John placed his light beside him in the bottom of the boat and stood up. "Why oona running so late today, huh?"

Gillam laughed. The fact that he and Queen Esther had spent the past two days together had spread like wildfire amongst the Edisto residents, black and white.

Gillam said, "Man, that's a devilish thing to say." The two laughed together.

Gullah John held a long pole with a metal hook on the end in his hands and used it to hold the boat to the dock. He laughed and the breeze picked up from the east when Gillam stood next to the vessel. It was a long rectangular box made from unpainted cypress wood. Gillam could smell the pine tars and resins Gullah John had used to waterproof the joints in his craft.

Gillam said, "This is a fine rig you got here."

"T'ank you kindly. Made it wit' me own hands. It four feet wide and twelve feet long. I use it when I forage in the island streams and coastal pools 'round here. Real good for oystering, shrimping, fishing and, today, oona see it great fuh duck-hunting."

"That's mighty fine," Gillam said. He swung the double barreled gun he carried over his left shoulder. A bag was looped over his right shoulder.

Gullah John pushed off from the dock and the boat moved into the channel. He sat on a middle board seat, laying his pole down. He lifted the lantern to his face and extinguished its flame with a quick breath. Gullah set it down behind him and moved the two oars into place. He maneuvered the boat farther out on the water.

Gullah John said, "We heading down this stream, the Dawhoo Creek, going straight across the North Edisto River to Leadenwah Creek. We gwine inland to the north. From there I know a little nook back in dere on Wadmalaw Island. A Polish buckruh named Sosnowski owns it. He let me hunt in dere anytime I wan'—he a good white man."

The oars splashed in the water. John put his back into

his work and the boat sliced through the water. "Mista Gillam, we'll shoot these scatter guns once each—dat four shots—and kill a hundred and fifty ducks."

Gillam said, "Sho' 'nough! Two shots apiece?"

Gullah John nodded his head in the gray morning light.

Gillam said, "What we gone do with so many?"

"I get two cents apiece for ducks at Bailey's Store on Edisto."

Gillam shook his head. He sat back, looked up at the fast-fading stars hidden by the towering trees on both sides of the Dawhoo channel. He smiled at Gullah John who returned his gesture.

"Two cents apiece for ducks." Gillam shook his head. "John, I could get used to living like this. I really could." He sat back and watched his chauffeur chart their way through the swirling eddies of the Sea Island stream.

31

THE LOB OF MONEY

Joseph sat at the small table in the kitchen at Queen Esther's Edisto Island cottage holding his Bible. Cuppie stood nearby at the black-and-white wood cookstove, her back to her young husband. His eyes followed her every move and her curves bounced with every motion. The smell of smoked bacon filled the room. She stooped down, opened the small oven to the left and checked on a dish inside. It was difficult to find a bad meal in the Low Country and Joseph had continued to put on weight. He was heavier and looked more like his old self every day.

Cuppie turned and smiled at Joseph and then moved back to her work. She said, "What you looking at, boy?"

He said, "The prettiest t'ing this side of the Ashley River."

She flashed him her brilliant smile and turned the last piece of the meat in her black cast-iron skillet. The utensil announced her efforts with a series of sizzles and pops.

Cuppie said, "Where you get that Bible?"

Joseph said, "It belonged to my friend Pete."

"I loved it when you wrote me about him in your letters. He sounded like a good man."

"He was. He was just troubled by the war and his hand in it."

Cuppie said, "Bet he t'ink a lot 'bout him causing y'all to be taken and sold as slaves."

Joseph said, "God know what he doing. We'd have never met if none of that had happened. You wouldn't be my pretty wife or fixing me shrimp grits."

"Let's use his name for our child's middle name, if it a boy."

He nodded. "What you gone use for the first?"

She said, "How 'bout Marion?"

He said, "That'll work for a boy or a girl."

She smiled at him again and added a bowl of chopped onions, garlic and a few red peppers to the skillet. The aroma leapt into the air and flew straight to Joseph's nose.

Joseph said, "Gal, what you doing ober der?" He rose, approached her from behind, and patted what was only his to touch.

She said, "Man, what oona up tuh?"

He put his arms around her waist and nuzzled his chin into the right side of her neckline. He said, "I learned something during my years on the road. If it ain't legal before God and man, don't do it!"

She laughed. "Papa Gillam sho got out of here early this morning."

Joseph said, "He met Gullah John at de boat dock to go hunting over on Wadmalaw Island."

She stirred the mixture in her pan and began to add

shrimp. She put in the largest ones first. They sizzled in the grease and added their distinctive aroma to an already delicious smelling room.

Joseph said, "Gal, I sho' liked watching you throw that shrimp net yesterday." He nibbled on her ear.

She said, "Quit, boy!"

Joseph said, "I left home a boy. I come back full-grown, with a man's appetites."

She leaned away from him and twisted her neck to look into his face. She pecked his lips with a kiss. "What do men like, mistuh?"

He said, "I t'ink you can answer dat for yo'self, after a few days of marriage."

She leaned away and looked at him again. Cuppie crossed her eyes. They both giggled and he pulled her against him in his arms.

She pushed him away and said, "Joseph, when you gone tell Miss Queen Esther 'bout what happened?"

His eyes widened. Joseph said, "Cuppie, now why you bringing that up?"

She said, "Cause you need to tell her and get it offa yo' mind."

"I don't want tuh tell Mauma 'bout dat."

From the door that connected the kitchen to the front room, Queen Esther Hale said, "What is it you don't want to tell me?"

Cuppie and Joseph turned to look at her. She stood just inside the room with both hands on her hips.

When Joseph did not speak, Cuppie said, "Mama Queen Esther—" It was the first time she'd called her that. "Joseph won't say it. He scared of Gullah John, but I want oona tuh know somet'ing 'bout the day Marion Crenshaw drowned in the tidal pool right out dere." She looked at Joseph. He turned away, but looked back when Cuppie rubbed the middle of his back.

Joseph said, "We was little and oona took us to First Baptist Church here on Edisto. They done a baptizing dat day. We played colored folks church when we got home, like we always did. Marion wanted to baptize, just like the preacher done."

Joseph frowned and chewed on his bottom lip. Cuppie moved a chair out from the table. He sat down and Queen Esther edged closer. She stood behind a chair on the other side of the kitchen table. The shrimp and bacon on the stove sizzled and Cuppie pushed the skillet onto a cooler spot on the stovetop.

Cuppie said, "Joseph, dis why you went away and stayed gone so long. It need to be told!"

Joseph nodded again. He said, "Mauma, Marion didn't drown by accident when de tide come in like I said back then. Gullah John come by when we were playing and...and he wanted to help put us under the water. He done all of...of us colored kids first. Then, he did Marion. Gullah John, he...he..." Joseph sounded like a child. Cuppie put her hands on his shoulders. Joseph said, "He held duh white boy under too long." He paused and swallowed hard. "Dat how Marion died. It was Gullah John dat done it."

Queen Esther said, "Why didn't you tell me before?"

Joseph shrugged his shoulders. He told what he'd

always feared, "Gullah John said he'd kill March and Dora if I ever tol' anybody what he done."

Queen Esther said, "Lord, help us. Lawd, have mercy. Gillam out with that fool right now."

In the distance, a woodpecker marked his territory by drumming on a tree. He issued a unique call.

Gillam said, "What kind of bird is that?"

"Dat a ivory-billed woodpecker." The Dawhoo current was incoming from the tide. Gullah John leaned into the oars working to get them to the North Edisto. "His wings almost big as a fish hawk's."

Gillam shook his head. He enjoyed another spoon of oysters and grits. For him, it was just another bird. He did not give it a second thought. They drifted inland toward the mouth of Leadenwah Creek across the channel of the North Edisto from the Dawhoo. A few flaps from Gullah John's right paddle guided their craft from the North Edisto into this side stream.

Edisto Island lay behind them and Wadmalaw sat on their left and right. The first light of day rose above the eastern horizon and both islands came alive with the natural sounds from the resident beasts and birds.

Gillam said, "Gullah John, I been meaning to speak wit' you 'bout two things."

Gullah John stared at Gillam but did not speak.

Gillam said, "What are your intentions with my daughter?"

Gullah John only laughed and offered no reply.

Gillam said, "And, why is it that my son Joseph, who

fears nothing, acts scared out of his wits every time you come 'round?"

Gullah John frowned. "So, you back now and want to be the big man, working t'ings out fuh yo' offspring?"

Gillam said, "Perhaps, perhaps. But, it could be that my inquisitive mind just wants to know."

"That's fair 'nough." Gullah John looked at the bank to their left. He took his hand off the oars and pointed into thickets.

Several brown birds moved amidst the naked bushes, green palmetto saplings and grasses. They were pigeon-sized, brindled brown in color, with long flat beaks, and big eyes. They walked through the brush in cadenced wandering moves. Occasionally, the birds would stop and rock back and forth on their feet, in a dance of sorts.

Gullah John looked at Gillam. He said, "Woodcocks. Pretty, ain' dey?"

Gillam nodded.

Gullah John said, "You know Marion Crenshaw my pappy?"

Gillam shook his head.

Gullah John nodded and looked surprised. He said, "My mauma said old man Crenshaw didn't know she Vesey's gal. Duh buckruh was so scared of Vesey that he sold her 'way into duh deep South cotton land when he found out." Gullah John stared at Gillam. "Meant to sell me, but I run off into the swamps to the south. They couldn't catch me and I ain' come back 'til during the war, 'cept fuh two times."

Dwight Fryer

Gillam said, "What dat got to do wit' Joseph being scared of you?"

Gullah John laughed aloud and his cackles echoed in the deep woods. "Mr. Gillam, oona know duh white folks used to go to the coast in the summer to avoid dying of a fever. They thought the air caused malaria fever, you know?"

Gillam said, "Uh-huh."

In the distance to their right, a drumming sound came to their ears from a woodpecker working on a tree trunk. A bird called, "Kent, kent, kent, kent." Another answered from their left with a similar pecking sound followed by the same call.

Gullah John said, "Dat a ivory-billed woodpecker."

Gillam nodded. He put an oyster into his mouth and leaned forward.

Gullah John said, "My mauma say Vesey tol' her duh mosquitoes cause malaria. Mauma tried to tell old man Marion Crenshaw dat 'bout the mosquitoes. He tol' huh she crazy." He laughed and continued. "After he sold my Mauma 'way, old man Marion Crenshaw shot his own brains out. 'Bout dat time, I slipped back onto Edisto. I went into duh Crenshaw place ober at Edingsville—my mauma say Vesey helped build duh house."

Gillam said, "Really."

Gullah John nodded. "Dat how he come to be my mauma's pappy. Her mauma jumped the broom with Vesey when he was out here working on duh Crenshaw house at Edingsville. That Vesey, he somet'ing else. Dat what my mauma say." He laughed and said, "Mr. Gillam,

I wondered if what Vesey tol' my mauma was right or wrong 'bout dem mosquitoes. Mr. Gillam, you ever experimented on t'ings in yo' smithy work?"

Gillam said, "Sure, John, I do all the time to find out how to get something to work."

"My job out here in duh woods and I wanted tuh know. So, I brung two jars of duh mosquito wiggles wit' me from the swamps when I slipped ober dere to Edingsville. It was just befo' time fuh dem to leave the water and fly. I poured one in the cistern and I put duh other under a bed in duh room wit' Claude Crenshaw's brats." He paused and looked into the woods on both sides.

Gillam said, "What happened?"

Gullah John laughed. He said, "Mr. Gillam, I b'lieve Vesey was right, 'cause two out a three of dem white children died with duh feber. Folks don' never get a feber at Edingsville, dat why duh white folks went dere ebry summer. Mr. Gillam, oona t'ink Vesey right or was he wrong?"

Gillam shrugged and looked at Gullah John. He did not speak a word.

Gullah John said, "It so many t'ings a Negro know that could save a white man if he'd listen." He laughed so loud that a group of sandpipers flushed into the air on their left. He said, "You know, the same t'ings can kill a white man if he don'."

Gullah John laughed again when they drifted amidst a group of giant cypress and tupelo trees on both banks. The large cypress limbs still held to the last of their foliage. The brown cypress needles floated atop the black swamp water in the Leadenwah. The leaves looked like bird feathers adorning both sides of the craft at the waterline.

Gillam said, "What's all that got to do with Joseph and how he acts 'round you?"

Gullah John guided them into a side channel off the Leadenwah. He said, "You ask yo' son 'bout dat. Be interesting to see what he say."

Gullah John laughed again, softly this time. He turned around to look ahead and guide the boat toward shore to the right. Gillam Hale wished he was back in Queen Esther's arms beneath the covers where he'd left her instead of in a cold boat with a maniac at the oars. He thought about all Gullah John had just revealed to him. Denmark Vesey had been right and he was also wrong. Gillam whispered, "I been wrong, too!"

32

ODD BEDFELLOWS

Claude Crenshaw said, "Dah, let's stop. I got to rest." He and Miss Grozalia had reached the first floor of Pine Glen. He looked back up the narrow stairs and said, "I seen the time I used to run up and down those."

"Oona run 'em again if you rest, lib right, eats good, gib up tobaccie and take strong drink in moderation," Miss Grozalia stated.

He looked down at the tiny woman. "Dah, how'd we come to this?"

She shook her head. "Don' ask what oona a'ready know."

His eyes widened and then narrowed. He nodded.

Miss Grozalia said, "Let's git oona in dis office to sit down."

Claude leaned on her, as he had for much of his life, and they moved from the foyer into a room just off the front door. No decorating work had been done on the room since its previous occupant had had it done by his slaves in the early 1850s. There was faded off-white paint on the waterstained walls. The plaster ceiling was cracked, but still sky blue. A faded mural of hunting scenes covered the entire wall to the left—armed hunters and their canine minions sought bear, fox, bobwhite quail, deer, ducks and woodcock in the colorful scenes.

Scuff marks on the heart-of-pine flooring from the boots of Union army soldiers and freedmen occupants during and after the war were clearly visible in the eastern morning light. The room was sparsely furnished—Claude had never restocked it after its antebellum trappings had been shipped north to a Union army colonel's home during the Edisto occupation. Claude Crenshaw had left the plantation safe open before the occupation. It was to the right of the table. Perhaps the weight of the big green contraption and its lack of contents had convinced the occupying soldiers to leave it behind.

Claude and Miss Grozalia made their way across the room to a small table. Claude said, "Wish I knew where Daddy's rolltop desk was the damn Yankees stole!" They turned and he was about to sit in his wheeled wooden office chair when Dora entered the room.

"Morning, Papa. Morning, Miss Grozalia," Dora said.

Claude looked at her. He smiled, a first in a while. He said, "Dora Crenshaw, as always, you a picture of health and beauty. How're you, darling?"

She walked over and hugged his neck. She was as tall as he. Their eyes met when she pulled back from him. She grasped his right arm and Miss Grozalia held his left. The two women eased Claude into the waiting seat.

"Papa, Uncle Bentley got some turtle soup. You want some?"

"Where he get a turtle this time of the year?"

Miss Grozalia said, "Geechee caught a big ole snapping turtle in duh late fall. We kep' him in a pen fuh a special occasion."

Claude Crenshaw looked at the woman who raised him. He said, "Dah, you jus' too good to me."

Miss Grozalia laughed and put her hands on each of his shoulders.

Claude rolled over to the safe and reached inside. He pulled out three thick gray ledgers. He said, "Dah, remember these?"

Miss Grozalia said, "Yo' fada wrote in 'em eberytime somet'ing bought or sold at Pine Glen."

Claude said, "Dora, these books tell the story of every financial transaction made at Pine Glen back through my grandfather's time."

Claude placed the books on his lap. He opened the one on top and thumbed through its pages. He said, "Dah, this is Marion Crenshaw's hand writing from the day he sold yo' gals."

Miss Grozalia said, "My Mae, Omega and Seven?"

Claude nodded. He pulled a few pieces of Confederate currency from the back of the book. They were twenty dollar bills. He turned them in his hands and looked at the illustration on the back side—a scene with slaves, the foundation of the Southern economy and much of the pre-Civil War U.S. capital sources. He marked the location with the paper money and spoke while he turned to the right page in the book.

"Dora, they were my sisters, my daddy's daughters by Dah Grozalia."

Claude turned and looked at Miss Grozalia. "Dah, why don't you go get me some of that soup while Dora writes a letter to that old bastard in Tunica to enlist his help in finding Mae, Omega and Seven."

The front door opened and two sets of footsteps sounded in the front foyer. A woman's voice called out. "Is anybody home?"

Claude coughed. He said, "We in here."

Marjorie and Charles walked into the office. The five occupants of the room stood still. Neither said a word until Claude finally broke the silence.

He said, "Marjorie, it's good to see you. Welcome back to Pine Glen."

Marjorie moved toward the middle of the room. She removed her hat and said, "It's good to be back." She looked at Claude and turned her gaze to Dora.

Dora said, "Pardon me." She began to leave the room.

When Dora neared her, Marjorie said, "Child, please don't leave." Marjorie removed her gloves and reached out for Dora's hand. She said, "I'd like you to stay."

Dora took her hand by the tips of her fingers, like a child might do. Marjorie stepped toward her and hugged her husband's youngest living offspring. Miss Grozalia smiled and Claude exhaled.

Marjorie said, "Claude, Millicent Baldwin had a stroke. She's dying."

Claude said, "I'm sorry, Marjorie. I know how much she meant to you."

Marjorie said, "Yes, she's loved me and taught me much over the years." She looked at Dora.

Charles said, "What smells so good in this house?"

Miss Grozalia said, "Bentley got some turtle soup in duh kitchen fuh oona."

Charles said, "Thanks, I lob all kinda critters."

Miss Grozalia said, "Well, Edisto full ob 'em and we got the right t'ing fuh oona, if oona wan' it."

33

SEPARATING SEED AND CHAFF

Separating seed from chaff is a necessary function. Since ancient days, indigenous peoples have stood on threshing floors, places where the wind blows the hull away from the valued grain. Sometimes these spots were in open-windowed buildings in high places. Other times they might be next to a humble rural abode.

That is where June Hale stood that afternoon. Earlier, she had used a wooden pestle and mortar to pound the Carolina Gold from its hull. She had grown the rice on a two-acre plot on her small farm at the southern end of Edisto Island. It had been produced by the rich and sandy soil, fertilized with every flood. The water, both from rains above and the creeks and ponds below, along with the sun and perhaps even the moon, fueled the production of this bounty.

She stood now looking out over the windswept Low Country plain dotted with palmetto trees and filled with the flowing sweet grasses she harvested for her basket work. A few remaining long-leaf pines framed the area. They were small, immature and would never rival their ancestors sacrificed for the flooring at places like Pine Glen and for the masts of tall ships abroad.

She looked at the dormant cropland, land the bluecoats had delivered to her from God. In a smooth motion, practiced by her so many times that it took no more effort than breathing, she placed the container on the smooth dirt and grasped the rounded Gullah basket. June bent over and poured her crop from the cylindrical container into a flat rounded winnowing basket.

June stood tall, just as women of African descent had done since the earliest times, when the Creator had first brought mankind forth somewhere deep in that native land. She looked out at the South Edisto River in the distance, winding its last leg to empty into the Atlantic.

She turned to the west and the southeastern wind blew onto the left side of her face. She tossed her harvest into the air in a smooth motion. Like all efforts, her fruits were a mixture of good grain and useless chaff. Like a conductor leading an orchestra, she counted time, silently. Into the wind, the rice and hull mix rose. The outer shell blew away; her rich grain fell back to the basket, captured by the low side walls.

It was a cold January day, but she and August sweated in the direct sunshine. He sat next to the wall of their tworoom home, watching her every action.

June said, "August, go out and hitch up the ox to the cart. After dat, we gone get our t'ings togedda. We gwine ober to Mauma's afta while."

The boy said, "Yessum."

She said, "Mek sho oona bring duh 'possum I caught

yestidday. He in a sack hanging up in the palmetto by the gate."

The boy nodded and he ran around the house toward an appointment he loved, driving to Queen Esther's house.

The wind had stopped blowing when Gullah John arrived just before three in the afternoon. He walked up the path from the river. He jingled the money in his purse, coins from the sale of the ducks and the ivory bill. He ensured June heard them.

Gullah John looked at the loaded cart a short distance from the house. August sat on the seat holding the reins. He opened his mouth to speak, but June interrupted.

She said, "Me and August going to my mauma's fuh a few days. Oona be gone when I come back."

Gullah John said, "What the hell you talkin' 'bout?"

She said, "Get out of my house tomorrow and fin' somewheres else to stay."

"I ain't going nowheres!" He stepped toward June; intended mayhem was spelled across his scowling face.

June picked up her pestle stick. The woman glared at Gullah John. He froze in his tracks. She said, "I know 'bout dem Crenshaw chillun."

He said, "You knot-headed wench! Oona know not'ing."

He moved toward her again. She drew back the stick and moved into a stance to hit him.

"Man, oona done hit us fuh de las' time. I'll knock oona into next yea' if oona eber touch me or my boy ag'in!"

Gullah John looked at June and then the large end of

her wooden weapon. He said, "Get yo' nappy head on duh wagon and git outa hea' den."

June backed away. She lowered her head, walked to the cart and climbed aboard. August did not speak. He popped the reins on the ox's back and they lumbered toward the north end of Edisto and Queen Esther's home.

Gullah John watched them move away. He walked over to his long gun. Raised it and fired into the air.

June did not look back. She smiled at August; he returned her expression. June's hands moved from her lap to her belly. It was already ripening with the fruit in her womb. Her seed had mixed with that of Gullah John one last time. The child would be born in her mother's birth month and would bear her given name as a middle one.

34

DOING CRITTERS

Gillam Hale stood on the front porch. He rubbed his sore shoulders. His name was on the property deed along with Queen Esther's, but he did not yet feel ownership. His breath left a trail when he exhaled into the cold night air.

A half mile away, the soft glow of a lighted lantern came to life from the direction of Pine Glen. It edged through the darkness with the cadence of tentative steps along a dim path. Gillam knew the one carrying the light was not familiar with the surface—it was not Claude Crenshaw. The lamp moved from the mansion through the woods at its rear and progressed along the walkway that came through the marsh to Queen Esther's home.

Laughter emerged behind Gillam from inside and echoed through the front surfaces of the house. The front door opened. Queen Esther stepped through it and closed it behind her. She pulled a white linen shawl about her shoulders.

She said, "Gillam, I have something for you."

Gillam turned toward her. The soft interior glow shone through cracks around the door. It formed a halo around her face and shoulders. He said, "Baby girl, I want whatever you got for me." They both laughed.

She said, "You still sore from rowing?" Queen Esther moved across the porch to where he stood next to the steps.

He nodded.

She said, "Well, I know oona gone wan' dis." Queen Esther reached up and placed something on his right shoulder.

Gillam's left hand moved to where she held the item. It was a large, thick cotton sock filled with a warm material. He clutched her hand and lifted the bag-like contraption to his nostrils. He sniffed at it through her fingertips. The smell of rice filled the winter air as if it was steeping moist, fluffy and hot in a tripod-hung pot at the end of a crop row over an open fire. Instead, it was hard and dry inside this heavy cotton material.

"Rice?" he said.

She nodded. "Carolina Gold's good for many things. I warmed this in a skillet to ease your pain from rowing all morning."

Gillam said, "Being here takes my hurt away."

She looked at him. "You sure?"

He nodded. "We got some things to unravel, but u'm mighty fine compared to how I been for twenty-five years." He looked into her eyes.

Queen Esther moved the rice to his arms, rubbing his biceps with it. An involuntary moan escaped his lips. She peered into the darkness behind him.

Queen Esther said, "Somebody's coming from Pine Glen."

He nodded. "Probably Dora and the young preacher. Surprised she stayed over there so long."

Queen Esther said, "'Specially after Miss Grozalia said Marjorie Crenshaw came earlier today."

Gillam nodded.

"That white wench used to call my children critters to my face." She shook her head and stared at the mansion lights across the marsh. A misty fog hovered over the wet places and moisture clung in the air. "I couldn't do nothing 'bout it."

Gillam said, "Now, we not speaking of that tonight, on such a happy day. Are we?"

Queen Esther smiled, but her eyes glistened in the dark. She massaged his shoulders and moved the now lukewarm rice around to the back of his head. Her fingers held it there and locked behind his neck. Gillam reached around her waist with both arms. He pulled her to him. She moved the grain to the left side of his face.

Gillam said, "Gal, I like what you doin' wit' dat rice."

They laughed and he kissed her again. She giggled.

"Gillam, you sho' know how to make me happy."

Gillam asked, "You sure 'bout the answer you gave me this afternoon?"

Queen Esther leaned into him. She nodded emphatically. "Absolutely," she said. "I made money in my restaurant, but I don't think I want to deal with all the trouble the whites will give me to open another one."

Gillam said, "It will be fine with me if you change your mind. I can stay here or in Charleston, long as I got you."

She smiled and they hugged again.

They turned to look at the lantern light across the way. It reached the halfway point and those carrying it had gained speed.

The rice almost fell. She caught it and slipped it inside the front of his shirt. She leaned into Gillam harder and alternated rubbing each of her cheeks against the warmth of the sock and his chest and neck.

Queen Esther said, "I despised rice when I first moved here. They eat it with everything—morning, noon and night." She sighed. "But, over the yea's, I came to be fond of it."

He kissed her again. Gillam took the warm rice and moved it across her forehead, cheeks and rested it on her neck. He said, "How you like rice now?"

She giggled as though she'd had too much wine. "Lob it."

They kissed and held each other in an embrace.

He asked, "When oona wanna git married?"

"Easter be a good day to jump de broom wit' oona again," she answered.

Gillam smiled. "Oona wan do dat we spoke ob fuh dis ebening?"

She leaned back and laughed at his attempt at Gullah. She passed the rice back to his chest. "Oona betcha, man. Gone be hot wen we mek dat fire." The two lovers laughed. They held each other and swayed back and forth, synchronized with the trees in the nearby brush. It was as if they forgot all that had occurred while they were away from each other.

The sounds of giggles, muted voices, and hurried footsteps on the resin filled pine board walkway interrupted their private moments. Gillam and Queen Esther turned to see Reverend James Frazee help Dora step from the wooden pier. They ran cross the yard toward the house.

Dora said, "Mauma, the doctor's at Pine Glen to tend to father and to March."

Queen Esther frowned.

She stepped closer to her mother. "March's all right. Sergeant Mueller whipped him 'cause he caught him wit' Sophia Cohan Smith, and…and he know what he done to help me last month."

Queen Esther opened her mouth to speak, but Dora interrupted her.

"The deal's already struck to straighten things out," Dora stated.

Queen Esther stared at her youngest.

"It seems Miss Sophia is going to sell her place on Sullivan's Island to Sergeant Mueller at terms he favors. He helped her bring March here after that arrangement happened. Now, here's what'll really open your eyes. March and Sophia are going to Europe together. My brother now has a rich Charleston widow on his string."

Queen Esther placed her hand over her mouth.

Reverend Frazee opened the door. Dora stepped inside and the young preacher followed, closing the door behind him.

The wind gusted across the marshes and onto the porch.

Gillam shivered. He said, "Gal, I don't want no secrets 'tween us ever again."

He reached for the door. She stopped him.

Queen Esther said, "I love you and I'm looking forward to spending the res' of my life wit' you." She gave him a joyful smile. "Let's see how these folks doing with the food and the negotiations."

He reached around to open the door. Together forever, the couple stepped into the front room.

Inside the house, Joseph sat hunched over a checkerboard. He said, "August, boy, where you learn dis game?"

Mr. Geechee spoke for his star pupil of many nights like these. "Son, tell him it was Br'er Fox dat showed you how ta mek the checkerboard moves!"

Gilbert walked over to where they sat at a small table in the front room. He pulled his watch from his britches. He looked over young August's shoulder before casting a smirk at Joseph.

Gilbert put his left hand on the boy's shoulder and said, "Y'all might say it was Br'er Fox that taught this boy, but I bet it was really Br'er Bear that done the real instruction."

Queen Esther and Gillam entered the room and looked around. Miss Grozalia and Cuppie sat in the sitting room near the stove. They were weaving Gullah baskets and barely looked up when the couple stepped through the front door. Mr. Geechee and Gilbert were watching young August master his Uncle Joseph at the table a short distance away.

Queen Esther walked away from Gillam toward the kitchen. She stopped in the doorway next to Dora and

Reverend Frazee. Queen Esther said, "June, you done in there? The folks out here ready to eat."

From the kitchen, June said, "We jus' 'bout done in here. Duh meats, rice, taters and veg'tables ready. We browning the gravy right now. Ain't dat right, Reverend Crenshaw?"

Reverend Charles Crenshaw looked up from his facts and figures toward June at the stove. He half smiled and then looked at Queen Esther. He swallowed hard before saying, "Dat sho right, wha' June said. We jus' meking the final details."

Gillam walked to stand next to Queen Esther. He stared at Charles.

Charles said, "She's agreed to sell her mineral rights to my brother. Reverend Frazee suggested it. We'll give her a fee for every ton we mine and restore the land after we finish digging out the phosphate rock. That place will stay in the hands of her and her forebears for generations to come."

Gillam stared at him again.

Charles continued, "It's all right here in the contract. I'll leave it with you for your review."

June said, "Reverend Crenshaw, oona got a stay fuh dinner and try everything I done cooked or I ain't signing not'ing."

She opened the oven and pulled a large cast metal pan from inside the stove. A large opossum surrounded by carrots, onions, garlic, greens and Irish and sweet potatoes filled the container. The flesh around its jaws had receded during its time in the oven; the beast's teeth now showed in a mocking smile of sorts.

Charles looked at the bounty. He said, "June, that'll be the best part of this negotiation. I don't do critters all the time."

June set her work on the stovetop. She opened a large pot of rice. Steam rose and its odor filled the room. She turned back and said, "Well, our new preacher done tol' us dat ebryt'ing the Lawd made is good. He preached dat sermon so good last week 'til it made us shout all ober duh church."

Reverend James Frazee said, "Let's eat. Sister June, I can't wait to have me some of that big fellow you got right there. A possum makes a fine meal. He's oily and the meat's white and kinda sweet, but you'll like it mighty fine."

June handed the opossum to Charles Crenshaw. He stood and moved through the group toward the table in the dining room. In assembly-line fashion, June handed the food to Dora, Queen Esther, Reverend Frazee and Gillam. She came in herself with piping-hot corn bread.

Queen Esther said, "Y'all come and get it."

"You won't have to call me twice. I'm so glad to eat something I didn't have to cook," Uncle Bentley teased.

Mr. Geechee said, "I bet that possum gone be the best t'ing on the table."

"You should a seen Mauma climb that tree yesterday and knock him to the ground before he could climb inside a hole in duh trunk. I didn't know she could move so fast," August said.

Miss Grozalia ran her hands across the boy's head.

They gathered around the table and, one by one, joined hands.

"Reverend Frazee, would you bless the food?" Queen Esther asked.

The preacher said, "Let's bow our heads. Lawd, make us thankful for this food which nourishes our bodies for Christ's sake. Amen."

June said, "Y'all get your plates and he'p yo'self."

Each person picked up an earthenware plate and began to dig into the Low Country delicacies. Charles Crenshaw put a bed of rice on part of his plate. He cut into the opossum and placed a hindquarter atop the fluffy white grains. He smothered it in brown gravy and stopped to fork a small bite of those three items into his mouth.

"Hmm," escaped Charles's throat. "This beast tastes good!"

Every person in the room, including Charles Crenshaw, erupted in laughter that lasted for several minutes while they moved about the oblong table serving themselves.

Joseph said, "Reverend Frazee, where'd you learn that blessing?"

June said, "Yeah, Pastor, I wanted to ask dat, too!"

Reverend Frazee said, "My mauma taught me. She wouldn't tell me his name, but she said my papa was a slave she knew briefly. He told her his daddy said grace that way."

Queen Esther, Gilbert, Joseph, June, Dora and Gillam exchanged looks. They knew that to be the preferred grace of Jerome, the Hale family patriarch, former slave and AME preacher. Gillam smiled and the others joined him.

They began to sit about the table. June entered the room with sliced red onions and shallots on a plate. Their odors mixed in with the smells of the various meats, vegetables, the corn bread, and the thick gravy. The room grew quiet and the only sound was the utensils clanging onto the pottery plates. Not one person in the room uttered a single syllable after they dug into their meal.

35

I CHOOSE YOU AGAIN

At Pine Glen, the doctor said, "He's taken quite a beating, but he'll be all right with a few weeks of rest." He looked at Marjorie Crenshaw and turned to Sophia. "You sure you don't know who did this to March and why?"

She shook her head and looked at the floor. The doctor knew she was lying and that neither she nor Marjorie would tell him the truth.

The doctor said, "Well, I had better be going. Marjorie, I've left plenty of laudanum for you to give March. He should sleep most of the night. I'll come by again tomorrow. Sophia, you take care."

Marjorie nodded and looked at the young man lying in the bed. Sophia sat down in the chair next to him. Marjorie followed the doctor from the room.

He said, "Marjorie, I'll let myself out." Marjorie stood there watching him descend the steps. A knock came on the door when the doctor was halfway down. The doctor opened it when he reached the landing in the foyer. It was Charles Crenshaw.

The doctor looked over Charles's shoulder. He said, "Charles, something's on fire back there!"

Charles turned around and stared across the marsh through the trees. He said, "Don't be alarmed. I just came from the Hales' home, conducting a little business for my brother. They decided to have a fire outside this evening after supper."

The doctor said, "That fire's mighty bright. They must be burning long-leaf pine."

Charles looked back. He nodded and made sure he spoke loud enough for Marjorie to hear it above. "They're burning that end of the pier walkway."

The doctor smiled. "Good night, Reverend," he said and walked into the brisk January evening. He descended the stairs to the ground, walked around to the other side, picked up the weight attached to the horse's bit, and climbed aboard. With that, he was off into the night.

Charles watched him depart before he moved toward his room and sleep.

Upstairs, Marjorie Crenshaw blew out the candles in the hallway and entered Claude's bedroom at the front of the house. Miss Grozalia had only made up two extra rooms and the unexpected visit by Sophia Cohan Smith and March Crenshaw required Marjorie to sleep on the cot beneath the window in Claude's room. She could not see in the dark room and stumbled when she bumped into Claude's bed.

Marjorie moved to the window on the left. She opened the curtains and undressed in the moonlight. She slowly removed her outer and under garments before walking over to the cot beneath the other window to retrieve her gown. Marjorie moved back across the room and stood there watching the fire at Queen Esther's home across the marsh. Her silhouette was visible in the orange glow of the fire and the white moonlight.

Across the room, Claude Crenshaw had watched her every move. He sat up in the bed admiring the curves of her body.

He said, "Marjorie."

She half turned. She said, "I thought you were asleep."

He said, "I was earlier, but I woke up when I heard the doctor and Charles talking."

She turned to look at him. The moonlight shone into his face and she realized that he was looking at her nakedness. She blushed in the darkness and the cool wind seeping around the one-hundred-year-old panes chilled her. These two had been married since childhood, but Claude had never seen her this way. His Southern thoughts on white women and the need to keep them pure had kept him from looking upon her unclothed. He had previously seen only women of color naked, those women totally under his control.

Claude said, "Marjorie, would you like to sleep here in bed with me?"

She stood there for a few minutes. She was cold, but she wanted to let him see her. Only Ethan Sneed had looked at her in this way before and she had always felt a certain shame afterwards. This man was her husband, and despite all that had occurred over the years, she wanted him to look at her. The sounds of her steps across the pine floor provided her answer. She slid into bed beside Claude. She turned away from him, but, much to his surprise, Marjorie snuggled her back close to him beneath the covers.

He turned toward her. He said, "Marjorie, I'm sorry for all I done. Can you forgive me?"

She did not speak. She moved backward, cuddling against a man who had not touched her since early 1858, just before their two youngest had died of a fever at Edingsville.

Claude said, "After I get better, let's sell this property and move to Savannah. Would you like that?"

She nodded and moved back again, pressing even closer into him.

Their private war with Claude Crenshaw having reached a truce, Dah Grozalia and Uncle Bentley had not fed Claude saltpeter in almost a week. Perhaps it was that, combined with the fact that he and Marjorie had never been this way before as husband and wife, naked together and unashamed. Perhaps it was that she had shown him what he had always wanted to see and the effect that picture had on him. It might even have been something divine that delivered this blessing.

Claude said, "Marjorie, I've never seen you that way. You're beautiful."

She laughed aloud as she had as a young girl when he'd taken her outside for a kiss during her first dance. She sat up and pulled her gown over her head, and quickly lay back against him again. He pulled the covers around her neck to warm her.

The smell of the Dah Grozalia's pine resin medicine

leapt into the air when she had thrown the covers back to disrobe. In the moonlight, Claude looked at the multi-colored maple leaves on the top quilt. He remembered who made it, but, more importantly, he also thought of who was here with him—his wife.

Clouds moved through the Low Country and blocked the moon from sight. The only light in their room came from the large fire that consumed the bridge across the wetlands. Claude and Marjorie Crenshaw knew how fortunate they were that evening. For the first time in their lives together, they would not waste this blessing.

Gullah John walked into the store on Edisto Island just after the clouds moved from before the moon. He expected to get paid the rest of his money for the ducks he had dropped off earlier in the evening. Instead, there was a surprise for him just inside the door.

The Edisto constable and Sergeant Mueller stood there. The sergeant said, "John Cotton, I want to speak wit' you about three sailors that are missing from a cargo ship. One of their bodies washed up on the Battery in downtown Charleston a few days ago."

Gullah John ran from the store door. He jumped from the porch and ran toward the nearby bushes. The constable stepped calmly onto the ground and leveled his Colt .45 at the fleeing man. He fired a single shot and, as usual, this lawman did not miss.

Across the marshland, a breeze picked up and fanned the bright orange flames. Their glow illuminated the area and shadows of the surrounding trees, Spanish moss, sweet grasses, bulrushes and cattails danced with the movement of the fire.

Gillam looked at Gilbert and Mr. Geechee. He said, "Gentlemen, thank you for helping me with this. It breaks a hold on our lives."

Mr. Geechee said, "Gillam Hale, dat a good t'ing." He looked back at Miss Grozalia. Reverend James Frazee helped her climb into the wagon for the late night ride home to Seaside. "It takes work, but it can be done. Don't oona forget dat I know." He looked at Gilbert. "Brother Gilbert, when you leaving fuh Cumberland?"

"Me, Gillam and Queen Esther will catch the steamer tomorrow afternoon to Charleston. I'll help them close down her restaurant and then Gillam's place. I figure to catch a schooner to the capital in a week and a train to Cumberland from there."

Queen Esther, Joseph, Cuppie, August, Dora, Uncle Bentley and Reverend Frazee approached.

Reverend Frazee said, "Mr. Gillam, I understand you and this lady want to recommit your wedding vows at Easter."

Gillam said, "Yessuh, we do." He spoke to the young man in the tradition of respect for a preacher, despite his young age.

Reverend Frazee said, "Mr. Gillam, Miss Queen Esther asked me to do it, but Miss Grozalia kept Joseph on the church roll at Bethel all these years. I've questioned him about his calling and, because he's had a great deal of training from the Episcopal preacher while looking for you, I believe your son can be licensed in the AME tradition in time for an Easter wedding on Edisto. What you think of that?"

Gillam began to laugh. No one spoke another word. They just looked at the fire and watched it miraculously consume only what needed to burn.

Queen Esther walked up behind Cuppie. She draped the new quilt she had been working on around the young woman's shoulders. She said, "Here's your first gift for the new baby."

Miss Grozalia said, "Geechee, come tek me tuh de house."

Within two months after the birth of Cuppie and Joseph's son, Miss Grozalia would die and the creator would receive her to sleep with her ancestors. Her family would pass Joseph and Cuppie's baby over her coffin in Gullah tradition. Mr. Geechee would bounce the boy on his knees for years to come. He would tell him stories about the family's history, and how love brought them together and gave them the strength to remain strong.

READING GROUP GUIDE

ABOUT THIS GUIDE

The following questions are intended to enhance your group's reading of THE KNEES OF GULLAH ISLAND by Dwight Fryer. We hope you enjoyed this historical novel, which brings to light issues of that time period, many of which are very relevant today.

STUDY QUESTIONS

1. Name the Charleston widows in the story and describe their fortunes.

2. Who was after their wealth?

3. Did March Crenshaw care about Sophia Cohan Smith?

4. How did losing his first children and Queen Esther affect Gillam's ability to leave Rena and Gill Erby? Discuss any parallels and connectivity seen in society today with parents leaving the home and their children.

5. Gillam instructed Media to send twenties to her cousin and he reported on her brother. What were the names of the cousin, brother and mother of Media whom Gillam spoke about to Media Coleman Sneed (see *The Legend of Quito Road*)?

6. Can you make an exhaustive list of the pearls in this book?

7. Who owned Queen Esther's building and what did that also entail for Queen Esther and the owner?

8. Discuss Queen Esther's quilts and the meaning behind them and their maple leaf designs.

9. How did Gillam's return heal June? Discuss the evidence.

10. Discuss the relationship between Gullah John and June. How, when and why did June get the courage to make a change?

11. What was the full name of June's son and who were his namesakes?

12. How does Queen Esther's question about Claude Crenshaw's Negro heirs affect Claude's thinking? Discuss the evidence that he has changed.

13. In addition to Claude Crenshaw, who knew the combination to the Pine Glen safe?

14. How common or uncommon do you think it was for white men to have liaisons with black women they owned or controlled?

15. Why did Queen Esther stay in Charleston and not return to Cumberland, Maryland?

16. Who were Gillam's son and grandson by Rena Erby? Discuss how Gillam's last lesson to that son affected the lives of that family (see *The Legend of Quito Road*).

17. Discuss Queen Esther's role in the Underground Railroad.

18. Discuss several nuances of Gullah culture.

19. Do you see any traces of the Gullah culture in your family or that of your contemporaries?

20. Discuss some of the valuable commodities and goods moved in and out of Charleston. Be sure to include human chattel, crop staples, manufactured goods, raw materials and transportation modes and routes.

21. Why was Gillam reluctant to go to Edisto Island and Queen Esther's home there?

22. Who was Media Coleman Sneed and what was her secret?

23. What did she know that surprised her husband?

24. What advice do you think Gillam gave her during their conversation at his home?

25. Discuss the AME Church and the Episcopal Church figures and congregations in the book. Include how they aided or fought against slavery.

26. Discuss the slave trade and its impact on Charleston. How did slavery impact the U.S. then and today? What are some of the things about slavery found in this book that are not in typical history textbooks?

27. Is human bondage still a problem today? If yes, discuss the similarities in how it is practiced today versus yesterday.

28. How did Captain Baldwin make the bulk of his money?

29. Discuss Miss Grozalia, her life, children, the fathers of those children and her use of sea rose tea and the Boo Hag lore.

30. Who was Mr. Geechee?

31. Discuss the economics and brutality of slavery. Include some of the slave prices, staple crops grown and impacts these financial matters had on both the black and white families in the novel.

32. What did Negroes say caused malaria and what did whites believe was the root of the disease?

33. How much did Claude Crenshaw pay for Queen Esther?

34. Discuss how the book impacted your ideas and thoughts about diversity, inclusion, privilege and oppression.

35. Discuss some ways news traveled in the Low Country.

36. Discuss the geography, flora and fauna of the Low Country.

37. Who are Mae, Omega and Seven and what happened to them?

38. What do you think happened to Jerome Hale?

39. Discuss how Media's true identity affected Rafe Coleman III.

These women are about to discover that every passion has a price...and some secrets are impossible to keep.

NATIONAL BESTSELLING AUTHOR

ROCHELLE ALERS

After Hours

A deliciously scandalous novel that brings together three very different women, united by the secret lives they lead. Adina, Sybil and Karla all lead seemingly charmed, luxurious lives, yet each also harbors a surprising secret that is about to spin out of control.

"Alers paints such vivid descriptions that when Jolene becomes the target of a murderer, you almost feel as though someone you know is in great danger."
—*Library Journal* on *No Compromise*

***Coming the first week of March
wherever books are sold.***

sepia™

www.kimanipress.com   KPRA1220308TR

Featuring the voices of eighteen of your
favorite authors...

ON THE LINE

Essence Bestselling Author

donna hill

A sexy, irresistible story starring Joy Newhouse,
who, as a radio relationship expert, is considered
the diva of the airwaves. But when she's fired,
Joy quickly discovers that if she can dish it out,
she'd better be able to take it!

Featuring contributions by such favorite authors
as Gwynne Forster, Monica Jackson, Earl Sewell,
Phillip Thomas Duck and more!

Coming the first week of January,
wherever books are sold.

"King-Gamble's engaging African American romance has broad appeal."
—*Booklist* on *Change of Heart*

NATIONAL BESTSELLING AUTHOR

MARCIA KING-GAMBLE

Hook, Line and Single

For newly divorced Roxanne, the new age of speed dating, singles parties and noncommittal encounters is all a bit awkward. Between keeping her business afloat and coping with a teenage daughter, Roxanne feels like a fish out of water. But she plucks up her courage and boldly goes where only singles dare to go—the world of online dating. Because maybe, just maybe, Mr. Right is out there looking for her....

Available the first week of January, wherever books are sold.

sepia™

www.kimanipress.com

KPMKG1180108TR

The inspirational sequel to

He's **FINE...** *But Is He* **SAVED?**

Acclaimed author

KIMBERLEY BROOKS

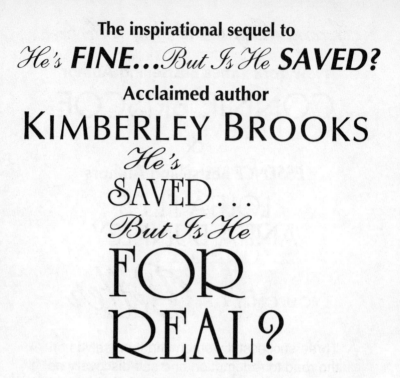

He's
SAVED...
But Is He
FOR
REAL?

An entertaining novel about men, dating, relationships and God.

Sandy, Michelle and Liz are three single girlfriends who are each struggling with their own issues with men. As each faces confusion, jealousy and loneliness, they look to the one Lord and Savior of all for help.

"Heartwarming and engrossing...
He's Fine...But Is He Saved?
engages you from the first page to the last."
—Bestselling author Jacquelin Thomas

Coming the first week of February wherever books are sold.

www.kimanipress.com   KPKBI230208TR

Because even the smartest women can make
relationship mistakes...

ACCLAIMED AUTHOR
JEWEL DIAMOND TAYLOR

You
DESERVE
MORE

A straight-to-the point book that will empower women
and help them overcome such self-defeating emotions as
insecurity, desperation, jealousy, loneliness...all factors that
can keep you in a destructive cycle of unloving, unfulfilling
relationships. Through the powerful insights and life-lessons
in this book, you will learn to build a relationship that's
strong enough to last a lifetime.

"Jewel Diamond Taylor captivates audiences. She moves the spirit."
—Susan L. Taylor, Editorial Director, *Essence* magazine

Available the first week of January, wherever books are sold.

NEW SPIRIT
TM